SHALLOW WATER

AMANDA J. CLAY

First Printing 2018

Florence & Reynolds Publishing

1

No matter how much tequila we'd had the night before, Aiden's penis was at full attention at the break of dawn, like a proud rooster announcing the new day. I felt it pressing into my backside as I slowly ascended from the depths of a fitful, inebriated sleep haunted by obstinate memories. I suppose that meant he was still here. While it was comforting to have a warm body beside me in sleep, sometimes it was just easier if he left in the night. Then we wouldn't have to stumble through the awkward feigned dialogue of "give me a call" and "next time" come morning.

What a specimen he was—tall and classically handsome but with the Devil-may-care-ness of a roaming artist. To his credit, he had the gift of music and prose—a man truly blessed by St. Cecilia. But beyond the prolonged eloquence of a gifted tongue, he'd always been a bit vapid. I suppose that's how it goes with men with whom you've got that raw, blood-boiling chemistry. Once the flame fades into its waxy bed, there's not much left but the wisp of smoke and the lingering scent of bergamot and clove. And as enticing as it is, no life was ever built on bergamot.

I rose from the bed, slick and sticky between my thighs, annoyed at having not peed after sex last night. Fucking tequila. I poured some raw cranberry juice and set a pot of Fair Trade Ethiopian roast brewing. The scabbed ink on my hip itched and burned, and I was hesitant to inspect it in case we'd done some damage to the fresh artwork last night.

I tossed two English muffins into the toaster—enough hospitality to be polite but not enough that Aiden would linger in hopes of conversation. I perched myself on my window seat, curled up my legs and stared down at the stirring downtown Austin beneath my little studio. Soon the streets would erupt with vibrant entertainment and eclectic culture. Restaurants would open their door to sling tacos and gooey queso along outdoor corridors. Quirky artists would add to enduring murals. Street musicians would showcase their homemade indie tracks and sell logoed tee shirts begging you to Keep Austin Weird. That was the thing about Austin--It let you create a soundtrack all your own.

Aiden finally stirred, pulling my attention away. One sleepy eye flitted open.

"Clara, where'd you go?" he half whispered.

"I was awake and in need of coffee. There's more if you want some," I said.

"Mmm," he hummed, opening his other eye. "Come bring those fabulous boobies back to bed."

My nipples puckered expectantly at the idea, but I resisted.

He could be such a child sometimes.

"Not a chance. It's after seven. I gotta get to the office. Chain restaurants across the nation are in need of my brilliant marketing copy. Besides I've already missed my morning workout."

"What's CrossFit compared to sweaty morning sex with moi?" he grinned.

I rolled my eyes. "Glad to see your ego is still intact. Pull yourself up and come have some coffee and a muffin."

Aiden lifted the covers to admire his persistent erection. He shook his head mournfully.

"Wasted. But I guess we banked enough until next time." He pulled himself up and started pulling on his clothes.

"You know how I feel about 'next times'," I said.

"Yes, yes, I know. Let's not complicate a simple thing." He laughed, so careless, as though nothing ever bothered him. "I think you just forget how fun complicated can be."

I'd solidly tried to mold something more tangible from the mess that was Aiden and me. But our life was an endless blur of too many cocktails as I stood on the sidelines while his band played. There was only so much of our time we could spend naked after all. I was trying to build a career; he was working hard to sustain his adolescence. We were doomed.

My one and only real Austin friend, Lola, was already sitting at Dolce Bistro on Fifth with a glass of Pinot Grigio and French bread when I arrived for our lunch date. An Austin local, she'd been the only one to talk to me in Freshmen English at UT. I was a weirdly old twenty-one-year-old fresh off a three-year international binge and didn't make friends easily. Her first words to me were something along the lines of, "well, you look like you've seen some shit." It was the first smile I'd had in a while.

I hustled across the street, tardy to our luncheon as I was to every appointment I ever had. Lola, an editorial assistant at a local magazine with a good eye for storytelling, was thumbing through her iPad and I hoped she was lovingly admiring the travel article I'd sent her for review. She looked up coolly and adjusted her Betty Page reading glasses.

"Nice of you to join me," she said dryly.

"Sorry, sorry. I know, I know. You really should just always make our plans at least fifteen minutes before you actually want me there." I caught my breath and sat down, immediately helping myself to her French bread.

"Pinot Grigio," I told the waiter as he walked by.

Lola raised her eyebrows in judgment.

"Hey, you're doing it," I said.

"I work from home."

"Kim's out of the office. And I'm sure she'd prefer I function today by whatever means necessary. I have a massive hangover. Fucking La Cantina."

"Think you might drink a little too much? It's Wednesday."

I glared at Lola. "I'm an independent woman, and I'll do what I please, thank you very much."

"And whom you please," she said with a little eyebrow jiggle.

"I'll have you know I was with Aiden, not some random guy," I added.

"Oh, yeah, that makes me feel so much better about it. Keep banging the guy who broke your heart."

"He didn't break my heart. He more just...wounded my pride."

She smirked. "Whatever you say."

The waiter returned shortly with my wine along with calamari and aged balsamic for our bread. Suits and heels scurried in and out of the bistro, balancing take-out bags and oversized iPhones as a hot wind picked up. The air clammed up, thick with humidity. The threat of a summer storm whispered down Fifth Street.

"So?" I asked.

"Hmm?" Lola picked at the calamari with her fork, gently dunking a fried tentacle into marinara.

"Don't be coy. What did you think? Does it work? Is it shit?" I took a generous swig of my wine, anxious to outwit my hangover. Lola pushed herself back a bit from the table. Her bespectacled eyes darted about the bustling midday street traffic.

"When did Austin become so pretentious? What is this, Dallas now? I blame the Californians. They all come to see the bats and stay for the men."

"Lola, don't avoid confrontation."

She sighed. "Okay, okay."

"It was that bad? Shit, even my best friend hates it." I laughed. "Just give me the bad news so I can get on with it and start drinking." The rapid knock of a margarita hangover was escalating, begging for entry. More wine. Needed more wine.

"Your writing is superb, Clara." Lola rubbed a set of cherry red-manicured nails over the slim iPad on the table.

"Don't fuck around."

"Anyone ever tell you that you have a foul mouth?"

"Every day. So you're serious? You really like it?" My heart did a little jump-skip.

"I did. I think it's a great start."

"You think I could actually sell it? To a magazine or something?"

Lola bit a matte lip. "Well..."

I furrowed my brow. "You know I hate verbal inter-jections."

"It's just not there yet," she admitted. I let out a breath. No one wants to hear their art is subpar, but I somehow already knew it.

"I'll scrap it," I sighed.

"No, Clara, don't do that. Look, the descriptions of Chiang Mai, the sights and sounds, the people. I really felt like I was there. I mean, no one can deny you've got talent. But this piece lacks...truth."

"Truth? It's not like I made it up."

"Not that kind of truth, Clara. I don't feel you in this. It feels like a beautifully written travel guide."

"And what should it feel like?"

"A glimpse into your soul," Lola smiled. My gut knotted and I shook my head.

"My soul is too dark to see into," I muttered. Lola snick-ered as if I was being melodramatic, but she didn't know the half of it. She didn't understand what drove me to Thailand in the first place.

"If you say so. But the world doesn't need another Lonely Planet contributor. It needs truth. Your experiences and how you feel about them are what set you apart from other writers. Don't discredit that."

"No one wants to read about my feelings."

"Are you kidding? You went through some serious stuff during those years. People will relate and eat it up."

I clammed up the way I did in the face of criticism, not wanting to open myself up to vulnerability.

"Or don't listen to me. Continue slapping marketing copy on Panera table tents and call it writing," Lola said.

I chewed my lip. I partly wanted to smack her, partly wanted to throw the iPad, partly wanted to just keep drinking. I wasn't ready to face what she was asking. I wasn't ready to go back there. But did I really want to waste away my years behind the gray cubicle walls of corporate America?

"Okay, I'll give it some thought," I said.

LATER THAT NIGHT, WITH A NIGHTCAP IN HAND, I STARED down at the little black words scattered across my laptop screen. I replayed my eastern adventures in my head. The striking temples and tropical hikes. Colorful markets and the sweet, spicy aroma of Pad Thai from street carts. Every smell, every noise, every pain. The burn of the needle, the taste of bile in my raw throat, the euphoria of too many Oxys on a Thai beach. Maybe Lola was right. I'd written the facts of my time there. Not the truth. Truth. How could I describe what I went through there? How could I bring the reader to my darkness without going back to the beginning? Without going back to a stormy summer beach. To a blazing bonfire and blurred impulses. The smell of the wooden floor in a lighthouse tower. To a lifeless girl in a watery grave, abandoned by those who were supposed to protect her.

A thump startled me from my whiskey drift into the past. I jumped, sloshing my drink on my keyboard.

"Shit." I scrambled to wipe it up, my heart beating a little faster. I glanced up to the window and shrieked. A shadowed reflection lurked in the night behind me. I flung around, grabbing for the large knife by my bed.

I exhaled, blood pulsing. It was only my navy throw blanket hung up to dry, freshly rinsed of the tumbler of tequila I'd spilled on it last night while Aiden was putting his mouth to good use. God, I was paranoid. I sat back in my desk chair and threw back the remainder of my whiskey.

My iPhone buzzed, and I yelped again.

"Fuck, Clara. Get it together."

The screen lit up with my Aunt Jo's California number. Strange. My mom's older sister never called me. I nearly brushed it off as a butt dial then glanced at the clock. Eleven p.m. on a Wednesday. That didn't bode well. I clicked the answer button.

"Aunt Jo?" I asked.

"Oh, Clara, sweet darling! Thank the Lord you answered," my aunt's melodramatic voice answered with the quasi Kentucky twang she still had, despite nearly three decades in Northern California.

"Is everything all right, Jo?"

"Well, honey, it's your mom. There's been a little incident."

"What? What's happened?" I sat up straight in my desk chair as my ever-paranoid mind raced with potential scenarios.

"She's all right, dear. But she's had a teeny, tiny stroke earlier this evening." She said it as though mom had no more than bumped her head.

"A stroke?" I nearly shouted, delirium, stress, and whiskey clouding my comprehension. "How?"

"These things happen with diabetics, honey. It's one of the risks."

"I know that, but what about her meds? Are they not working anymore?"

"I don't know much, unfortunately. The doctors are looking into it. It's possible she missed a few doses or something else she took got in the way."

My head spun. That made zero sense. My mom had

been a diagnosed Type 1 Diabetic since her teens. I doubted she all of a sudden became careless with her meds.

"But she's fine?" I said.

"She's been stabilized, and there shouldn't be any permanent effects. But, Clara dear, she's been asking about you."

"Can I talk to her?"

"Not just yet. She's sleeping. Quite an ordeal, a stroke. I know you're busy, but can you come home? She should be able to come home tomorrow."

The words struck me in the lungs, knocking the air from each vessel. Home? I hadn't been to Point Redwood in eight years. Not since...

"Jo, I..." I searched for an excuse big enough to justify not going to see my sick mother. I sighed.

"I know what it means to you. But think of your mother. Isn't it time you face down your ghosts for her sake?" Jo said.

Every ounce of me screamed to argue, make excuses, hang up the phone and run to bury myself under the covers.

"Pick me up at the airport?" I said instead.

2

A unt Jo was an incessant stream of chatter and mindless anecdotes on the two-hour drive from the tiny Santa Rosa airport up the coast to Point Redwood—population 1,000—nestled in the cliffs of the remote Mendocino coastline of Northern California. I tried my best to engage in conversation, but the looming fate of stepping from her Volvo onto the soil of my childhood had my mind wound into a labyrinth.

The car veered from civilization, winding up the misty coastline of HWY1, through redwoods and eucalyptus, darting in and out of tiny towns boasting the best clam chowder. As we made the final descent through the Mendocino forest toward the coast, the stormy Pacific unfolded along the horizon like a vast, gray welcome carpet. The lighthouse caught in my peripheral and I resisted the urge to shut my eyes and sing to avoid taking in the sights and sounds of this place.

Playground, secret woods, gas station.

As we drove past St. Thomas High School, nausea

threatened. That's when I finally closed my eyes and started humming. Aunt Jo didn't notice.

We finally came to the woodsy dirt road that led to the remnants of my childhood. Our little house hadn't been updated much over the years—its sea-worn frame nestled in a tangle of overgrown brush. I took a deep breath as I exited into the brisk summer night, feeling a rush of emotions as my feet touched down on the rustic bed of my past.

The house was tidy but smelled medicinal and stale, as though it hadn't been aired out in a month.

Mom was in her bed, propped up by a tower of fluffy pillows—courtesy of Aunt Jo's TLC, no doubt. The same rustic crucifix hung on the wall above her head. When I stepped in, her heavily lidded eyes beamed and her mouth curled into a thin smile. She was frailer since the last time I'd seen her the previous summer when she'd come to Austin—her cheeks paper-thin and her wrists like fresh, spring twigs. I hoped it was from the past twenty-four hours and not a slow deterioration I had missed in my absence.

"Clara," mom said softly. I came to her bedside and took her frail hand in mine. She looked to her sister. "Thanks for getting her, Jo."

Aunt Jo nodded. "Would you like some tea, Ginger?"

"That'd be great, thank you," mom said.

"Hey, mom. How ya feeling?" I said, kneeling down.

"I've been better, I've been worse. Doc says I'll be fine though."

"What happened?"

"Not quite sure. I take proper care with my insulin and you know I never touch sugar. Oh, sure, I like my wine on occasion, but doc has always said I'm allowed in moderation."

"Are they running more tests? Should you get a second opinion?"

She waved her hand dismissively. "Don't worry yourself, Clara. They're running some tests, and I'm sure there's a reasonable culprit. In the meantime, I'm to rest, and Doc O'Brien will be around to check in."

My heart warmed a little to think of our small-town doctor who still made the occasional house call, his little spectacles wrapped around a bald round head.

I squeezed mom's hand and forced a smile. "Well, I'm glad you're okay."

"And I'm glad you're here, Clara honey. Sorry it took me falling down to get you home."

Guilt clutched my heart. "Yeah. Me too, mom. Me too."

3

Dark hair sprawled in a shallow grave. Midnight waves, ebony in the moonlight, lapping, over frozen flesh. White eyes, empty and cold.

I lurched from sleep on the brink of vomiting and drenched in sweat. I heaved, catching my breath. Fucking nightmares. I wiped my forehead and took a mental assessment of my location. Right. Point Redwood. Home sweet home.

The promise of a warm day peered in through the blinds, basking the hangover of my childhood in soft white beams. I glanced around the small room, relatively untouched in the past years. Amateur artwork and world maps hung in place of movie posters and volleyball trophies or whatever normal kids had in their rooms. I never had enough friends in the normal classification to really know what their rooms might have looked like.

I reluctantly pushed my body from bed. Mom had set up an art easel and a work desk and upgraded the bedding and window dressings, but most of my belongings remained. A bookshelf of classics and travel guides I'd never use, my first award-winning poem written in precise calligraphy framed on the wall, a montage of photos. I glanced over the memories captured in faded color. My best friend Ruthi and I in our plaid skirts and Oxford blouses. Pink streaks in my blonde hair in rebellion to our Catholic school homogeny. Her brother Sean's navy polo untucked, a rip in his khakis. His dark hair disheveled over wily blue eyes and a boyish smirk. I fought a tear.

I looked at the next and my heart nearly stopped. I picked up the picture frame and dabbled in that faded memory. Ruthi and I on the beach that last spring break, Sean in his army fatigues, one arm around either of us. We were so hopeful. Smiles all around. Did we know that in a matter of months it would all be over? We should have lived so much after that. Should have studied and laughed and stumbled home drunkenly arm-in-arm, inconsiderately singing show tunes to the chagrin of everyone around us. I closed my eyes and pressed back the tears. I set down the photograph. I wasn't going back there today.

After I'd caffeinated and fixed mom some local, organic scrambled eggs, we sat in the kitchen finishing our coffee over a game of Gin Rummy.

"What will you do today?" Mom asked.

"Whatever you need me to do," I said. I drew a card from the deck.

"Oh, that's sweet, honey. But I don't need much of anything. You should see the town a little. It's really come on these past years. New little boutiques up and down Main. Some really delicious restaurants."

It was nearly impossible not to smile at mom's unwavering enthusiasm for a town that shit on both of us.

"Oh? Maybe I'll drive down then," I said.

Mr. Muffins mewed off key at my feet, and I reached down to scratch his ancient kitty head.

"This guy is still alive, huh?"

Mom shrugged. "It would appear so. He'll outlive us all. They even have a little gallery of local art."

"Hmm?"

"In town. Had one of my paintings in there for a bit. Sold it to a tourist."

"Oh. That's great, mom. I'm glad you're still painting. You're so talented." It was a compliment I didn't have to force with her. Raw talent was just truth. Truth.

She gave a little happy hum and discarded an eight of hearts.

"Have you seen Sean?" Mom said.

My lungs tightened, and I paused mid-draw. I'd been afraid to ask what had happened to Sean, where he'd gone after the army. I didn't want to picture his life now. Settled with a pretty wife and a litter of ankle biters in some quiet suburb? Some mindless corporate job in San Francisco? I wanted to remember him as the boy who said he'd love me forever. But that was a different life.

"No," I brushed it off. "When would I have done that?"

"Clara. Don't you think he'd love to see you?"

"Is Sean even in town?" I said, a little bitterly. Even his name on my tongue stung.

Mom looked up at me as if I'd asked my own name.

"Didn't you know?"

"Know what, mom?"

"Oh, that he came back a couple of years ago."

The air went from my lungs. Sean was here? A mere mile from me at this very minute? Why would he ever come back to this place?

"Oh, I...didn't know," I said, trying not to react.

"I'm sure after being over there in the Mid East, he needed the comfort of home."

The cold comfort of ghosts. I knew he'd been to combat shortly after everything had happened here. I used to think getting sent to Iraq—that desolate, war-torn wasteland—was a blessing for him. Something to distract him from the hell that had become our town. Much the same way I'd run off to Asia. But maybe he'd only marched off to face another hell.

"He set up with a little business downtown. I think he has a little house off Mountain House Rd.," Mom went on.

What would that be like? To have gone so far—to the ends of the world, to the depths of civilization—only to return to the thing that broke you? I laid down a three-card straight and discarded.

"Rummy," I said unaffectedly, pushing out thoughts of Sean.

Mom shrugged and made a little quip.

"Glad to see you haven't lost your edge. He looks good."

"Who?"

"Sean."

"Geez, mom. Are we still talking about him? Sean is ancient history."

She quipped again and pursed her lips in amusement—a whatever-you-tell-yourself kind of expression.

By noon, the air in mom's house was suffocating me so I figured I might as well check out the town I once called home. I pulled on some skinny jeans and riding boots and a fitted tee shirt and headed out. I stopped short, remembering I'd need a light coat, even in summer, and grabbed my leather jacket.

The coastal air ripped through my lungs as I stepped outside. I breathed it in deeply, almost tasting the eucalyptus and sea salt. Summer on our little slice of coast could be winter anywhere else, but it lent a certain respite from the sticky days of Austin. Summers in Austin brought the siren's call of sultry nights and frozen margaritas to free you from the doldrums of monotonous life. But it was also a vortex of Texas brimstone. Some cleansing sea air was much in order.

Borrowing mom's little Ford SUV, I headed down the road into town. Waves of nostalgia flew by me as I sped down the winding, tree-lined road, still damp from the morning mist. I found parking near the tiny town square, and I sat behind the wheel for a few moments, taking it all in. It was surreal to be back here after eight years. It all seemed like a distant dream now—some childhood memory you weren't quite sure actually happened but still replayed vividly in the moments between dreams and the dawn. I took a breath, grabbed my purse and stepped out into the familiar unknown—the contradiction in that thought not lost on me.

The midday sun danced off the remnants of the misty morning, sending shards of platinum light dancing down the old sidewalks. Despite the summer sun, a chilly breeze swept by, climbing up my spine. I wandered in and out of a few summer tourist lures—the one time of year the town showed vibrancy. It hadn't changed much, although a few boutiques and cafes had indeed popped up along the main square, lending a quaint little vibe to the mundane. I passed a young mother pushing a baby stroller. Her eyes darted to me, looking me over then lowering with wariness. Who did she see? An old man coughed as I passed by. Two boys on bikes gave me amused glances. I felt curious eyes on me every time I passed another person. My paranoia festered like a wound inside me.

Did they remember me? Of course they did—everyone remembered who Clara Kendrick was—they would forever need someone to blame for what happened here. But did they recognize me? It's difficult to judge how much we change over the years. After all, we only see the gradual shifts each passing day in the mirror—a slight new angle, a new freckle, a subtle line. Day by day, these little things creep up. What does eight years of physical evolution look like in one fell swoop?

My phone buzzed.

Mom: Can you get my prescription from Wilson's?

Me: Sure. Anything else?

Mom: And a ginger ale.

Me: Sure.

I WOULD NEVER ADMIT IT TO MY FOURTEEN-YEAR-OLD SELF, but I was relieved to find slivers of my childhood still intact in Point Redwood. Wilson's Drugstore stood faithfully at the corner of Main Street and Ocean as it had for some hundred years—the way any good small-town pharmacy should. I closed my eyes and could still smell the saccharine aroma of cheap ice cream and hear the bad Beach Boys covers that always crooned in a low hum throughout. A few kids burst out of the door with ice cream cones, nearly knocking me over. I stepped in, jingling the little bells tied to the door, and inhaled the blend of sugar and medicine.

Despite the weather outside, you could always tell it was summer in Point Redwood. The shelves were well-stocked, signaling the onset of anticipated tourism. Come winter, every shelf would be a skeleton, a few lingering candy bars and dated magazines hanging from its bones. I ducked my head as I brushed past patrons browsing face wash and batteries, hoping the years had changed me beyond recognition. I had certainly changed on the inside.

"Clara?" a chipper bird voice said.

Fuck.

I stiffened, found the fake smile I used with my coworkers and lifted my head. A compact brunette in yoga pants and a high ponytail was staring at me with disbelief, her big doe eyes looking anime against her tiny features. I thought fast and hard.

"Gina," I said after a brief pause, thankfully recognizing the tell-tale beauty mark under her right eye.

"Oh my God!" Gina squealed. "I had no idea you were back in town!"

And I had no idea you stayed.

"Yeah, I just came in last night kinda unexpected. Family thing," I said.

"I heard your mom took a spill. So sorry."

"Thanks, Gina. Um, how've you been?"

She still had the porcelain skin and tight frame of her former ballerina self. I won't go so far as to say we were friends, but over the years, Gina was at least nice to me. We'd had a team project once in sixth grade, and her mom had me over for dinner. That was before I became the pariah of Point Redwood. Bad influences didn't get invited to slumber parties and Sunday dinners.

"I go by Georgina now, if you don't mind. It's my real name, isn't it?" She laughed a little, bright white teeth beaming. "Things are good. I've been back here a few years now."

"Are you still a dancer?" I bumbled, having no idea what else to say. I was terrible at small talk.

"Oh, I danced for a bit in college but ended up getting

my teaching credential. You're pretty much dead as a balle-rina at twenty anyway. I teach 3rd grade at St. Thomas now, if you can believe that."

I could.

"Cool. Well, it's good to see you. I gotta get some things for mom," I said.

"Oh right, well, don't want to keep you then. Hey, are you around for a bit? I'd love to know what you've been up to all these years. How about a drink before you leave town?"

Can't. Books to read. Memories to dodge.

I waited for her to recant her polite offer.

"Uh, sure. I can do tomorrow, I guess," I said after a moment when it appeared she was quite in earnest.

Georgina beamed.

"Perfect! I'll have Jim watch the kiddo. Here." She reached into her purse for a paper and pen and jotted down her number. "Text me tomorrow afternoon sometime and let me know."

I wanted to slap myself for saying yes. Why would she care what I was up to, anyway? So she could talk about my downward spiral at her next book club? Hate to disappoint you bitches, but I am not, in fact, a crack whore.

I walked over to the pharmacy counter, patiently waiting my turn as a few old ladies diddle-dawdled over small talk with the pharmacist. I stepped up and smiled politely.

The pharmacist gave me a quizzical look, which quickly faded to disbelief.

"Holy hell. Be damned if it's not Clara Bell Kendrick," he said.

God, I fucking hated that nickname. Was I a cow? I

smiled at the ginger-haired pharmacist, mind computing quickly to place him. Ginger, freckles, small nose, nice eyes. Basketball. Old money. Sean's grade. Miles? Niles. Nigel. Nigel!

"Nigel," I said warmly, praying as always that I was right. His face lit up, and I exhaled a little.

"Back in town?" he asked.

Unless I'm a hologram.

"Yeah, for mom."

"Yeah, sorry to hear she's ill. I always liked her." His tone implied, despite what everyone else thinks of her.

"Yeah, thanks. You're a pharmacist now," I stated, equally as obviously and dumbly.

"Sure am." He pointed to his nametag. "You here to pick up her prescription?"

I nodded, and he pulled up the records on the computer.

"All right, looks like we have Pradaxa. One dose, twice daily with food," he said matter-of-factly. "Pretty simple, but call me if she has questions. No copay, so if you could just sign here, you're all set."

"Thanks, Nigel," I said putting my mark on the receipt. I had a thought then but wasn't sure if I wanted to go there. He sensed my hesitation.

"Something else?" he asked.

I glanced behind me and seeing there was no line, went for it.

"Doc O'Brien says mom's stroke was a complication of her diabetes. But she's taken those meds for thirty years or more. Do you think—think anything could have been wrong with her insulin?"

"Do you mean the wrong dosage?" He sounded a little offended that his staff would make a mistake.

I bit my lip. "Possibly. Or even that it could have been

ineffective or a dud or something? It's just strange that all of a sudden this would happen after all this time."

Nigel blew air through his lips and gave a little shrug.

"I'm not her doctor of course, and O'Brien is a good man, but it's more likely that she'd missed some doses and messed up the effectiveness rather than any kind of defect with the medication. Those things are really rare, even for a little small-town place like this."

A line started to form behind me.

I nodded. "Of course. I'm sure you're right. Well, good to see you. Take care."

"You too, Clara. Give your mom my regards."

I strolled down Main St. back toward mom's car, a sense of unease festering in the pit of my stomach. It was unfounded maybe, but to me, the picturesque façade of this little tourist trap town was still a portico to the dark strata that lay beneath.

4

Stupid girl. Stupid, stupid girl. Being where she doesn't belong.

I feel the soft flesh of her neck between my fingers as I squeeze and think about her. Think about why she's back here. Think about what she deserves. How this soft flesh in my grip should be hers instead. I feel the fragile bones collapse beneath my pressure. The blow to her head has stunned her like a helpless animal, and so she doesn't squirm.

The little girl's eyes glass over as her shock fades to fear, then to eternal darkness.

I hate her even more for making me do it.

The next morning I sat sipping bitter black coffee and picking at a wheat bagel smothered in whipped cream cheese, debating how soon it would be acceptable to get the hell out of this town. Sure, I guess coming home had been a nice break from the monotony of my boring job, but if I were going to take a break from life, I'd just as soon be in a jungle halfway across the world. Mr. Muffins purred at my feet, nudging me with a discordant mew at my indifference to him.

"Oh, quit your whining," I said, picking him up and setting him on my lap. "So needy in your old age." I scratched his head, and he nuzzled into my belly contentedly.

I picked up the daily Mendocino Independent on the table, smiling at the feel of a real old-fashioned newspaper in my hand, and scanned the front-page headlines of the open B section. County Fair was in full swing. Don't miss the FFA auction. Expect higher gas prices. Prepare for another drought. I flipped it back to the front page.

The tidal wave of memories barreled toward me,

crashing with ferocity against my composure. The recall went feral inside me. The air fled my lungs, and I struggled to re-inflate them. I scanned the article and chills scuttled up my spine.

Mom came shuffling into the kitchen, her little walker scraping across the linoleum. Her hair was knotted on top of her head, wisps of silver and blonde nudging toward freedom. Her fuzzy cotton robe looked comically regal engulfing her frail frame, but I couldn't find laughter.

"Morning, Clara. Did you get some coffee? I've been up for a while so it might be cold." She stopped. "Everything all right, dear? Looks like you've seen a ghost."

Not far off, Mom. I didn't answer right away. My eyes went back to the paper.

Point Redwood, CA—*Local teen girl found dead on Bronner Beach.*

"Have you seen this?" I asked.

Mom bit her lip nervously then said, "Hmm? Oh, yes terrible thing. So sad." Mom moved to take a seat at the kitchen table across from me. She reached for a section of the paper and went about reading as if a bomb hadn't just gone off in my gut.

"Bronner Beach," I said almost under my breath. Almost unable to utter the words.

Mom pursed her lips and instinctively averted her pale blue eyes.

"Very sad."

"That's all you have to say?"

"This has nothing to do with Ruthi, honey. That was many years ago. It's tragic, yes, but a tragic coincidence. Nothing more."

The body of a teenage girl was found early this morning on Bronner Beach in the coastal village of Point Redwood.

Local police are ruling it a homicide. No suspects reported as of yet. The victim's identity has not yet been released, but sources have confirmed she attended St. Thomas High School locally.

In an instant, I was back there. Back on that beach. Ruthi's vacant eyes staring up at the pale moon. Sean falling into me as his shouts shattered the still small hours of the summer night. I pressed my eyes closed. This couldn't be happening again. Who hates this town that much?

Drunken Mermaid at 6 p.m. I groaned, thinking about the any number of old acquaintances I'd likely see at the local bar. My prayers that the traces of long tequila nights and tattoos would have aged me out of recognition were clearly misled, given Georgina and Nigel's insta-reaction earlier that day. I'd tried so hard to be invisible after everything that happened with mom years ago, and then Ruthi's death had to make mine the most recognizable face in town. People never forgot something like that in a place like this.

I hadn't been able to shake the news of that girl's death all day, but if I let it consume me, then I might never emerge from the dark place again.

I stared at my open suitcase and the few items I'd haphazardly thrown together when I got Jo's late-night call. I chewed my lip, scanning my outfit options. I naturally wanted to look my best in the event of running into people I knew, but I also didn't want to seem like I was trying TOO hard. It was just Point Redwood, after all. Eventually, I slipped on my favorite dark wash skinny jeans (which Aiden affectionately referred to as my butt snuggers) and a V-neck tank top that somewhat concealed my imposing cleavage in the event that the middle school bra-snapping brigade was still at large. Some childhood anxieties never disappear. I pulled on some stacked boots and fixed up my face and hair a little.

After tucking mom in with hot chamomile tea and Netflix, I headed into town to see what a summer night in Point Redwood had to offer.

I didn't know what to expect upon entering the Drunken Mermaid, formally Pirate's Cove. I remembered the place as a declining spot for weathered fishermen and other locals winding down on Friday nights or a place to snag some mediocre chowder from a can during the day, but the upgraded exterior suggested someone had finally given the dilapidated staple a little TLC. New thatched layers had replaced the weather-worn shabby shingles clinging to distant memories. The windows once etched with salt and cracks, had a pearly sheen. A few patrons sat at the mellow bar, coddling tall pints and picking at bowls of pretzels. The sun was preparing to settle into its bed for the evening, relinquishing its duties for the day. The glow of the impending sunset seeped through the windows, dancing on the polished wooden bar and reflecting off the antique anchors and seaside treasures adorning the wall.

I spotted a few faces that conjured memories from my youth, but they were like aged masks of their former selves. I'd done my best to forget those faces, anyway. Crime victims will often tell you how they'll never forget that face. But who wants to remember the likeness of your tormentor?

Are you a whore like your mother?

Where'd you get that bruise? Dad get bored with your mom?

How much did your boob job cost?

As if fourteen-year-olds got their tits done.

Shake it off, Clara. You got this.

Georgina sat at a bar stool, fingering a glass of white wine and chatting to the young female bartender whose face I knew, but couldn't place. As my heeled boot clicked against the wooden floorboards, a few salty old timers looked up with suspicion. I smiled, happy to see a little Point Redwood flare still intact. After a split-second inspection, they indifferently turned back to their beers. Georgina saw my approach and waved eagerly. I took a breath and said farewell to my anonymity for my duration in town.

"Clara! So glad you came." Georgina hopped up and gave me a light, friendly hug. Her teeny frame barely made an impact against my hardened torso. Her dark curls bounced as she pulled away.

"Hey, G. Thanks for the idea," I said. I had to admit that Georgina's bright smile was infectious.

"Do you remember Olivia Baxter?" She said, turning toward the bartender.

Olivia Baxter. Tall, cute nose, dark eyes. Edgy look. Olivia Baxter. Chubby girl. Girls' locker room. Period panties. Viral photo. Shit, yes, Olivia Baxter. I tried not to laugh as I extended my hand.

"Yeah, hi. Good to see you. Not sure we knew each other well," I said.

Olivia shrugged, all traces of the timid fat girl long gone or well-hidden beneath eyeliner.

"Yeah, if you weren't relentlessly teasing me back then, then you probably wouldn't know me," she said, half smiling. I knew that feeling. I saw the thoughts in her shadowed eyes. Yeah, I know some cheerleader texted nude pics of my fat ass to everyone, but your best friend was murdered, so I think you win.

I smiled back, and we shared a brief fuck Point Redwood moment.

Sorry you're still here, my eyes said.

Sorry you had to come back, hers said.

"Nice tats," Olivia said, nodding approvingly to the shoulder-to-elbow ink of my left arm half sleeve. I smiled and noticed the Asian lettering on her forearm.

"You too."

"Drink?" she asked.

"Jameson, rocks."

Olivia nodded and gave the bottle a heavy hand.

"SO WHEN DID YOU GET ALL OF THOSE?" GEORGINA SAID A little scandalized, nodding toward the half sleeve of memorialized memories on my arm.

A sultry Chiang Mai night. A frozen Berlin escape. A Point Redwood basement. Buzzing, pain, forgetting.

"Just over the years. It gets a little addicting."

"You're nuts! I couldn't even bring myself to get a double ear piercing," Georgina laughed. "Although I did birth a human."

"Fuck, I'll take a needle to any part of my body over that," I laughed.

"Well, you've got the arms for them, anyway. I mean, you're in some seriously good shape, Clara." Georgina shook her head, smiling. I blushed a little.

"Thanks. Working out is good therapy."

"Okay, but seriously, how'd you get that ripped and keep your boobs?" She said through a chuckle, a small blush lighting up her pale cheeks.

I laughed as well. "Cursed, I guess. These bitches won't go away no matter what I do."

"I sort of want to hate you, but how could I possibly hate someone so dang cool?"

I was cool. Imagine that.

I raised my glass, and we clinked. It was good to laugh with an old friend in an old place. Wipe some of the rotting memories away and replace them with something lighter.

The night went on, a lot more enjoyable than I'd cantankerously imagined it would. It was nice to have a female to commiserate with, even if the conversation bordered on the mundane. We all needed a little nothing in our day sometimes. Conversation with other women tended to intimidate me. I was a little different--I had a lot of scars. And they didn't always know what to do with that. I also had a low capacity for mindless bullshit. I didn't care about The Bachelor or spa days or what so-and-so meant when she said whatever to you at the last party, and now she hasn't liked any of your Instagram posts in a week.

Chatting with Georgina wasn't like that at all. We conversed on about the routine unfoldings of life, sure. Georgina married a boy she met in college who was fascinated by small-town life and liked the idea of running his Internet startup from the chilly beach. Little Eli came along shortly after, rounding out their little world. Now she taught the future of tomorrow all they needed to know and had dinner with her parents every Sunday. Blissful domesticity.

"What's that like? Teaching here in PR, I mean. Seems like nothing's changed," I said.

Georgina shrugged. "That's pretty much true. A lot of the same players as always, just a grown-up version of the game. A lot of the same cliques still apply. Kind of comical, really."

I shuddered, thinking about the grown-up version of our high school mean girls.

"I don't know how you could stand it," I said with a smile but more serious than not.

"I just don't let it get to me. The moms can be pretty intense. For people whose lives haven't really amounted to all that much, they can be pretty damn competitive. From everything from who gets to be Mary in the Christmas pageant, to who memorized their state capitals first, to how well their kid's shoes match their lunch box. The moms care more than the kids, I think."

"Sounds terrifying," I said.

"Oh and there's this one little trio. Mother Mary help whoever crosses them. It's like the other moms need permission from them to plan their kids' lunches."

"A little Mama Mafia."

Georgina laughed so hard she snorted.

"Oh Lord, yes," she said, wiping a tear. We laughed hard for a moment before regaining composure.

"So you're in Austin? Never married?" Georgina said.

"Never married."

"Seeing anyone at least?"

At least. Did my semi-regular trysts with Aiden save me from the Ninth Circle of Singledom?

"Oh, not really." I heard my own voice creep up an octave. "I work a lot."

Georgina nodded and didn't press the issue. Suddenly, her attention pulled away to something behind me. She let out a little amused snort.

"What is it?" I asked.

"It's just entertaining to watch the girls practically fall off their bar stools when he walks in."

I turned to see what had caught her notice, but

somehow I already knew. I felt it like a summer breeze. I smelled him. My heart stopped. My gut turned. My breath fled.

Sean.

Sean, effortless in country boy chic, was walking through the room. Plaid work shirt rolled to the elbows, Levis and worn-out boots. Corded forearms detailing our memories in sharp brush strokes. I looked away and focused on my Jameson. Sultry amber dripping over crystal ice. How long had it been since I'd felt the rush of him?

"Clara, everything okay?" Georgina asked.

"Yeah, fine," I muttered, not looking up. Georgina glanced back to Sean, then to me then finally it clicked.

"Oooh, right. I completely forgot."

"Forgot?" I looked up at her, incredulous.

"About Sean. And you."

How could the woman fucking forget? Sean and I were basically the same person our entire adolescence. I held back an angry retort and breathed. Did I really care whom she loved in high school?

"Yeah, you know we were a thing back in the day," I said casually. "I haven't seen him since…" Since the day I left. "It's been a long time."

Georgina smiled understandingly, smooth porcelain doll cheeks barely making a line.

"Those were rough years for you," she said with heartfelt compassion. I choked down a wave of unwanted emotion.

"Yeah," I manage to say with composure. "But it was a long time ago."

I dared a glance back up at Sean. He was offering friendly hellos to everyone he passed, looking strangely confident in his surroundings. He smiled playfully at two middle-aged women at the end, who erected their spines and thrust out their busts in response.

"Looks like he comes here often," I said more to myself, but Georgina perked up.

"Huh? Oh, well it's his bar. Didn't you know?"

I raised my brows. "Like his spot?"

She laughed. "No, like his bar. He bought it a couple years back and really fixed it up. You might not remember the old place, but it was a real hole."

Sean's bar. Not only did Sean come back here, but he also bought a business. Set down roots.

"I did not know," I said slowly. I tilted the rest of my whiskey down my throat and tried to breathe normally.

Sean turned then and saw me. The wide grin on his face fell flat in an instant. Our eyes locked. The shock of his electric stare knocked me from my equilibrium. A million things unsaid hung in the air between us. He took a step toward me, and I stiffened. I wasn't ready for this. I would never be ready for this. He came all the way then, bridging the gap, his blue, almond eyes unsure of what he was coming toward.

He stopped a foot from me. His gaze took me in, then ran down my figure, stopping to linger on where my breasts tested the fabric of my thin tank top. I imagined my face was a pale blank canvas as I stared up at him.

The boy I knew lingered in the man before me. Those same eyes, that same firm jaw—both hardened with the weight of burden. The softness of his boyish countenance had been usurped by a jaded observer. Had I been a brick in that consignment of strife?

My eyes raked over his toned physique—sculpted shoulders dipping into a tapered waist. I enjoyed the way his figure was still all lean sinew—like that of a runner or outdoorsman—signaling his structure came from real life physical assertion and not simply powerlifting and ten pounds of white meat chicken per day. But my God, it was strange to see the boy converted into a grown man, the soft lines hardened and worn. Did he think the same of me? Had all trace of my youth been left at a rest stop somewhere in my past?

He stared at me, cold and calculating.

Did I blame him?

My arm burned anew with memory and empathy. Every painful memory I'd tried to burn out with needle and ink flared to the surface as if still raw and bleeding in a Chiang Mai bar.

As if feeling the sting himself, Sean's eyes fell to the colorful swirls of my left bicep. The questions danced in his sapphire eyes. What did it all mean? What were these stories on the Illustrated Woman? I would never be able to confess the truth of every stroke. How could I? How do you really explain a feeling? That under the skin, blood-boiling, heartbreaking reality of a raw soul? We can't because the truth is too agonizing.

I snapped back to the moment.

"Sean," the word slipped out of my mouth timidly. My recognition gave him the proof he seemed to be searching for. Emotions waged war on his expression until they relented to anger.

"What are you doing here?" he said with a mixture of confusion and irritation.

"My mom...she, um, she's sick." I blabbered.

"Yeah, I heard. Sorry to hear. But why are you here? In my bar."

I struggled. Would he really believe that me walking into his bar was happy happenstance?

"I was meeting Gina for a drink," I glanced back to her for a lifesaver. She smiled brightly.

"Hi Sean," she said, chipper. He stared at her then nodded in recognition.

"Hey, G. How're you doing? Where's Jim?"

"At home with Eli. Needed a girl's night out."

Sean smiled thinly then turned his eyes back to me. "Okay, then. Good to see you," he said stiffly and turned to go.

The words nearly knocked me to my knees. That was it? Eight years and a 'Good to see you?' I sat, patiently waiting for more, but he didn't offer an addendum.

"You all right?" Georgina asked.

"Yeah. Fine. We just...there's just a lot of history there that we've never really worked out. It's complicated."

"Things around here can never be simple."

"Do you see him often?" I asked.

She shrugged. "A bit. He and Jim—my husband—they're friends. We hang out with them every so often."

"Them?" I shouldn't ask, but I couldn't resist the burning question. "So he's seeing someone then?"

Georgina looked a little uncertain.

"Oh, um. Yes. Tabby Gates." She said the name almost under her breath, so it took me a moment to make the connection.

Tabby Gates? Head cheerleader, choir singer, virgin-club, saccharine Tabby Gates? With my Sean? I almost laughed, thinking she had to be kidding.

Every thought running through my brain must have been apparent on my face.

"Yeah, I know what you're thinking. But she's a lot different now than you'll remember her. Still a bit of an uptight perfectionist, but she's less...in your face about it. She's a sweet girl, really," Georgina said.

I took a breath. I wanted to protest the absurdity of that statement but caught myself. I didn't think back on Tabby as a sweet girl, trailing behind her trio of haughty, self-righteous bullies. But hadn't we all changed so much? Wasn't the Point Redwood we all knew just a shadow of a memory?

"We go to the same yoga studio," Georgina added.

Of course you do, woman. There's only one. Likely owned by another ex-cheerleader.

"Oh," I offered meekly. "How long has that been a thing? She and Sean I mean."

"Hmm. I think a couple of years. Right around the time Sean moved back here."

She squeezed my hand.

"I'm sorry, I didn't even think twice about meeting up here. It's been so long, and this is just really the best place in town nowadays. We always come here, really. I never thought after all this time you two wouldn't have...that there'd be..."

"It's okay," I interrupted her. "It's just been a long time since I've even seen him. Just kinda strange. Hey Olivia, another?"

I sat sipping my drink, processing, as Georgina distracted me with chatter.

Did I really expect I wouldn't run into him if he were in town?

Whiskey finally broke down my resolve, and I was determined to have a conversation with Sean. Just a normal conversation, like normal people who haven't seen each other in years have. I found some courage, excused myself from Georgina, and moseyed up to the end of the bar where Sean was doing some paperwork.

"Hey," I said softly.

His sharp eyes flicked up, and he stared at me silently.

"Hey." His tone was flat. I struggled through my buzz to find the right words, but none would come.

"Did you want something?" Sean asked.

"I just wanted to...say hi."

He sat up straight and set down his pen.

"Didn't we already do that?"

Just like Sean to make everything difficult.

"I just...can't we just talk for a minute?" I said.

"What about?"

"Anything. How are you? What have you been doing? I can't just sit there drinking and gossiping like you're not standing thirty feet away from me for the first time in eight years."

He leaned back in his stool and considered me. I was suddenly self-conscious about whether my intoxication was showing.

"I'm fine. I live in Point Redwood, and I own this bar. Anything else you'd like to know?"

For years, I'd imagined what it would be like to see Sean again. But this wasn't exactly what I'd envisioned. For starters, he was angrier than I'd anticipated. The years had hardened him into a steel shell of the already ornery boy I'd loved a lifetime ago.

"I take it you're still angry," I said.

He laughed incredulously and shook his head. Then he reached over the bar and grabbed the bottle of Jameson, filling up a tumbler neat. He took a deep swallow.

"I'm not angry, Clara. There's nothing left to be angry about. The past is the past. I've moved on. You should too."

"I have!" I added, too severely.

He nodded, impassive.

"Good."

I wanted to bolt, but I wasn't ready to pry myself away. After so much time, I still felt a magnetic pull toward him. I finally turned, not knowing what else to say.

"I just…" I struggled against the tide of confusion in me.

"I have work to do," he interrupted me. "If you need anything else, Olivia can help you. But I'm really not in the mood for nostalgic chit-chat, okay?"

I opened my mouth, then shut it. I nodded.

"I never meant to hurt you, Sean," I said as I turned to go.

"Tell your mom I hope she gets better soon."

I glanced back, but he had his head in the paperwork again.

WHEN I GOT HOME THAT NIGHT, BUZZING WITH THE BURN OF whiskey, I climbed onto my bed. I texted Lola. She didn't know everything about my past, but she knew enough to know I sported some pretty deep scars from this place.

Fuck this town. Seriously.

Lola: Write it out, girl.

I pulled out my notebook and pen. Old school. I could barely form the thoughts in my swirling mind, but they needed to come out. They flew from my pen, liberated onto the page. Truth? You want truth, Lola? Seeing Sean was like seeing a piece of your insides you mislaid somewhere along your journey and thought was forever lost to you, lying on the side of the road. Seeing it, reaching for it to slide it back into place and make you whole again, and it just slipping through your grasp. There's some fucking truth.

But he'll never look at me without seeing Ruthi. There's some truth.

This town will never forgive me for letting her die. There's some truth.

Reckless daughter like reckless mother. Truth. Truth. Truth.

My hand cramped, and I leaned back on my pillow.

My phone buzzed. A little message banner popped up.

When you coming back? Missing those tits.

Aiden. I laughed incredulously at his oblivion. So simple. A welcome distraction.

Me: Not just yet. Being a good daughter.

Aiden: I can be your daddy.

Gross, I laughed out loud. I might have daddy issues, but not those kinds.

Me: If you want to play daddy, try the Alpha Phi house.

Aiden: I love it when you talk dirty. Want a dick pic?

I laughed and set my phone down. He did know how to brighten my mood, the beautiful, overgrown child. I could have used his arms around me then, pulling me into his warm body. The feel of his hard dick pressed against my backside. Quite honestly, I was more likely to win in a street fight over Aiden, but even a strong woman wants to feel arms around her at night.

I closed my eyes and leaned back into my pillows. I slipped my hand under the band of my yoga leggings, down in between my thighs and pictured Aiden's taut form on top of me.

Point Redwood, CA—*Police have identified 16-year-old Hannah March of Point Redwood as the victim of a homicide. March was found dead early Saturday morning on Bronner Beach, a popular site for camping and local parties.*

March suffered a head wound, but officials are ruling the official cause of death strangulation. March had not been reported missing when her body was discovered. Anyone with information is urged to contact Detective Ricky Lindsey at the Point Redwood Police Department at 707-323-6696.

HANNAH MARCH'S DISTANT EYES STARED AT ME FROM HER school photo on the front page of the Mendocino Independent. Her dark hair tumbled around her shoulders, and her pale face was ethereal. An uncanny resemblance to my best friend.

Same look, same death, same place. A tragic coincidence?

"Did you know her?" I asked, looking up at mom who was sitting across the kitchen table from me. With barely one thousand people in town, everyone knew everything about you here. Why was mom not more upset?

Mom shook her head. "Not directly, no. Family was new to town."

"New to town? Why on Earth would a family with a teenager just up and move to Point Redwood?"

Mom shrugged narrow shoulders and smiled thinly.

"Beats me. I don't know why folks do what they do. Maybe they just longed for a quieter existence. Small towns are quite en vogue these days."

A quieter existence. This place would never be such a thing for me. This place would always scream with the clamor of raucous memories.

"I'd seen her folks just recently in church too. Such a shame," Mom said.

I snorted. "You still go to St. Thomas? After all the shit this town put you through."

Mom gave me an incredulous look. "Clara, honey. You don't turn your back on God because of other people's mistakes."

I stood and fetched another cup of coffee. I walked back to the table and stared at the paper again. I scanned the faded black ink. The coroner put the time of death at 3 a.m. My heart contracted, then rolled in slow, steady beats. I was suddenly cold and flushed at the same time.

"Clara. Clara, what's wrong? You're pale as milk," Mom said.

"The time," I said, softly. "She was killed at 3 a.m."

I flicked my eyes to mom, who stared at me knowingly. She'd already connected the dots; I could see it in her pale eyes. When you're so close to such tragedy, you remember those minute details like time of death.

"A coincidence, honey."

"Look at her, mom. She looks just like Ruthi. What if..." I couldn't bring the words to fruition on my tongue.

Mom reached across the table and took my hand with a gentle squeeze.

"A coincidence," she repeated.

Her calm indifference set a match to my temper.

"Mom," I snapped. "How can you think it's a coincidence? Same manner of death, same looking girl, SAME TIME? They never found out what happened—"

"Calm down. Don't get worked up about something that isn't anything. How do they know exactly what time she was killed, anyway? I know it's strange, and I can only imagine the memories it brings up, but it's just a coincidental tragedy."

Tense silence danced between us for a few moments as we sipped our coffee. Anger stewed in me at my mother's lack of sympathy to what this meant to me. At my sacrifice in even being home to begin with. Even back then, she hadn't fully understood what I had lost. Why I had to stay away. Why the guilt consumed me to the point where I couldn't even look anyone in the eye.

I pushed up from the kitchen table forcefully.

"I'm heading out," I said.

"Where to?"

"I don't know. Just out," I said like an insolent teenager. Nothing like being back home to reignite your repressed adolescent angst.

Mom gazed at me with such understanding, I suddenly felt guilty for my petulance. How did moms know exactly how to push your hidden buttons?

"Sorry, mom. It's just difficult being back here. And this," I nodded to the paper, "Who would do this? Who would do this to this town again?"

"Don't go chasing ghosts where there aren't any," Mom said and turned back to the paper.

8

I left the house annoyed, frustrated, angry and quite honestly, a little scared. Though I couldn't quite identify what I was scared of. My usual coping methods knocked—find the nearest bar, ice my brain with a stiff scotch and text Aiden. Drunken fuck my way to oblivion. But Aiden was 1,700 miles from here—likely sleeping off a hangover pretzeled around a UT freshman. And there was no way in Hell I was distracting myself with any male from this town.

Not even Sean? My subconscious poked. Especially not Sean.

A few minutes later, I found myself sitting at Patsy's Beachside Café, sipping house white wine (more acceptable before noon than scotch, I figured) and jotting down words in my notebook. Being back here was proving more overwhelming than I'd anticipated, but I couldn't let this anger and fear consume me.

It was strange to curiously watch the town go by—a town that was home for eighteen years but now felt like a fishbowl. People watching had become one of my favorite pastimes in Austin. Sitting on the sidewalk outside a little café, watching the world pass by. Those decked out in polished suits, ready to conquer the day; those flaunting their aesthetic apathy. Was it ignorance or uncaring? I would watch the entire world go by in those moments— the way the men glance when they think you're not looking. The way the man with flowers willfully looks straight ahead. He won't be accused of unfaithfulness. The oblivious teen girl on her phone, the distracted mother, the asshole who cuts you off. Strolling, jogging, strollering, sauntering. We all have our own pace.

In my hometown, the same patterns rang true, if on a slightly smaller scale. Humanity in its many forms. My little town was a time warp in the center of a modern world.

My thoughts drifted to the days following that horrible night eight years ago, as they often did once a healthy buzz kicked in.

"They'd found tearing and evidence of sexual assault," they said of my best friend, as though it were a poorly scripted primetime crime drama. I'll never forget those cold, medicinal words for as long as I live. Or forget the chilly interrogation room as Sean and I sat, zombies, being questioned for hours. The same question asked twenty different ways. It didn't change anything. We didn't know anything. And where were we? What were Sean and I doing? In the lighthouse, you say?

Yes, in the lighthouse. It's all our fault, officers. Death by neglect.

"Clara?" a high-pitched voice rang out. "Clara Kendrick?"

I looked up from my notebook and wine to see a woman my age with a mop of curly brown hair looking down at me dubiously from a narrow, marsupial face. Her arms were loaded with shopping bags. I stared at her, trying to place the familiar aspect.

"Oh my God, look at you," the woman said with a hint of amusement as if the sight of me sitting there with my notebook and wine was extraordinarily scandalous.

"Hi," I said awkwardly, fumbling for her identity. The computer in my brain went into overdrive. She must have gone to St. Thomas, but I couldn't place her.

"You don't recognize me, do you?" she said, mock pouting.

Why do grown women pout?

I began to make an argument to the contrary, but it was futile.

"Sorry, no," I admitted. "I haven't been back here in a long time."

"It's Maryanne. Danson." She added when the first name still didn't ring a bell. Then it clicked. Maryanne. Yearbook. Drama Club. Mean Girl Groupie.

"Oh, wow. Hi," I said, once I placed her. "I'm sorry, you look...really different."

"Losing 100 pounds will alter your appearance slightly," she said smugly. She twisted with a slight show-offy turn in her hips.

"I'll say. You look great, Maryanne. Good to see you," I pulled my features into a smile.

An awkward pause seized the moment, neither of us having much to offer up by way of scintillating conversation.

"And look at you. Haven't changed a bit. Well, except for," she glanced down at my arm sleeve disapprovingly. "A few more of those. So edgy." She gave a little shoulder raise and a nose scrunch that bordered on distaste.

I pursed my lips into a placid smile, not appreciating her judgmental gaze. I knew one didn't get half her arm inked and not expect people to look, but admittedly, the judgment got really fucking old sometimes.

Our conversation hung suspended in the air for a few moments as I grasped for small talk that wouldn't come. She simply stared at me uncomfortably in anticipation. I was about to blow her off when the silence was broken by another woman our age approaching, holding a bag of groceries.

"Sorry that took so long. They had to find the cheese in the back—" She paused when she saw me, then shot me a bright white, welcoming smile through glossy pink lips. "Oh, I'm sorry to interrupt. Hi there." She extended her hand, then hesitated as realization dawned in her wide brown eyes.

My mental computer didn't need to work—there was no mistaking this one. She had changed over the years, to be sure—her coiled, Shirley Temple blonde curls now lay in more mature waves, a cleaner shade of blonde than my own dirty swirl of caramel and wheat. She was well-dressed in a floral, ladylike boatneck sundress and ballerina flats. An understated yet deliberate gold cross hung around her neck —a grown-up version of the Virgin Club president I remembered. Prettier than she'd been, or maybe just less juvenile. Her expression fell, and her doe eyes exuded something like anxiety.

"Tabby," I said, more dryly than I'd intended. "Nice to see you."

I took her hesitant hand in a firm shake. She studied my face for a moment as if to confirm my existence.

"Clara," she said gingerly, "I didn't know you were back in town."

Why would you? Everyone kept saying that as if it should have been on the downtown bulletin board.

FOR ONE WEEK ONLY: SHE'S BAA-AACK! COME
SEE THE GIRL WHOSE BEST FRIEND WAS BRUTALLY
MURDERED GRADUATION NIGHT!

It was hard to look Tabby in the eye with anything
resembling friendliness. Irrationally, I fumed at the idea of
her with Sean—my Sean. Don't be ridiculous, Clara.

"Yeah, just for a few days. Family stuff," I said.

"Oh, yes, I heard. Very sorry to hear." Tabby simpered
and shifted uncomfortably, her unease giving me a dollop of
satisfaction. I half-heartedly wondered if she was still a
virgin. If she wasn't, I bet she only did missionary.

"Thanks."

"You look...well," she said, awkwardly fumbling with the
tension.

"Thanks. You too." I wasn't lying. Much to my dismay,
she did look good. Slender and polished, ladylike, tasteful
makeup and pink nails, unblemished skin—Virgin Barbie.

The uncomfortable silence dragged on until I finally
said, "It was good to see you. Maybe I'll see you in church."

Tabby flicked her eyes to Maryanne. I could read her
face. Is she joking? Is she making fun of us? Yes, on all
accounts, ladies.

"Please give your mom my regards," Tabby said.

I smiled and stared until they fumbled an awkward
goodbye and went off about their day. I slammed back my
wine and rubbed my head. If Sean was spending his time
with that, then he was not the man I remembered. I chided
myself. You don't remember a man, Clara. You remember
a boy.

~

AFTER I FINISHED AT PATSY'S, I WANDERED THE STREETS FOR A

bit. The warmth of the summer day suddenly faded, and a violet haze spread its wings across the sky, turning the air with a chilly wind. I shivered against its onslaught.

"Odd weather," a husky voice said.

I snapped my head around. An old man with leathered skin and the crooked hands of a fisherman stood beside me. A tattered cap was pulled down around large ears, and he leaned on a cane, like a little caricature. He just needed a pipe.

"What's that?" I said, lost in my examination of him.

"Strange the way it turns like that. One moment we're basking in the simplicity of a summer day, then next someone brings a tempest with them."

He stared at me for a moment with dark, beady eyes—not smiling, nor frowning—just impassive. My skin prickled.

"Best get in somewhere safe, hmm?" Then the old man turned and wobbled in the opposite direction, his cane tapping against the sidewalk.

I shivered. This town was messing with my head.

I was browsing books in the little local bookshop, trying to shake off the old man's cryptic musings, when my phone rang. Mendocino number. I hesitated but answered.

"Hello?"

"Hi, is this Clara Kendrick?" a deep male voice said.

"Yes."

"Hi, Clara. I'm Detective Ricky Lindsey from the Mendocino County Sheriff's Department. Hope you don't mind, but your mom was good enough to give me your number."

"Um, ok," I said, nervously running my hands along used book spines.

"I was hoping you could come down to the Point Redwood Police Station to answer a few questions."

My heart thudded. "What about?"

"The murder of Hannah March."

I nearly dropped the phone.

"Miss Kendrick?"

"Why?" I asked dumbly.

"We just want to ask you a few questions. I assume you read about her death in the news?"

I closed my eyes and breathed into the phone, fighting down the spins.

"Miss Kendrick?"

"Yes, I did. But, why do you want to talk to me about it?"

"Please, just come down here. It's best we discuss it in person."

"Um, yeah, okay. I can be there in about ten minutes."

"Do you know where we're located?"

I fought down a ferocious laugh. Yes, sir. I'm quite familiar with the place.

9

The Point Redwood Police Department stood inconspicuously at the edge of the main drag of town. It hadn't changed much since my time sitting in the waiting room, staring down Officer Rhodes while I waited for mom to pick me up after my latest infraction—truancy, stealing cigarettes, drunk in public. Rookie Rhodes would sit in his chair, arms crossed and a little smirk playing at his yummy mouth. If it hadn't been for Sean, I would have absolutely tried to seduce Rhodes, and I'm reasonably certain I would have succeeded. He wasn't exactly an all-out perv, but back then he was twenty-three, with a set of muscles that suggested the testosterone was racing through his chiseled body at octane speeds. I think he would have found a way to justify sleeping with a sixteen-year-old girl with the body of a porn star. Okay, maybe I'm giving myself some credit here, but let's just say I was well-developed early on. Statutory lines are a little more blurred in small towns with low inventory.

Sean and mine's complete obsession with each other

through our teen years was seen as a glaring problem to a lot of busybodies. Concerned teachers and distant aunts and people I barely knew would lecture me on the merits of being free at my age. It was worrisome that I was so attached to a boy when I was still so young. I shouldn't compromise my virtue!

What they all failed to realize was that my uncompromising dedication to Sean probably kept me out of a lot of strange beds in an attempt to reconcile my adolescent rage and hormones. An indignant teen girl looking to numb the pain could do a lot worse than a steady boyfriend.

The low chatter of police banter and the smell of stale coffee and greasy junk food assaulted me as I stepped through the front door of PRPD.

I stepped up to the receptionist sitting behind the front desk. She glanced at me over her spectacles, recognition and censure flickering in her eyes.

"Um, hi. Clara Kendrick," I said.

"Mmm. Yes, you are." Her eyes ran over me. I shifted on my feet.

"Um, I'm here to see Detective—"

"Clara!" A bawdy male voice interrupted. A salt and pepper mustached detective in a gray suit and polka dotted tie walked over, waving. He had such a clichéd look about him, my mind instantly started turning him into a cartoon.

"Detective Ricky Lindsey," he extended a large hand.

"Hi," I said, timidly taking his shake.

"Thanks for coming down, Clara. This shouldn't take too long. Follow me this way, please."

I followed Lindsey through the small station, subtly glancing around to catch familiar faces, lying to myself that I wasn't looking for Rhodes. Would he still be here? And how old would he be now, early thirties? Would he still be hot or was he really only hot through the looking glass of teenage lust toward one in uniform, just out of reach? I wondered if he still had a thing for young girls. Was I still young enough?

Lindsey led me through the station to a private back room. I stepped in and yelped when I saw Sean sitting in a chair, drinking coffee from a paper cup. I took a breath, pressing my hand to my chest.

"Expecting someone else?" Sean said dryly.

"Not expecting anyone at all. But certainly not you."

"Please, have a seat, Clara," Lindsey said. "Coffee?"

I shook my head. "No, thank you."

He stepped around the table to the opposite side and sat. He set a file on the table, then folded his hands on top of it and looked at Sean and me in turn, not saying a word.

"You gonna tell us what this is all about?" Sean finally said.

"I'm sure you read the news this morning. About Hannah March."

My heart clenched. I knew what he wanted to speak to me about but hearing the words turned my stomach.

"Yeah, terrible. What's that got to do with us?" Sean said.

Lindsey's eyes darted between us. He opened the case file to reveal grisly photographs I did not want to see.

"Did you know her?" Lindsey asked.

"No," I said.

"Not really. I've seen her at Mass," Sean said.

Mass? I shot him a questing look. Grownup Sean went to Mass?

"Mmm, hmm. There's no real delicate way to put this. Hannah's murder is identical to your sister's," Lindsey said.

I felt Sean's tension and the shift in his body.

"Yes, it's hard not to see the resemblance," I said, softly, trying not to look at the grotesque images in front of me, nor those long-buried in the recesses of my memories. Sean's eyes hit the table.

"So?" Sean asked. I knew this side of him. The side behind the stone wall.

"You were there when your sister was killed, right?"

A sour taste climbed up my throat. Sean and I spared each other an uncertain glance. What was Lindsey getting at?

"Not exactly," Sean said.

"Can you be more specific?"

"Well, we uh, we were at the beach party, of course. But we didn't see anything." Sean scratched the back of his head. I watched the veins in his neck pulsing.

"But you two were the ones who found Ruthi's body, correct?"

Lapping waves. Tangled hair splayed out in a shallow pool. Moonlight dancing off pale skin and sand. I closed my eyes.

"I'm sorry, but why is this relevant?" I interrupted, my own nerves mingling with mounting anger.

Detective Lindsey stared at me for a prolonged moment. "I'm just asking questions. So you found the body?"

Sean took a calming breath and nodded. "Yeah. We lost track of her during the party, and we found her body on the beach."

Lindsey glanced down at his notes. "Blunt force trauma. Ligatures around the neck. Water found in lungs. Possible sexual assault. How'd you lose track of her?"

My stomach twisted, and my heart increased its rhythm in ascending staccato. Those words—now nothing but scribbled notes in a dead case file—described the moment that had altered my world forever in the space of a heartbeat.

"I think I can speak for Sean as well when I tell you that night was the worst night of our lives. And we don't care to relive it. We already went through this pointless song and dance eight years ago," I said.

Lindsey sighed and leaned closer, resting his clasped hands on the table.

"Forgive me. I'm sure it's difficult. But your sister's case remains cold. And this case has uncanny similarities. We just want to see if there are any patterns. See if the police missed anything back then."

"Aren't you the police?" Sean said dryly.

"I wasn't on your sister's case." Lindsey was cool and collected as he met Sean's glare.

I opened my mouth to protest the whole thing, but Sean rested his hand on my thigh, sending an unexpected jolt through my body. I looked to his hand, then to him. He quickly retracted it.

"We get it," Sean said, his voice trembling ever so slightly. "We want to help. But there's nothing we can tell you today that you can't read in the case file."

"Maybe there are details you remember now that you may have overlooked back then. Someone you may have remembered acting suspiciously. I'm sure your heads were cloudy back then. You were drinking that night, right?"

Sean sniggered caustically and grimaced.

"If you knew how much booze has been in my system over the last eight years, you'd be surprised I still remember my name."

"Don't you want to solve your sister's case, Sean? And you, Clara? She was your best friend, wasn't she?" Lindsey's tone climbed.

"Yeah, sure I do. We do. But what makes you think you'll have any more luck nearly a decade later?" Sean said.

"Because, as much as it's difficult to say, this girl's death may very well provide needed additional clues as to who would have gone after Ruthi. It might be the same goddamned guy."

I chewed my cuticle until I tasted blood, but felt no pain.

Lindsey sighed, growing visibly frustrated. He flicked his eyes to me.

"When did you arrive in town, Clara?"

"Thursday morning."

"And you haven't been back to Point Redwood since...?"

"Since..." I searched the air. "Since that summer. I think I left in August, once the investigation gave us the green light and we could leave town."

"So you arrived after eight years on Thursday, and the body was found Saturday morning."

"So?"

"Interesting coincidence, don't you think?"

My heart dropped into a hard knot in my stomach.

"What the hell are you implying?" Sean said, coming to attention in his chair, palms on the table, corded forearms pulsing.

Lindsey held up his hands. "No need to rile your temper, Sean. Just questions. Seeing if there might be some pattern we're overlooking."

"What pattern?" I snapped. "For God's sake, I'm in town because my mom had a stroke!"

"Are we under arrest of any kind?" Sean asked.

"Of course not," Lindsey said.

Abruptly, Sean stood, taking my hand to pull me up. "If you have more questions, you can call my lawyer."

I hesitated, my eyes darting from Lindsey to Sean.

Would that make us look guilty of something? Sean's icy eyes were unwavering, so I found my breath and nodded to Lindsey.

"Detective," I said.

We turned to go.

10

"Are you all right?" I asked Sean as we stepped from the little station out into the brisk summer day. The fog was rolling in as the day relented to the afternoon lull, casting an eerie haze over the streets. He let out a slow, guttural laugh. His hand traced the fatigued shadow across his jaw.

"No, of course not. You?"

"No," I shook my head. "Not really."

"Fuck, Clara. I can't go through all this again. I can't relive it. And what if they start questioning mom and dad? You know they will."

"I would expect it sooner rather than later."

"Mom can't handle this shit. She's never been right since...that night."

Had any of us been the same since that night on Bronner Beach?

"Do you really think it's connected?" I asked.

He paced in a little circle, running his hands through his charcoal hair.

"Hell if I know."

"It is uncanny though, isn't it?"

He looked up at me and stared hard, eyes like sharp blue steel going right to the center of me.

"Yeah," he said softly.

It was like the rustic stitches holding that wound closed were being slowly ripped, one stitch at a time, so that we felt each prick. Each one delicately slit at the seams, slow and deliberate.

We stood in silence for a few minutes in front of the station, staring out over the horizon at the breezy coastline.

"I almost forgot how pretty it can be here," I said almost to myself.

Sean let out a short grunt. "Like a postcard."

"It's nice to see it hasn't changed much," I said, ignoring his sarcasm.

"Funny thing to say, considering you couldn't have gotten out of here fast enough."

I rolled my head toward him and glared. "Don't abridge the story like that, Sean. You were more than happy to see me go. As was your family."

"They were just heartbroken, Clara. It wasn't personal."

"Sean, don't. I know how your mom felt about me. How she felt about my mom."

"It's water under the bridge. Those grudges died with Ruthi. Mom didn't have the capacity for anything but grief after that."

We let the subject drop. There was nothing more to say. He was right about water under the bridge—but with all the shit we kept throwing under there, the bridge was about flooded.

"You want a drink?" Sean finally said.

"A drink?"

"You know, the thing that obliterates our pain and common sense."

I burst into laughter. I don't know why. It just rolled up from my gut and exploded through my mouth. The absurdity of everything. Sean looked annoyed, but then his lips played with a smile.

"Glad I entertain you."

I composed myself. "Sure, why not? I could use a drink."

"Come down to my place. The bar, I mean."

I nodded, and we got into our perspective cars.

I followed Sean's truck down the dirt road and through town. We came to the fork in the road that led down to the beach. His truck idled there for a moment—the storybook wooden signs pointing in either direction, testing our composure. Did he ever go back there? How could he?

Finally, his truck pushed through and headed down the road to the bar.

"I don't open up until four tonight, so we'll have the place to ourselves for a bit," Sean said as we walked through the front door of the Drunken Mermaid.

The bar had the eerie feel of absent patrons. Like something plucked from a Stephen King mystery. Fitting, considering the circumstances.

"Have a seat."

I took a seat at the long wooden bar. It was an uncanny feeling, sitting at a bar in my hometown. I still felt like some prying-eyed, nosy townie was going to tattle to my mom about me drinking. You never quite feel fully adult amongst the remains of your childhood.

"Whatcha drinking these days?" Sean asked, filling a low ball with ice and Jameson.

"That'll do," I nodded toward the bottle. He slid the drink to me and fixed another for himself. He took a long sip, then rested his elbows on the table.

"Look, I'm sorry if I was a jerk the other night when you came in," Sean said. "You were the last person I expected to see, and it kicked up some dormant anger I guess."

I looked into my drink. "It's ok. I get it. So how'd this all come about, anyhow?" I asked, looking around the room. Sea-battered anchors, fishing nets and quirky signs hung on the rustic walls beside framed photos of the high school football team and the 4th of July parade. He'd done a good job of sprucing it up without losing that stubbornly old-fashioned Point Redwood charm.

"Needed something to occupy my time," Sean said.

I shot him a skeptical look. "Want to share any more details than that?"

"Maybe not." Then he sighed and looked around. "It's not much of a story really. I came back from the army a couple of years ago, not really knowing what to do with myself. I always thought I'd get a degree after but...I didn't have it in me for school after combat. Not after everything I'd seen. The army didn't go exactly the way I thought it would when I enlisted. Probably never does for anyone. Anyway, this place came up for sale. It was pretty run down but," he shrugged.

"It was kind of an impulsive decision, to be honest. I remember unlocking the doors for the first time and thinking, what the Hell did I just do?" He laughed a little.

"But..." I searched for delicate phrasing. "Buying a business is a hefty investment, Sean. An impulsive decision?"

"You want to know how a twenty-four-year-old without a job could afford it?" he smiled slightly. I blushed.

"Well...I wasn't going to ask outright."

"I had some cash saved from the army. I was deployed for most of my time so, even though the pay is shit, it adds up when you're not spending it. And then Gramps passed away a couple years ago. Left us a bit. Not much, but it was enough to buy this old shit shack. Sam Turlock—the owner —had let it go pretty badly, so the building wasn't worth much."

"I'm sorry, Sean. I didn't know Robert had passed." Of all the Killarneys, Old Grandpa Robert was always the kindest to me. Gentle eyes, a little gruff, great stories that were most certainly embellished.

Sean shrugged. "Thanks. We were expecting it. The lung cancer finally did him in."

"But why..." I stifled the words. It wasn't my business.

"Why did I come back," he finished for me. I nodded.

"It wasn't really planned. When I got out of the army, I came back to figure out what to do next. I had no direction —just this piece of paper thanking me for my service and enough nightmares to last the rest of my life. Mom's depression had gotten really bad—she was just this shell of a woman. And Dad was living at his office, avoiding it all. I felt like I couldn't leave her. I was just going to stay for a little bit and see if I could help her get well. Work and save a little money. Then this came along..." he nodded out toward the empty room. "And here I am."

"And how is she now? Kendra, I mean."

He shrugged. "Every day there are challenges, but she's a world from where she was. She and dad have gotten better, too. For a while, I thought it would tear them apart. They say losing a child is the death of a marriage."

"Do they know about Hannah March?"

"Of course. Hard not to know something that big in a

town this small. But we haven't talked about it. Honestly, I don't go over there much these days."

I sipped at my drink, unsure of what to say next. I had been alone in my grief over Ruthi for so long, I had forgotten that anyone else in the world shared my pain. No matter how much I'd suffered through it all though, I couldn't imagine the sheer agony of losing a child.

"So...Tabby," I said, changing the subject. Sean raised a bushy black eyebrow, the ghost of a smile playing at his lips.

"You don't waste any time getting the dirt, do you?" he said.

"Mmm." I smiled.

"What about her?"

"How did you two come about?"

I pictured Tabby—mop of curly blonde hair and high-necked sweaters. Always on time, always polite—even when her pack of bitchy friends wasn't. What did my rugged biker boy Sean see in her? Had he changed so much? I wasn't the same wild child, I knew that. We all have to grow up some-time. But I wasn't about to resign myself to the entirely mundane.

"She's a good girl," he said without much emotion.

"That doesn't exactly scream passionate love," I said.

He stared into the amber liquid in his glass.

"You know as well as I do that passionate love is a ticking time bomb."

I didn't argue.

"Is it serious?" I asked as nonchalantly as I could.

"Why do you care?" he said a little too harshly. His sharp jaw was clenched. *Did* I care?

"I..." I stumbled with incumbent words. "I guess I don't. I'm just being conversational."

I averted my eyes and tried to focus on something else.

Even after all these years, Sean's presence still suffocated me in a way that was both overwhelming and addicting.

"Do you see a ring?" He said, his lips curling into an amused half smile.

"Sean, it's not like I wouldn't expect you to be with some-one. Hell, I'm surprised you don't have a whole litter running around this town."

"Many have tried," he grinned. My stomach clenched at the sight of that grin—straight white with a subtle front gap.

"So, no future with Tabby?" I pushed, not really wanting to replace my face with another's, but female curiosity winning out.

"It's not really your business, is it?"

"I guess not. She just seems..."

"Seems like what, Clara? Seems like a nice girl?" he snapped.

"I just remember her differently, is all."

"People change. You're not the same. Clearly."

The emotional walls we had seemed to breach went up again, quickly.

"I'm sorry. I just...I still care about your happiness, Sean."

"Yeah, sure you do. Save your concern for someone who needs it." Sean tossed back the rest of his whiskey. He filled his glass again.

"Are you seeing anyone?" Sean asked after a moment, a little salt mixed with his tone.

I thought of Aiden. Long-haired, carefree, brilliant Aiden; all bronzed canvas and laughter. I shook my head.

"No one of consequence."

Sean snickered at my response. "I suppose there are a lot of inconsequential men roaming around wherever it is you've been, then."

I ignored the jab.

"Austin. I've been in Austin."

"Right. Thought I heard that."

"And no, it hasn't been in the cards for me," I said. "And why do *you* care?"

He smirked. "I try not to."

"It's so strange to be back here," I said. "Strange seeing you, this different version of you."

"Life goes on without us."

"I did miss you, you know. Leaving wasn't easy," I said softly, whiskey chipping away at my defenses.

Sean grunted. "Don't say sentimental shit for my benefit."

"I'm not."

His blue gaze shot up to meet mine.

"Then sorry you had to miss me."

It was a very Sean answer. He had a tender core, I knew. Deep crevices full of lightning and fire. But it was deep, deep down in a dark place that most would never see. To most of the world, he was an impenetrable fortress of pure steel.

I'd breached those walls once upon a time. But I had the feeling the fortress had long since been reinforced.

"You still write?" he asked, obviously changing the subject.

"Yes." I heard the hesitation in my own tone.

"Not quite sure?"

I thought back to Lola's comments. *There's no truth to it.*

"I mean, I try. I'm working on some pieces. Some things about my travels."

"I heard you saw the world. Must have some pretty good stories."

"I suppose I do. But lately, I've lacked the inspiration."

"Maybe you aren't writing the right thing then."

I gave him a curious look. "Meaning?"

"The Clara I knew never lacked inspiration for anything in life."

"Back then, the Clara you knew lived a different life."

"Looks like you've done some living, if those are any indication" he eyed my left arm. I instinctively stroked the artwork with my own hand.

Unexpectedly, he reached out and touched my bicep, gently running his fingertips along the illustrations. My stomach contracted at his touch, and I pressed my eyes closed.

Then he gave the muscle a little squeeze and laughed.

"Damn. You could probably kick my ass."

I laughed and opened my eyes. "I work out a bit."

"That's more than a bit."

"It's kind of a hobby, I guess. Hobby slash therapy. Beats the whiskey."

"Amen to that." He picked up his glass and raised it in salute.

We sat silently for a few moments, things left unsaid swirling in limbo.

I finally broke the silence. "Look, Sean, I'm not about trying to make things weird between us. I know...I know it's complicated and you've probably tried to forget about me."

"You give yourself a lot of credit. Just like always."

"That's not entirely fair," I protested.

He shrugged. "Since when is life fair?"

I swigged at the whiskey.

"Okay, fine. Well, then at the risk of giving myself credit, I'll try to stay out of your way, okay?"

"Probably best."

I pushed myself up from the stool. "I should go."

He nodded curtly. We had an awkward moment of silence and then I grabbed my purse.

"Clara, wait. It is good to see you. I wasn't sure how I would feel if I ever saw you again. And I wasn't sure I ever would. Never thought you'd come back here."

"And how do you feel?" I asked in a low tone. Tension crackled between us. I could feel the threat of some confession.

He chewed his lip and stared at me with those icy blue eyes. "It's just good. Drive safely."

I nodded to his back and left.

11

I left the bar fuming, a cocktail of frustration and despondency sloshing around in my belly along with the whiskey. I couldn't stand to go home just yet, so I drove around the woodsy roads for a while. I wasn't in the habit of driving after more than two, but this was Point Redwood. You only got a DUI if, 1—you were sloshed enough to take out a light post; 2—the cops were looking for an excuse to lock you up.

Fuck this town. Why did I have to be here?

As I pulled back through town, the flicker of neon at Hardy's Market winked at me.

With a fifth of Jameson, I pulled the car up to the beach and made my way to the hood. I sat, bottle to my lips, looking out at the endless ocean--a view that stretched into the unknown like the vastness of dreams.

The blanket of night was falling when I finally, quietly, stepped through the side door of my house, feeling like my teenage self again, sneaking in after a night out with Sean. It wasn't that late, but mom crashed pretty early these days, and I neither wanted to wake her or answer questions about my day.

I was too wired to sleep.

I needed to hit something.

I dug through the garage until I found the beat-up old boxing bag the therapist gave dad years back. *Here, Michael. When you feel like punching Ginger, punch this instead.* Wasn't all that effective.

I'd discovered the catharsis of punching an inanimate bag in Thailand about month six into my journey of self-destruction in a foreign land. One of the local bartenders—an American educated Thai man who went by the name of Jimmy Boy—picked my limp body up off the floor for the umpteenth time. He brought me back to his place to sleep it off. I woke in a bamboo tree house to a throbbing hangover and a pair of boxing gloves dangling in my face.

"What the hell are those?" I grumbled.

"Your new outlet," he said. *"Unless you'd rather just kill yourself. In which case, you can do it at another bar."*

I hate to say dramatic things like *Boxing SAVED me.* But, there might be some truth to it. I didn't have this Come-to-Jesus moment and throw away the bottle for life, but when my fist connected on that canvas for the first time, pain rippling up my forearm, I actually felt the anger oozing out of me. The sadness dripped from my pours and the rage burned the surface of my skin. Despite my churning stomach and pounding head, I hit that bag until my knuckles bled and my arms burned, and I collapsed into a pile of exhausted, frustrated tears on the bamboo floor.

"And now you have Tom Yum," Jimmy Boy said, handing me a steaming bowl of soup so spicy I could taste the peppers through my skin.

I think the detoxifying effects of the soup saved me nearly as much as the boxing did.

Since then it's been a little bit of an obsession. Hitting that gym floor every day at daybreak is necessary to keep the little balance my life has. It's what keeps me from that third glass of whiskey on a lonely, dark night. I can't hear my internal demons so loudly when I'm grunting and sweating. It gives me control over something. And it's a hell of a lot cheaper than some pretentious therapist.

I strung up the old bag on a hook on the garage ceiling. I flexed my knuckles—no gloves, damn. I took a deep breath and let my fist fly. Pleasure and pain rippled through my body at the feel of skin on canvas. No longer caring if I woke mom, I yelled from the bottom of my gut. I yelled until my throat burned and punched until my knuckles shredded against the bag. I collapsed to the concrete and cried, pain rippling up my spine, down each extremity.

What the fuck was I doing back here? Why did I ever come back? Mom had Aunt Jo, she'd be fine.

I had tried so hard these past eight years to fill that emptiness inside me with anything I could. Thick whiskey and warm bodies, adrenaline rushes and bad decisions. The pounding of fists against canvas. Anything to dull the pain —to make me forget. To make me feel something other than loss.

I'm not so self-deluded as to think I'm the only one who's ever lost someone. So many people have lost absolutely everything they've ever known. And maybe that's why I still linger in this place of darkness. The guilt of my own self-indulgence. But I was doing okay. I was surviving and moving on. And then this shit had to happen. I had to get dragged back into this painful web. My breath heaved as I fought down my tears. What happened to the strong girl who'd survived? How had she faded into this weak pile of woman on a garage floor?

I found my breath and composure and hoisted myself back to my feet, swaying a little as I found balance. Fuck this. This wasn't who I was. I was controlled, tough. This wasn't going to be the thing that broke me. Not Sean. Not this town. Not some twisted bastard.

I stumbled back into the house and collapsed in a fitful sleep.

12

Sitting on the tailgate of Sean's truck parked at the top of Mountain House Road, I took a swig of the Don Julio, the burn only a low smolder now that I'd grown used to the taste. I liked the way it burned. Tequila and Sean. I stared at him poking the small campfire, Garth Brooks humming from the stereo of Sean's old blue Chevy. He may be old, but his music never ages. Garth I mean. I don't care what anyone thinks. There, in that peaceful slice of serenity away from home and school and the bullshit, I could forget how fed up I was with my everyday life.

People always tell me how teenagers are such a pain—we're weird and emotional and unbearable. It never made any sense, but I guess I get it now. I mean, it's fucking hard to be fifteen. The world forces you to grow out of the things you loved as a child—your dolls die in your hands and I'm bored with everything and adults don't seem to get it. They don't get why we don't want to watch Disney films or go church or sit around and talk to them. Because it's *boring*. We need some excitement in our lives. Sometimes I envy the athletes in school. I mean, yeah, they can be a little intense

and all school spirit and shit, but at least they have something to occupy their time. I think I could have been a pretty
good athlete. If dad wasn't an abusive prick and mom hadn't
done what she did with Bill Connolly and everyone in town
didn't hate me. Whatever. Fuck them. I've got Sean.

Sean finished with the fire and stood, his strong figure
silhouetted in the glow of the crackling flames. My tummy
fluttered, and I had to force a breath. He came toward me,
slowly, deliberately.

"You look so pretty in this light," he said.

My cheeks flushed with blood, and I resisted the urge to
lower my gaze in embarrassment. There was nothing to be
embarrassed about. He was there with me. We were there
together.

"Thank you," I whispered to the night air.

He stopped just in front of where my bare legs were
dangling from the tailgate. His eyes darted down to where
my mini skirt stopped, and a little smile played at his lips.
His gaze climbed up my figure and rested on my chest. I
wanted to squirm under his approving stare, but I clenched
my abs and stayed still. Boys at school stared a lot, and I just
rolled my eyes at them and brushed them off. But it was
different when Sean did it. When he did it, it warmed me
from the inside.

I still couldn't believe sometimes that we were here
together, like this. I'd known him forever as Ruthi's older
brother. He'd always been our third half, but now we were
something so much more. Now I can't even remember life
without his touch. I know Ruthi was weirded out by it, but
she was being cool because she loved us both.

The air was damp with the onset of fall—Indian
summer finally passing the torch to autumn. Sean leaned in
and grazed my trembling lips with his, the burn of tequila

dancing at their surface. The distant lights danced below us. Coastal fog crept in, surrounding us in a protective embrace. His hands settled on my hips, pulling me toward him. My bare skin slid across the cold metal of the truck bed—tiny goose pimples colliding with beads of sweat.

Our lips danced, our bodies flush and pulsing with nerves and want. I knew it was right. Tonight was the right time, finally. With his lips on mine, he eased me back onto the blanket in the truck bed. It wasn't good. It wasn't clean. But it was perfect. I have no regrets.

13

The next morning, I woke up before sunrise, poignant memories of Sean churning in my groggy mind with nauseating cadence. I knew I couldn't stay. I wasn't prepared to deal with this place, with Sean, with the memories. And sure as hell not another murder investigation for a teenage girl.

When sleep was a lost cause, I pulled myself up, knocking Mr. Muffins off my stomach with a kitty shriek. He hissed and swatted at my back as I sat up.

"Sleep in your own damn bed, cat!"

I grabbed my Nikes and pulled on my windbreaker. Despite the cloud of hangover and sleep deficit, I stepped into the bitter morning.

My feet hit the sand in a mindless rhythm, muscles pressing down hard into the packed grains of damp shoreline. The morning tide crept up, chasing me as I sprinted. I breathed in the salt and eucalyptus and clean air, letting it scrub my lungs. The wind tore through my tied back hair and nipped at my skin, scouring the previous night's whiskey and fear from my body.

I reached the turn in the beach, the winding curve that would take me into Bronner Cove and down to the lighthouse. I stopped, the memories pounding against my wall of fortitude. I looked out at the vast expanse of waves stretching into the unknown. How far could I swim until my strong arms gave way and the mysterious depths of the sea overtook me? I often had bizarre thoughts like that. If I jumped from the bridge would I really die? I plopped down into the sand and closed my eyes, reflexively taking what serenity the ocean had to give.

The stench of gas explodes in his nostrils as he reads the words splashed across makeshift banners slung over crumbling 13TH Century brickwork. He coughs, sweat and glaring sun conspiring to blind him in the turmoil. The clamor builds up around him, closing in. Smoke and screams and tears. Flames devouring ramshackle buildings. Gray rubble walling up around him, trapping him in the inferno...

Sean awoke with a start, his naked body drenched in sweat. He caught his breath and ran his hand through his damp hair.

"Fuck," he muttered. The clear images and sounds still danced in a slow reel in front of his eyes.

He shuddered. It had been a while since the nightmares had visited him in the darkness. The relentless terror. He understood why so many turned to booze and drugs or the business end of a pistol when they got back. It was like living it all over again, every night. If it hadn't been for what had happened to Ruthi, he might have done the same. But he'd rather face the ghosts of war in his dreams than the image of her dead body.

He reached for some water by the bed, then checked his phone. 3 a.m. He lay back against his pillow and found his composure, but his nerves were too rattled for sleep. He resigned himself to getting up and making coffee.

Sean sat by the window, reading Cormac McCarthy until the first signs of the day unfolded below. He missed early mornings--small hours of daybreak while the world holds its breath for dawn. Even as a teenager he'd been inclined toward mornings—the brisk bite of the coastal air and the quiet of a sleeping beach. He remembered basking in the gray mist with his sister, who suffered from insomnia her entire life. When she couldn't sleep, they'd slip out of the house and spend those quiet hours on the beach, lost in thought. God how he missed that girl. He'd never forgive himself for what happened to her. And warranted or not, he wasn't sure he'd forgive Clara either. Somehow, they seemed equally guilty.

His phone buzzed, startling him back to the present. Probably Olivia. Something wrong with the end of the night cash out? Dammit. He could always rely on her when he needed her, but she didn't always pay attention to details.

The picture on the screen knocked him in the gut. Clara. All of Clara, flesh and sinew wrapped around some beefy, long-haired surfer looking guy. In a very compromising position. Who the fuck would send this to him? And who was that guy? The desire to snap the stranger's neck over-took him. He stared at the snapshot. Clara's toned body straddling a tan, hairless torso. Her inked arm wrapped in her own hair, those full lips parted in ecstasy. The guy had a firm grasp on one of her perfect, full breasts. His stomach threatened to unburden its contents.

He tossed his phone onto the coffee table and fought down the rising anger. Who would send that? Someone trying to hurt him? Maybe Clara really did have a boyfriend and she was hiding it, but he somehow knew about Sean. It made no sense.

He shouldn't even care after all these years but seeing her again was like a sledgehammer to his dormant feelings —everything from anger to longing. He slammed back his coffee, already itching for something stronger. No, fuck that. He wouldn't be driven to drink before daybreak by some sick fuck. He'd sweat it out.

He threw on his trainers, running pants and sweatshirt, put in his earbuds and took off running down Mountain House Road to the calming rhythm of acoustic beats. As if he needed one more haunting image to torment his sleeping mind, now he got to picture Clara being manhandled by some hairless man baby.

His feet hit the pavement in rapid cadence, pounding out the persistent image with each stride.

What right did he even have to be jealous? It's not like he'd even spoken to Clara in nearly a decade. Did he think she'd sworn off sex? Not like he hadn't had his share of encounters. Hell, more than his share. And he had Tabby now, and that was good. She made him happy. Happy-ish. She kept him on a good path, and there was something to be said for that. There was a reason he and Clara didn't work out. Nothing good could come of so many terrible memories. What they'd shared had been great—thunder and lightning, crashing waves, a calm breeze in the lull—but it was just a memory now. Just a slice of some past life. The ghost of people they no longer were.

The road curved at the foot of the hill and he let his feet carry him mindlessly until the paved road faded into a sandy path down to the beach. The sun finally peeked out of a misty gray fog, raining shimmering rays of luminescence across the pearly sand. It was mornings like this that kept him here, in this place. This beach had been the scene of his worst nightmare, and yet it still gave him solace. Maybe Tabby didn't know how he could still look at the lighthouse or walk past the cove but somehow remembering that place kept Ruthi with him. He didn't want to forget. He couldn't let her disappear forever.

A figure up ahead caught his attention. Blonde ponytail whipping in the wind, ample breasts bouncing with each stride. A smile tickled his mouth. Christ, she'd gotten sexy. Not that she wasn't beautiful when they were young but, well, they were young. The lines and curves of age and the strong corded muscles, her obvious resilience and defiance of the onslaught of life. Warmth spread through his extremities as he watched her jog the misty shoreline. It was everything he could do not to snap a video on his phone. Instead, he quickened his pace to catch up.

"Hey!" He called when he got closer. Clara didn't stop but turned her head slightly. Surprised at seeing him, she lost her balance and tripped on a strand of beached seaweed, tumbling to the damp sand with a yelp.

Sean stifled a guttural laugh as he hurried to help her back up.

"Christ, you scared the shit out of me," she said, laughing.

"A little jumpy these days, Clara Bell."

He extended his hand. She rolled her eyes at him but accepted the assistance.

"Don't call me that," she said.

Sean raked his eyes over her—sweaty hair and rosy, wind-kissed skin, tight muscles curving sharply. It was difficult to maintain his anger with her when she was there in front of him like that. Then his mind flashed back to the image on his phone and fury welled up inside him. He dug his nails into his palm to maintain composure.

"Everything okay?" Clara asked.

"Hmm? Oh, yeah fine. Just had a rough night's sleep."

"Didn't know you were a morning runner," Clara said.

"You never bothered to ask," Sean said, grinning.

She gave an abbreviated laugh and shook her head.

"Well, I assumed the proprietor of a late-night establishment wouldn't make it out of bed at the break of dawn."

"Can't say I often do. Hell, some Saturdays, I'd be just going to bed right about now. Part of the job I hate the most, really. Especially after the army. Nothing like going from 5 a.m. attention-ready to 2 a.m. last calls."

"Talk about opposites."

"You always up this early?"

Clara shrugged. "A lot of the time. Helps me stay on track. Get my head straight for the day."

"Something we could both use right now," Sean said. He scratched the back of his neck and took a breath. Should he tell her about the pictures? How could he? It was probably just some jealous guy. Did that mean she had a stalker?

"Hey, I'm sorry about how I was the other night," he said instead.

Clara raised her brow. "And how's that?"

"I don't know, I guess I was harsher than I needed to be. This is just all very raw and surreal. I don't really know how to react to it all. Truth is, I've blocked out a lot of that pain over the years. And now it's like it's all coming back to the surface."

Her tawny eyes glazed over, and he thought she might cry. In a moment, they were clear again.

"We're both under a lot of stress." She arched her back in a bendy stretch. "Look, Sean, if it makes you feel any better, I was in no way prepared to face all of this either. Coming back here, this murder thing. Least of all facing you."

Her eyes dropped to her trainers. She traced her foot through the sand sheepishly.

"Seeing you, here in this life, it was like someone took a sledgehammer to my reality," Sean said.

"I'll leave as soon as they let me. I don't know how you've managed to make a life here, but being here is just too damn hard for me."

"I get it. I guess there's part of me that feels like being here is being close to her. I don't want to abandon her memory."

Clara's head shot up, and her eyes narrowed at the supposed implication.

"I didn't mean it like that," Sean said. "That wasn't a personal attack. We all have to deal with things in our own way. For you, it's making a life somewhere else. For me...I don't know. I guess for me, for now, it's carving out an existence here."

Clara turned to the swaying ocean. Her gaze traced the lines of the horizon. She nodded slowly.

"We must let go of the life we have planned, so as to accept the one that is waiting for us."

Sean laughed. So like Clara to find philosophy.

"I've got to get back. Nice to run into you," Clara said, with the formality of someone who doesn't want to confront the uncomfortable.

Sean nodded. "Sure thing."

She smiled thinly and took off running.

14

When I got back home, Mom was in the kitchen, sipping coffee and reading the *Mendocino Independent*. Her little spectacles sat on her nose, making her look like an adorable grandmother and not the whimsical beauty who had garnered so much attention all of Clara's youth — both praise and ridicule.

"Morning, sweetie," Mom said, chipper. "You're so good, getting up to work out so early."

I smiled thinly.

"Yeah, thanks." I poured some coffee and sat down at the table across from her. I stared into my cup for a few minutes, searching for answers in the black hole before speaking.

"Mom, I'm sorry, but I can't stay here anymore. I need to get back."

"Oh?" She didn't look up from her paper.

"I need to get back to work."

She nodded. "I would imagine."

"Why are you taking that tone?"

She set the paper down and looked up at me.

"You want to tell me what it's really about?" she asked.

"What? It's not *about* anything, Mom. I have a job," I knew I was coming off like a bratty teenager, but I didn't want to verbalize the truth of things. I didn't know how to verbalize them.

"Is this about Sean?"

"Why do you think everything is about Sean?"

She stared at me calmly.

"Because for nearly two decades, daughter mine, everything in your life has been about Sean. I'm making an educated guess."

I collected my breath. The woman had a point. An infuriating point.

"It's not just Sean. It's this murder. The police questioned us yesterday. Me and Sean."

"Whatever for? You had nothing to do with it."

"Trying to find a link to...to Ruthi. I've spent too many years getting over what happened here to have it all reopened. I can't go through it again."

"Seems to me that wound never closed."

I glared at her. "What would you know about it? You didn't give a shit back then. Why should you now?" I regretted my words instantly, but neither of us could deny the truth in them. I saw the regret flash in her eyes, and I balanced between guilt and satisfaction.

"Clara, that's not fair. Things were different back then. I wasn't in a good place. But that doesn't mean I didn't care."

"Oh, and what place did your *bad place* put me in? Didn't make it any easier on me."

"I've apologized for what you had to endure because of my choices."

I bit my lip. "It doesn't matter."

Mom's lips trembled slightly, but she didn't argue with me.

"If you need to go, then you should go. I'm fine now. Aunt Jo overreacted anyhow. I'm sorry you had to come in the first place."

My defenses went down. Shit. I sighed.

"Mom, she didn't overreact. You had a stroke, that's serious. I'm glad I came." I tried to smile.

"Me too, sweetie. It was nice to see you."

"This is a process for me, mom. I'm trying."

"I know. Will you be able to get to the airport? Not sure I'm up to driving just yet."

"Yeah, I'll figure it out. I'll get someone to take me, or I think there's a bus."

I stood and turned to go.

"I know things weren't easy on you, Clara. Even before Ruthi's death."

I paused, my heart clenching.

"I know I wasn't a good mother. But it doesn't mean I didn't love you."

No, but you left me to fend for myself! You didn't care what your actions did to me! You made me a pariah! But that wasn't fair, I told myself. What would you have done, Clara? If that were your husband at the end of that drunken fist every night, you'd have sought comfort somewhere else too.

Tears welled up, and I left without response.

15

The next flight out of the tiny Santa Rosa airport to Austin was in two days, so I begrudgingly made peace with forty-eight more hours of Point Redwood. Easier than trying to get all the way to the San Francisco airport. Per usual, mom was lights out by eight, and I had nothing to do. I poured a glass of red wine and tried to read a cozy mystery from her shelf but couldn't focus. And did I really want to distract myself with more murder? In the end, I decided I'd mosey down to the Mermaid and see if Sean was feeling friendly. I knew I really should stay away, but I needed a friend at that moment. I needed someone who understood without me having to explain it all. I threw on the one dress I'd brought with me and my stack-heeled riding boots, tousled my caramel waves and swabbed on some lipstick and eyeliner.

THE BAR WAS MILDLY CROWDED, HUMMING WITH THE ENERGY of locals winding down. Nothing over the top, but enough noise to give you comfort. No one likes a quiet bar--it's depressing and unnerving to sit in silence. You can sit alone and lose yourself in the drum of strangers. I cozied up to the bar, nodding to a salty pair chatting over pints. Olivia was there, elbows on the bar in a way that squeezed her boobs together "unintentionally." Yeah, I invented that trick. She smiled when she spotted me, giving me a little wave and a mouthed "one second."

I sat and observed the little world of Point Redwood.

"You don't quit, huh?"

I turned, and Sean was standing behind the bar, plaid shirt rolled to his elbows, little clichéd bar towel over his shoulder. I laughed.

"You trying to be a caricature?" I said. His icy stare either didn't compute or didn't find the humor.

I cleared my throat and sat up a little straighter, pressing my chest outward in reflex. When in a pickle, show some tits. His eyes darted instinctively to my cleavage, and he gave a slight, amused head shake.

"What are you doing here?" he asked.

I shrugged. "Just needed to get out of the house. Felt like a drink."

He nodded and without asking, poured Jameson neat.

"So much for leaving me alone," he said it with a little smile that lightened the tone. He slid the glass of whiskey to me. I smiled and sipped.

"Thanks. You know I'm terrible at self-control." I raised up the glass.

He chuckled genuinely then.

"Of all people, I know the extent of that truth. I might just have a clean rap sheet if not for your lack of self-control."

"Don't you dare go blaming your mistakes on me, Sean Killarney."

We shared a quiet moment of smiling and memories.

"How're you feeling?" I finally asked.

"I've been better. It's just really surreal. No real other way to say it," he said.

"Yeah. I know. Have the cops talked to you at all today?"

"No."

"Me neither. Hopefully, they'll drop it."

"Doubt it. Dad called and said that Lindsey guy asked if he could come by the house. Mom's freaking out. Dad's afraid it'll send her into a backward spiral." Sean shook his head, frustrated. He poured himself a couple whiskey fingers and took a sip.

"I sometimes forget, what this must be like for them," I admitted.

"Look, just so you know, I'm not upset you're here. I know what we said yesterday, but well, I'd be lying if I said I wasn't happy to have you in here. I like seeing you," Sean said. I felt my cheeks lighting up with a rosy blush. "But Tabby's coming by in a bit. I don't know how you feel about that."

My heart dropped into the whiskey puddle in my stomach, struggling to keep from drowning.

"Oh," I said, shrugging nonchalantly. "Yeah, that's nothing to me." I buried my face in my low ball.

"Just didn't want you getting weird. I know it's been kind of a sensitive time with everything."

His concern warmed my extremities. Or it could have been the liquor. Maybe a little of both. But that was Sean. He was scrappy and hardened and made of steel, but he had a soft heart. He was a caregiver. He'd been the best big brother anyone could have hoped for. Even Ruthi, at a tender, volatile age, knew that. He'd been my solace in so many dark times dealing with my parents.

"Thanks for the heads up. I'll probably head out after this, anyway."

He gave me a wry look, eyebrows raised.

"Just one more for good measure then," I said.

Sean smirked and tilted the bottle over my glass. "Yeah, as if just one more was ever your strong suit, Clara."

He gave me a tiny wink and headed down the bar to take care of other patrons.

"So that's the infamous Clara, huh?" Jim said from his barstool, tipping his Bud Light into his mouth. Sean eyed his friend warily, chewed his lip, then nodded.

"The one and only."

"Georgina told me about her. Interesting girl."

"That's putting it mildly, Jim. You've got no idea."

Sean sipped of his own beer, swishing the hops around in his mouth for a moment before swallowing. She looked damn good, no denying that. The raging fire that died in so many with age had only spread in Clara, fanned and coaxed by the bitter winds of experience.

"Pretty cute," Jim said.

Sean shot him a wary glance.

"What?" Jim said, laughing. "Does that offend you?"

Sean's face relaxed. "No. Of course not. Yes, she's..." Cute? No. Puppies are cute. Clara was fucking bewitching. "Yeah, she's nice to look at. Always was."

"Looks like she could kick my ass though," Jim said.

"Probably could, city boy."

"Sooo..." Jim started with a hesitant tone.

"Yeah?"

"Are there, you know, sparks?"

"Sparks?" Sean cocked a dubious eyebrow. Sean wasn't a sharer to begin with and certainly wasn't about to talk about confused hypothetical feelings toward his high school sweetheart.

"Old flame comes back after all these years. Has to stir up something," Jim said.

"Dude, Jim, it's been like, ten years. We were a high school thing. That's not exactly serious." Sean almost believed the lie.

"Besides, I got a girlfriend. Clara and I are soggy shit under a forgotten bridge," Sean continued.

Jim gave a little shrug and polished off his beer.

"Always the stoic," he said.

Sean sighed, then pulled another beer for himself out of the cooler. Nothing about Clara being back spelled anything but disaster.

ONE MORE TURNED INTO THREE AS I TAPPED MY BOOT TO THE rickety jukebox and drifted to another time and place. Laughter, classic rock and top-40 blurred together into an unmelodious cacophony that was somehow comforting. I swayed to its cadence, whiskey lightening my soul.

I should have left when I had the chance.

"Clara Kendrick?"

I turned into the boyishly cute face of yet another past memory standing next to my bar stool. Soft brown eyes against a tanned backdrop. Hair like milk chocolate. This one was easy.

"Jerry Knox," I said, smiling, half wondering if he and Sean still had it out for each other. He was nautical chic in a polo, slim shorts and Sperry top sliders.

"Wow, I haven't seen you in...what, ten years?" He said, looking me over approvingly.

"About that I suppose."

Eight years, three weeks and six days to be exact.

"You look incredible," Jerry said, wasting no time. "God, what do you, work out like, every day?"

He had the slight lilt of booze on his tongue, and his body shifted ever so slightly as his eyes darted up to mine.

My cheeks warmed at the compliment. Feed me more, small-town boy.

"I try," I said.

"What brings you back?"

I told him about mom, to his feigned concern.

"So," Jerry said, running his hand through his hair. "Maybe we can get some dinner before you go. Catch up on life."

My flirtation waned. It had been nearly a decade since Sean and I had it out over Jerry Knox's flirting back in high school. As if douchey, jock-head Jerry was ever my type. And frankly, I didn't owe anyone anything, let alone Sean. But the thought of going out with Jerry still triggered feelings of betrayal in me.

"Oh, um, I don't know if I'm really going to have time. I sorta have some family stuff to deal with, and I won't be here all that long."

Jerry shot me a coy little grin and shrugged. His confident air had only increased over the years, it would seem.

"Too bad. Maybe I can get your number in case you change your mind?"

I gave a small smile. "I don't think so, Jerry."

My rejection bounced right off him.

"Boyfriend?"

I debated it, then nodded. "Something like that."

"Too bad. It was good to see you, Clara. Take care."

"Yeah, you too." I watched Jerry saunter away through the bar and take a seat with some other vaguely familiar faces in the far corner. I exhaled deeply.

"You're sure popular," Sean's voice said in my ear, a note of mockery in his tone.

"I think novel is more the idea." I pressed my glass to my lips.

"Small towns do get boring."

I turned and glared at him. "Have a problem with me catching up with old friends?"

"Friends," he repeated dryly. "Doesn't Jerry wish."

"I take it the years have not mended your fences."

"Meh. I still don't like the arrogant shit, but you learn to live with people in a town like this, you know that. Can't sweat the petty shit in such close quarters. And he and his friends are good business."

"That's why I prefer big cities. Won't Tabby be here soon?" There was venom on my tongue, and I was suddenly aware of a simmering pot of jealousy deep in my gut.

Sean considered me but didn't answer. He walked away and back to the other end of the bar.

As if summoned, Tabby stepped in a moment later. Her shoulder-length hair laid in perfect curves and she'd donned a sensible dress draped over a twiggy silhouette. Flat, non-descript boots. Blah. She was just so boring. I didn't realize I was staring so obviously until Olivia smirked in my ear.

"Trying to see if death-by-glaring really works?" Olivia said. I snapped my head up to her.

"Huh? Oh, shit," I laughed. "If only, right?"

"Oh, she'd be dead," Olivia smiled.

I turned back. Tabby noticed me too, then, and for a

moment our eyes locked. There was a hint of suspicion in her stare. Nervous that I was so close to Sean, perhaps? She didn't have a reason to be, but I still enjoyed the thought of it. The possessive teenage lover was still rooting around within me somewhere. Tabby beelined to the opposite end of the bar, where Sean came around and gave her a chaste peck. Tabby pulled back, looking a little affronted. By his muted affection perhaps? He pulled her into an embrace. I looked away, unable to stomach the sight of them together.

"If it makes you feel any better, she's pretty boring," Olivia said.

I smiled. "It does a little. Not a fan?"

"She's all right. Can't say we've ever been friends, really. But then again, I was never one for a lot of friends back in the day. Knowing Sean a lot better nowadays, though, I really don't see them together. Can't keep a guy like Sean on such a short leash—not sure how or why he puts up with it."

"Short leash?" My interest peaked.

Olivia tilted her head to the side. "Can't seem to let him out of her sight. Always hanging around here. Which would be normal if she wasn't so uptight all the time. What's a prude like that doing hanging around a bar, ya know? Sometimes I swear she just orders a drink for show. I don't know, maybe there's more to it. Maybe she's better in bed than you'd think."

I snorted, and she grimaced. "Shit, sorry. Slipped out," Olivia said.

"Do you, um, think they're serious?"

"What, like marriage serious?" She raised an eyebrow.

I nodded.

"Who knows? Not a lot to choose from if you're going to stick around this town. So I guess she's not a bad choice, either."

Olivia looked at me, a little pity in her eyes. Did she ever lose someone? A first love? They say it happens to everyone, but that's not true. Some people are lucky and get it right the first time. Sometimes a breakup with the wrong one just fades away painlessly. Sometimes people just never find someone special and so, while empty, their heart's intact. I had a hard time thinking of Sean as the wrong one. Or even the right one. I used to think he was just the only one. Olivia held the bottle up with a little inviting shake, and I nodded, sliding my glass over.

I didn't really want to stay. But I didn't really have anywhere else to go.

"Thanks," I muttered.

"No matter how much time goes by, that shit is always hard to stomach," Olivia said.

"Hmm?"

"Seeing the ex move on. Especially when it's the first time you've seen in 'em in a long time. You kinda hold on to this picture of them. Like a little time capsule, you think no matter how much *you've* changed, they're going to be right as you left them."

I mulled over that. She was pretty spot on. I glanced back to Tabby. God dammit, why did it bother me so much? Is this why they say you need closure in relationships? Otherwise, you just dwell on *what ifs* forever? I watched Tabby chatter on mindlessly with another woman, tossing her hair and making overly dramatic expressions, and my distaste for everything about her festered and multiplied like bacteria.

"Who's she with?" I asked Olivia. Why do I care?

Olivia glanced to where Tabby and the other woman sat at the tall pub table.

"Don't think anyone you'd know. Name's Tina. She married in."

"Who?"

"Chase Branson."

"Oh," I nodded, trying to remember who that was. "A couple classes above us?"

Olivia nodded.

"Let me guess, they go to the same Pilates class?" I said snidely.

Olivia grunted. "Doesn't everybody?"

LIFE IN THE BAR WENT ON, AND I GOT DRUNKER. REAL DRUNKER. Sean eyed me warily every so often as he walked by. He gingerly tended to Tabby, and it was obvious he was feigning more business than actuality in an effort to defuse the awkward situation. I really needed to just leave, but I couldn't pull myself away. Moth to a flame. Moth to a train wreck more like it.

A couple more drinks and I was ready to brawl. A few times Sean flicked his eyes to me with a, *why are you still here* look? Why? Who the fuck knows? Because I was drunk and had nowhere else to be. And because part of me didn't want to leave him alone with Tabby. I wanted them aware of me with every tender touch and every little peck. I wanted her bony ass shifting uncomfortably in her seat, knowing I was behind her, watching her every move. That's right, sit up straighter. Flip your hair. Don't laugh too loudly. Maybe you should Instagram your fucking beer.

What is wrong with you, Clara?

The thing about exes is you feel this entitlement. Like he was mine first, bitch! But that's absurd. You can't own everyone, Clara. You gave up your rights. I was like a spoiled, selfish child who discards her toys and then can't stand that another child has dusted them off and given them new life.

I glared at Tabby, her hair a cleaner, softer shade of blonde than mine. Her brown eyes a little lighter than mine —more reposado than anejo. In every way, she was a tamer, safer version of me. With an internal grin, I wondered how many pull-ups she could do.

"Hey, you all right, Clara?"

I wobbled my head around to see Olivia's concerned expression.

"I'm fine," I heard the slur of my words. "I'm fine," I repeated, trying to straighten them out.

Olivia filled a cup with club soda from the fountain gun and set it down.

"Sip on that for a few. Keep hydrated."

I took a heavy sip and tried not to watch Sean chatting with Tabby, carefree and fancy-free.

My gaze flicked to Jerry Knox. I tilted my head and considered. Hmm. Jerry. Knox. I could go there, I guess. Why not? He was cute-ish if a little douchey for my taste. Not like I had the best judgment in men to begin with. I'd done douche before. Jerry caught my gaze and gave me a wily little smile and a head nod. I averted my eyes in that *Let's see if you can do better* way and turned back to my drink.

Olivia snorted audibly. I glared.

"You don't get to judge," I muttered. She shook her head and walked down the bar to attend to two briny locals.

This wasn't going to go well. I just needed to go home. But first, I needed to pee. I slid from my bar stool, swaying a bit, and balancing on my heeled boots, walked through the bar to the back. I made an obvious attempt to *not* look at Tabby as I swept past.

I relieved myself in the rickety little one-stall bathroom,

then straightened up in the mirror. Don't you love how women in movies always splash water on their faces to collect themselves? Like, you're not wearing mascara and three layers of foundation?

I opened the bathroom door, stepped back into the bar and bumped into Tabby. The whiskey knocked me off balance, and I stumbled.

"Shit, sorry," I said, a little slurred.

She raised an overly plucked blonde eyebrow at me. "Mmm." Was all she said. She pushed past me.

"Bitch," I muttered, regretting it a second later. She spun around.

"Excuse me?" Her arm went to her narrow hip.

I'd gone too far now to back down. "I said, don't be a *bitch*."

Her little pink mouth dropped like a codfish. I had the urge to press her chin up with my forefinger. We stood deadpan for a moment. I didn't know my next move, but I did know I was now fired up, justifiably or not. I stood a little straighter, stretching toned, strong shoulders, breasts high. Tabby's eyes flickered a little, then she tilted her head and glared.

"I see you're still the hot mess you always were," Tabby said calmly.

"And you're still waving your judgment wand at everyone I see," I said, glaring at the gold cross over her chest. I had the urge to rip it right off her neck.

"Why are you even here, Clara? Sean doesn't want you lurking around. It's pathetic."

She'd hit a nerve. I stepped into her face. She wobbled slightly but stood her ground.

"You don't know the first thing about Sean!" I snapped, teeth gritted, ready to pounce.

"And you would? When was the last time he's heard a peep out of you? You don't know what he's like anymore. You remember a dreamy, love-sick teenager. Not a man who's made a life."

I stood, fuming. Whiskey coursed through my veins, fueling the anger.

Tabby took her cue and went on. "What are you trying to accomplish, anyway?"

"Why don't you just mind your own business," I said and turned. Enough of this shit.

"He doesn't worship at your feet anymore. No one does," she said to my back.

"Hey, what's going on?" I felt a hand on my arm.

I spun and met Sean's disapproving eyes.

"Nothing," I snapped, tugging my arm away.

"I think you should go, Clara," Tabby said smugly, hand on her hip.

"Don't tell me what to do." I made a slight lurch toward her, and she cowered back.

"I don't know what you two are arguing about but cut it out. I don't need a scene in here," Sean said.

I felt like I was being scolded by a teacher.

"Sorry," I huffed and turned. Sean said something to Tabby, but I ignored it.

I plopped down angrily on my bar stool.

"Another," I said to Olivia. She gave me an uncertain look.

"How about water?"

"How about you don't tell me what I want, *bartender*?" I snapped.

She rolled her eyes at me. "Whatever." She haphazardly filled a glass and flung it my way.

I threw it back in one swoop.

"You've had enough, Clara," Sean said, stepping up beside me. My sight was blurring, but I could still make out the disdain in his eyes. When did you get so fucking judgmental, buddy?

"Will everyone please stop tell me the fuck to do," I slurred out.

I think he might have laughed, but it was quickly overshadowed by his grip around my bicep.

"Watch out, I lift," I garbled out, trying to flex the muscle beneath his steel grip.

"I'll be careful. But you're going home."

"Hey, I can take her," Jerry's voice joined in. Sean turned and glared viciously at his formal rival.

"We're fine. I got this," Sean said through a tight face.

"You want to go somewhere else?" Jerry said to me. I pursed my lips and shrugged.

"Yep," I said.

"She's going home. Now," Sean said sternly.

"Am *no*," I protested.

"Sean, she can't drive," I heard Olivia say, although I now couldn't find her in the swirl of bar and noise.

"I'm aware, Liv. Cover things while I take her home."

"I'll catch you later, Clara," Jerry said, and I wiggled my fingers at him in a seductive wave.

Sean pulled me along.

"Ooh, coming home with me? You remember the way," I purred, pressing my palm to his cheek. He swiped it away.

"Knock it off, Clara or I'll knock you out."

"That's more like it," I said. After that, the world went dark.

16

I really don't like the feel of that girl's soft neck in my hands. The feel of her trachea collapsing under the weight of my gentle pressure. My thumbs press into her flesh like butter.

She begs. Please, please don't! She squirms beneath me, but the blow to her head has rendered her useless.

I watch her eyes bulge with fear, then gloss over as the life escaped her. But I had no choice. Why did she have to come back here? I can't bear it! She should have known better.

I'm annoyed I have to do this again. But that's how it goes. Kate was a stupid girl anyway.

17

I stared at the scribbled writing on the bathroom wall of the St. Thomas girl's locker room. So people actually did write your name on bathroom walls. Huh.

For a good time, call Clara Kendrick. Gives good head. What a waste of time. For one, no phone number. For two, it was the girls' room so, was the author expecting I'd be receiving female solicitors? I shook my head. No creativity at all, ladies.

I shrugged it off and washed my hands.

The door opened and the sound of little heels clacked across the tile.

I didn't bother looking, but when I glanced up into the mirror, three girls were standing behind me; two with menacing looks and one with a wary expression. Sandra, Maryanne, and Tabby. I internally groaned, really not in the mood. I continued my business until one of them let out a high-pitched quip. I turned.

"Can I do something for you?" I said.

Sandra, a tall, willowy brunette, stood conspicuously in the middle with a look of authority about her. One overly plucked and painted-on eyebrow was slightly arched as she looked me over, arms crossed over her white button-down uniform blouse.

"You *have* to tell me where you shop, Clara," she started. "I can never seem to find such slutty workout clothes."

I swallowed the anger bubbling in my throat. My eyes instinctively darted to the mirror to catch a glimpse of my double D boobs peeking out the neckline of my running tank top. I know, I know, bitches just be jealous. But it didn't lessen the sting of insecurity.

"I wouldn't imagine you'd need a sports bra with such small boobs," I said with a flat smile. Sandra's smirk turned down. I grabbed my bag and started out.

The mean girls didn't move out of my way.

The shorter, fat brunette, Maryanne, looked as though she was trying to faithfully mimic Sandra's demeanor, while Tabby, the demure blonde with the Shirley Temple curls, looked uncertain about everything transpiring.

"Can you please move?" I said, trying to mask the irritation in my voice. Girls like that were just easier to ignore than confront.

"I don't know what Sean sees in you," Sandra continued, taking an aggressive step forward. "He could do so much better. Don't you think, girls? I mean, if she's anything like her mom, she's probably giving it up to guys all over town."

Embers smoldered in the pit of my stomach.

"Don't talk about my mom," I said through a clenched jaw.

"Or else what?" Sandra sneered.

I clenched and unclenched my fists. Breathe in, breathe out, Sean had said.

"Hey, Clara, I've been looking for you."

I exhaled and turned sharply to see Ruthi in the bathroom doorway.

"Sean's waiting for you," Ruthi said.

I glared at the threesome of bullies and pushed past.

"You guys are such freaks," Sandra said with disdain as I left.

18

My head throbbed like two arms of a vise were slowly tightening around it. I flitted one eye open and the sharp glare of morning seared my iris. I slammed it shut again. Fuck me. What happened last night?

I moved my tongue around my mouth and tasted the bitterness of bile. I remembered throwing up in Sean's truck. Then absolutely nothing. Did he drive me home? The panic of unknown set it. It's the worst feeling imaginable to wake up and not remember what had happened to you. Certainly wasn't the first time.

Without warning, the assault of memory came at me—a strange hostel bed stinking of sweat and sour Hungarian beer, sore and sticky between my legs with someone else's vomit on the floor. I understand why it breaks women, I really do. But it didn't break me—just bent me to the brink. In the end—once I found clarity—it woke me up. Because I could have died. That drunk frat boy on European vacation could just as well been a sex trafficker or some sadistic bastard who gets off on torture porn. I was intact and alive.

The worst thing was not knowing exactly what happened. Sure, he'd wiggled his little appendage in me. I knew that well enough—a girl just knows that. But how did it all go down? Was it just him? Did he use a condom? I didn't get to know. Was it worse to have the unimaginable happen to you and remember every grisly detail, or to have known it must have happened but for the memory to have never imprinted? I don't blame myself for some asshole's warped sense of morality, and I'm not one to say that women are ever to blame, but in this case—in my case—I could have prevented it had I been just a little more careful.

I snapped back to the present. This town was fucking with my head, and I needed to get out, ASAP.

I pushed myself up and reached for my phone. A message from Georgina was bannered across the screen.

If you're still heading out tomorrow, I'm going to SR to do some shopping. Can drop you off at the airport.

Life saver, that woman. Maybe I'd take her tiny butt back to Austin with me. Put her right in my carryon.

I typed back. *That would be great. You're the best!*

Mom was in the kitchen, per usual, sipping coffee and reading the *Independent*.

Her face was annoyed as I trudged in.

"And how are we this morning?" she said with a note of irritation. I groaned.

"Please don't say anything. I feel bad enough," I grumbled, shuffling to the counter to pour a cup of coffee. I plopped down at the table and rested my head in my palms.

"I would imagine. You were blacked out drunk when Sean brought you in last night. Although it was nice to see you two together, the circumstances were not ideal."

"Yeah, I know. Had a rough night."

"You shouldn't drink like that. You know better."

"Mom, seriously, please don't. Things are a little stress-ful, okay? It's not good for me to be here."

"So you've said. Leaving soon, then?"

I nodded. "Tomorrow morning. Georgina is going to take me to the Santa Rosa airport on her way to go shopping."

"I'm sorry to see you go, Clara."

My heart clenched a little. She was so frail and fragile looking. I felt like a horrible person, leaving her while she was still in recovery. Oh, who was I kidding? This was mom —self-preservation was her top skill.

"You going to be okay, mom?"

"Of course. Jolene fusses over me like a mother hen."

I smiled lightly. It would have been nice to have an older sister to fuss about me.

My phone buzzed. My stomach clenched as Lindsey's number lit up my screen. I stared at the flashing numbers, too numb to react.

"Clara, honey, who is it?"

I took a breath and answered.

"Hello?" I said meekly.

"Clara, this is Detective Lindsey."

"H...hi. What's up?"

"I'll get right to it. I'm afraid there's been another murder."

I fell into a kitchen chair and went numb. I didn't say anything.

"Clara?"

"Um, yeah. That's terrible."

"Yes. And unfortunately, it matches Hannah March's death. Same Modus Operandi."

My heart hammered. Sweat dripped from my palms, and I almost lost the grip on my phone.

"Look, I'm sorry, but we're going to need you to come back down to the station and answer some more questions."

"I...I don't know anything," I mumbled.

"I want to believe you, Clara. But, for now, we need to ask that you stay in town."

"What? No, I can't," I nearly shouted. "I'm leaving. I have a job."

He sighed. "I understand. But we're dealing with multiple murders here. The investigation takes precedent."

SEAN WAS ABSENT THIS TIME. I GUESS THEY FIGURED THEY didn't have luck with the two of us in arms so they'd peck away at us individually and see if we cracked.

Detective Lindsey greeted me at the front desk and led me back into an interrogation room.

"Thanks for coming in, Clara," he said as I sat.

"Didn't have a choice, did I?" I felt like shit and was in no mood to play demure.

He raised a quizzical eyebrow at me saying, *Is that really how you want to play this?*

I sighed. "Sorry, rough morning."

"You look tired. Want some coffee?"

I nodded, and Lindsey stepped out and came back momentarily with two steaming mugs. Ceramic, not paper. What's your angle, buddy?

"So," he began.

"So."

"What are you not telling me?"

"What?" My head throbbed until my eyeballs felt like they might burst. "Why do you think I know something about any of this?"

"You don't think it's a little strange that these murders—two young girls brutally killed exactly like your dear friend—start the day you get here?"

"Of course I think it's strange, Lindsey. But that doesn't mean I know why they're happening."

"Do you think it's connected to Ruthi?"

I bit my lip and thought carefully before answering.

"I couldn't be sure." I paused. "But if I were you, I'd be making that connection."

"So if you were me, where would you go from here?"

I grunted, frustrated. "How should I know? Believe it or not, I copywrite chain restaurant menus for a living, not solve murders."

"Where were you last night?"

"What?"

"Last night. Where did you go?"

"What makes you think I wasn't at home with mom?" I said.

"Were you?"

I hesitated, then shook my head. "No. I was at the Mermaid."

"Sean's bar."

"Yeah."

"Can people corroborate?"

"What? Of course they can. There were like, a hundred people there. But why would they need to? Am I a suspect?"

"Not at all, Clara. Just asking questions."

"'K, well, I'm getting a little sick of your bullshit questions. I don't have any information for you. I didn't even know those girls."

"How do you know?"

"Huh?"

"I haven't said who the second girl was."

Lindsey stared at me with eyes that dug right through you. Expressionless and silent. I squirmed in my seat. He'd done this before.

"I don't know any girls in town anymore. Who was she anyway?"

"Kate Gordon. 17."

Lindsey's expression remained stoic. We sat in silence. An excruciating ticking clicked in my ear. A toilet flushed. He tapped his pencil.

"Have you questioned Sean?" I asked when I couldn't bear the quiet, not knowing what else to say.

"Should we question him?"

"That's really annoying, you know."

He raised a skeptical eyebrow.

"Answering questions with questions. I know you're being the big bad policeman right now, but I'm not an idiot. I've seen *Law and Order* like 1,000 times," I said. That made him smile.

"I want to work with you, Clara. Not fight you. Don't you want to solve your friend's murder? Don't you want to help us stop this guy from killing any more girls?"

I laughed, incredulous. "Sure. Sounds like a plan." I sipped the crappy coffee and chewed my lip.

"All right, in all honesty," I said. "What do you really hope Sean and I can do for you?"

Lindsey leaned back in his chair and studied me. I wanted to squirm under his gimlet eye, but I held strong and kept my core tight.

"I need to understand this town," he said.

I couldn't control myself and laughed. "Why the hell would I know anything about it? I've been gone for eight years."

"That's exactly why. You have perspective. You aren't so

caught up in the workaday world of things that I think you can give me some clear insight into these people."

"*These* people?"

"C'mon, Clara. You've been out in the great wide world. You know things never change here. But people do grow used to things, too close to things. They become blind to the matters right under their noses. You have not."

I chewed on his words for a moment. I hated to admit it, but he had a point.

"So how does Sean factor in? He's been back for years now. Dating the town sweetheart," I added cynically. I noted Lindsey's smirk and added a point in his column.

"Sean can offer a slightly different perspective, having left but being back for a bit. And, as you so graciously pointed out, he's been dating the town darling. He may know more than he realizes. And he runs the hottest bar in town," he added with a little jest. "Surely he hears some gossip."

I didn't respond. I realized that in all reality I knew nothing about Sean anymore.

"And of course, you're both linked to Ruthi's murder. Which at this point, we're calling connected. Can we just rely on your help, Clara? Can we call on you when we want to run something by you? Need to know about a certain character?"

"Like whether it was the pharmacist with the syringe in the cloakroom?"

Lindsey did not look amused. He resumed tapping his pencil.

I had the gnawing suspicion that his motives ran a lot deeper, but I nodded anyway.

"Sure. You have my number. That all?" I stood to leave.

Lindsey nodded. "That's all. We'll be in touch."

I left the station with something rotten festering in my gut.

19

The summer night was flawless—the precise blend of sultry and calm that a June night should embody. A warm breeze teased the pulsing waves and called to us as it whistled through the old coves of Bronner Beach. The evening sky faded into a vibrant painting of fiery reds and serene blues. It would have been a crime not to celebrate its perfection—and our freedom—with revelry.

"I regret ever knowing either of you," Ruthi mock pouted as I pulled her reluctantly down the sandy bank to the graduation party on the beach.

"I was there when you were born, so not a lot of say in the matter," Sean teased. Ruthi glared menacingly at her big brother.

"C'mon, toughen up. Don't let those bitches dictate where we can go. We never go to any of the parties," I said. With her social anxiety, I knew it was hard for Ruthi to be out in big social settings and we had all but dragged her from the house with the promises of grand memories to be made. I was determined to cement at least one good high school memory before we left this place forever.

"For good reason. People are terrible," Ruthi grumbled.

"And normally, I would wholeheartedly agree. But we. Just. Graduated!" I shouted to the wind. "Soon the assholes around here will be distant memories."

"And we never have to listen to Father Richard's Mass again," Sean added, poking Ruthi's side.

Ruthi's sour expression melted into glee.

"I can't even believe it," she said, shaking her head, long dark tresses whipping in the sea breeze.

I squeezed her hand. "Bright days ahead, my friend. Big, bright days. College and freedom, here we come."

I looked to Sean, a glimmer of jubilance in his blue gaze. Freedom was at our doorstep. He'd waited so patiently this past year for me. I knew it was frustrating, having to come back here to see me. It was all going to be different now. In two more months, I'd be at CSU, Long Beach and Ft. Irwin would be a short drive away. I knew there was the chance that he could be transferred to a different base, but we'd figure it out. At least we wouldn't be in Point Redwood.

Bronner Beach was a buzzing hive of giddy teens inching toward inebriation. I'd be lying if I said I wasn't a little nervous too—I hadn't been to a party in...I couldn't even remember. We had occasionally gone when Sean was still here, but since he'd graduated, it just wasn't worth it.

A keg was set up around a young bonfire, with an assortment of people perched on blankets around it. Jake and James Rhymes were strumming up a slow acoustic melody on their guitars and those already half in the bag swayed to the tune.

"You know they'll break this thing up before it's even dark," Ruthi complained.

"Oh my God, Ruthi, you are being such a baby," I laughed. "No one is going to harass seniors on graduation night."

"Rhodes is probably down there, looking for a date," Sean said wryly.

I chuckled. "Sean, give me that flask."

Sean pulled the whiskey flask from his pocket and handed it to me, which I then promptly shoved in Ruthi's face. "Have a shot and Re-LAX."

Ruthi sighed but acquiesced.

"Hey, hey! It's the American hero!" A male voice shouted.

Jerry Knox, a boy from Sean's grade who he sorta had this frenemy thing with, walked over to us, beer can raised high in salute. Sean smirked but returned the salutations with a small gesture.

"What's up, man?" Sean said, shaking Jerry's hand.

"Expected you to be in uniform," Jerry said.

"Nah. Going undercover civilian. Back in town?"

"Yeah, little bro graduated. Can't let him get shit-faced unsupervised tonight," Jerry laughed. He seemed to just notice Ruthi and me then. "Oh, hey girls. Congrats on the graduation. You must be fucking flying to be out of this place."

I didn't miss the sly little once-over he gave me.

"C'mon, we all have to do a shot." Jerry motioned for us to follow.

Sean looked down at us and shrugged a *why not*. Ruthi exhaled a breathy groan.

"I got you," I said, linking my arm through Ruthi's. "You're going to be fine. We're going to have a great night, I promise."

Ruthi took a swig from the flask, gagged, and forced a smile at me.

20

Sean was sitting at a little wooden table outside the front entrance to the Mermaid, a cup of stiff black coffee in hand and the morning news on his iPad when the police cruiser pulled up. He glanced up and saw the smug face of the overly testosteroned Ryan Rhodes.

"Morning, Sean," Rhodes said, walking pompously over to him, thumbs in his belt loops.

"Rhodes," Sean said, sitting up straight. He met Rhodes' eyes with a gimlet stare. "Bar's not open yet."

Rhodes gave him the ghost of a smile. "On duty."

"Sure thing."

"Have a minute?"

Sean considered an excuse but shrugged. "For PRPD? All the minutes."

Rhodes sat in the wooden chair opposite Sean.

"This about the murders again?" Sean asked preemptively.

Rhodes nodded.

"There's something she's not telling you, Sean," Rhodes said, tapping his fingers annoyingly on the table.

"Who's not telling?"

"Clara."

"And what's that?" Sean retrieved a cigarette from his shirt pocket.

"You can't smoke within twenty-five feet of a public doorway, you know," Rhodes said.

"It's my bar."

"Not your sidewalk."

Sean fingered the cigarette and stared Rhodes down, but relented and slipped the smoke back into his pocket.

"So what is this big mystery about Clara?"

"Not sure yet."

"You're real fucking helpful," Sean said.

Ryan Rhodes examined him. Sean never did like the asshat. Always making eyes at Clara when they were young. Total perv. And he just had that dick cop air about him. Sean wasn't anti-police or anything stupid like that. Actually, he held them in high respect. In a real city, it was a hard job. In his army days, he'd been military police himself. But respect was not what he had for smug prick Rhodes.

"She's hiding something, and we're going to find out what. She's not the girl you think she is."

"And what would you know about her? You haven't seen her in the past eight years any more than I have."

Rhodes' mouth twisted. Not a smile exactly, but a wry acknowledgment.

"It's not too hard to find out about people these days. C'mon, Sean, she's back in town five minutes after eight years, and two girls are brutally murdered just like your sister. You don't think that's strange."

"I wouldn't presume to make assumptions," Sean said, trying not to let Rhodes dig under his skin.

"You know she has a boyfriend?" Rhodes went on.

The words twisted with bile in Sean's gut. The sordid picture on his phone burned in his pocket.

"I didn't. You do?"

"She does. Handsome fella."

"So what? I've got a girlfriend."

"That you do. Glad you remembered."

"Are you here to preach morals at me? Can't say I've seen you at Mass lately," Sean said.

Rhodes laughed slightly. "Not here to preach. Just want you to know the kind of girl you're dealing with. Did you know she was nearly kicked out of UT for assault?"

Sean wanted to laugh, trying to picture soft-tempered Clara physically hurting another human. Although he had to admit, she wasn't exactly soft anymore. She'd grown a protective shell around herself.

"So what? I'm sure there's a story there."

"Always is," Rhodes said. "Look, I get it, Sean. Tabby's a nice girl, but she can be a little uptight. Hard to live up to her high expectations all the time, I'm sure. And Clara's a hottie. Always was. Bad girls just have that irresistible draw about them, don't they?"

"Yeah, I'm aware of your notice. Always did have a thing for the young ones."

"Hey, my hands are clean of Clara Kendrick. Even if I'd been inclined—which I wasn't, given I'm well aware of the laws of both morality and legality—she had nothing but eyes for Sean Killarney back then. I guess not so much anymore, from what I understand. I hear the boyfriend's a musician. What is it with women and guitarists?"

Sean dug his fingernails into his palm under the table to keep his reaction at bay. Rhodes was just trying to get under his skin. Get him to admit something that wasn't true.

"I don't know anything about it, nor do I care. And if you

think you're going to bait me into something by appealing to some dormant feelings for Clara, you're wasting your time."

"And what is it about sensible guys that makes them lose all common sense for a nice set of tits?"

Sean chewed his lip. "You would know."

Rhodes stood, a cynical smile playing at his lips. "I would have thought the army would have knocked some of that naiveté right out of you."

"What's life if all skepticism?"

"Watch yourself, Killarney. And don't say I didn't warn you."

21

So, I was stuck in Point Redwood for the foreseeable future. Nightmares really do come true. Well—I guess Austin and I could use a break. I'd had a hard time staying in one place anyway. I was doing my best because at some point you have to grow the fuck up, settle down, whatever. At least that's what they tell me. I guess Austin was as good as a city as any to put down some shallow roots. Good weather, good music, nice people for the most part. Easy Southern livin'.

I fired off a text to Georgina. *Change of plans. Thanks for the offer, but I'm sticking around PR a few more days.*

Georgina: Hope all is well, but YAY for me!

I laughed, not quite getting what it was she saw in me.

I pulled out my laptop and opened up my work Webmail. Despite my Out-of-Office status, work emails were piling up. Copy edits from clients. Announcement from the CEO about mid-year performance. Invitation to an office baby shower.

I began an email to my boss, Kim. Then I realized that I was going to have to just call her and explain. *I'm in the middle of a murder investigation and am detained in town until further notice* was a bit much for a work email.

I explained the high-level details over the phone to Kim, and we looped in IT to get me set up to work remotely. As much as work was the last thing on my mind, I couldn't really afford to go without a paycheck indefinitely.

My phone buzzed.

Lola: *Hey girlie. How's the writing going? I'm sure being back there is shit but just remember, it makes for good storytelling later on. Perfect people tell no tales, right?*

I smiled and wrote back: *I think it's dead men tell no tales, but you're close.*

Lola: *Just don't stay there forever, okay? Austin needs you!*

I closed my work email and pulled up my Gmail. The first subject line jumped right out at me.

ACTION REQUIRED—Your Cloud drive has been hacked

God dammit. How can they make cars that drive themselves but can't seem to figure out how to keep con artists in India from getting into our personal storage? Well, they were in for a whole lot of nothing but travel shots and probably a series of dick pics from Aiden.

I sighed and logged out and pulled up a search browser. The details of the murders flashed through my mind in stark images. My thoughts went back to the cove on graduation night. My stomach turned over with unease as I rifled through the blurry details. I didn't want to believe there was a connection, but how could there not be? Lindsey was convinced—I saw it in his eyes. The whole *we need the local girl as our eyes and ears* things was just a little too cliché crime novel for my taste. I stared at the blank browser, my fingers grazing the keyboard.

If these murders really were connected to Ruthi, was she the first victim? Or were there more?

Where to start? I typed in *Murders*.

Teen girl murders.

Thousands of Google hits. What was wrong with this country?

Beach murders, teen girls.

Mendocino teen girl murder.

I narrowed and scrolled through ghastly images of innocent life cut short until a headline finally caught my attention. Nine years ago, a seventeen- year old girl was found dead on the beach on the Lost Coast, a remote stretch of land straddling Mendocino and Humboldt Counties, murder evident. Contusions and strangulation. Samantha Bellows. Same wild dark hair. Same pale complexion. Same far-off eyes. Case remains cold. Uncanny. I fingered my phone. I didn't want to but...I texted Sean. *You need to see something.*

22

"So what exactly are you saying, Clara? That this is the same killer?" Sean asked.

I leaned back, shrugging. "I don't know but...but isn't it weird? Same M.O., same age. And, fuck, Sean, look at her."

Sean's blue gaze flicked to the image of Samantha Bellows on my iPad screen, then immediately flicked away. I knew what he was thinking. It was hard to look at—like looking at Ruthi all over again.

"And you think...that it's somehow connected to us? To you?" Sean said.

"I don't want to think that, but it can't be a coincidence. Almost one year before Ruthi. It's too similar."

"I think you're being a little paranoid. This is all getting to you. There are a lot of murders in this country," Sean said.

"Don't patronize me, Sean." I sighed. "I don't know. I... maybe this whole thing is crazy. But it has to mean something, right?"

"Possibly," Sean said, resting his elbows on the bar top and steepling his fingers. "But if this murder is related, why wouldn't Lindsey ask us about this? Why didn't we hear about it when Ruthi died?"

"I don't know. Maybe back then the jurisdictions weren't talking? I get the feeling he thinks...maybe that we were involved, somehow."

"That's insane," Sean said.

"I know! Of course it is. To even think that we would..." I shuddered. "We need more evidence. Need to dig deeper."

"That would be a start, I guess," Sean said.

"Will you help me?"

"Help you how?" Sean asked.

"Dig up some dirt. Do a little investigating of our own."

Sean's eyes looked torn. "Clara..."

"Please, Sean. I need someone. I can't go through this alone. And there's no one else but you."

I thought back to the days of suffering my grief alone. Being lost in a dark hole, watching the world go by above me. Dying a slow death and no one could see me. If I had to go back into that hole again, I don't think I would come out. Before I realized what I was doing, my hand was clasped over his. His eyes flicked down to our hands entwined. He turned his hand over and took mine. Tiny bolts of energy went through me and for a moment I thought I could stay in that position for eternity and nothing else would matter.

Sean exhaled deeply and searched the air. He finally nodded.

"Yeah, okay. I'll help you look into it. I guess it does involve me, too. But let's take our time with this. Don't do anything irrational." He squeezed my hand a little tighter.

"Like what?" I almost laughed.

"Hmm, like, I don't know, breaking into Mr. Fraser's office to write *cheater* across Sandra Irving's English essay."

"I only did that once, and she *did* cheat off me! I couldn't just let her get a good score."

He gave me a knowing glance, his expression warring between stern scolding and all-out laughter. A blush rose up on my cheeks to see those eyes fixed on me again.

The sound of timid footsteps grabbed our attention. He pulled his hand from mine quickly.

"Sean," a high-pitched voice interrupted. My stomach dropped.

We turned our heads to face Tabby walking through the bar. Pink-lipped, tight-faced, in some kind of Mennonite dress.

I needed to be nicer.

"Hey, Tabs," Sean said, his voice quivering slightly.

Tabs. I restrained my vomit. Tabby glanced to me with an acute brown eye.

"Hi Tabby," I said, forcing a weak smile. I was suddenly mortified by my behavior the last time I'd seen her.

She stared me down but didn't answer.

"What are you doing here?" Sean asked.

"I've been texting you all morning. As I was driving by, I saw your truck here. I figured you were doing inventory. Or something," she said suspiciously, her eyes running over me. I instinctively pulled up the neckline of my tight tee.

Without any real reason, I felt guilt gnawing at my bones. As much as I disliked the idea of Tabby, I didn't want to be *that* girl.

"Oh, sorry. I didn't see you'd texted," Sean said—a lie if I had to guess. Phones were a necessary appendage to all of us. Tabby knew it, too.

"What are you all up to?" Tabby said, her exaggerated squeal revealing her insecurity about seeing us together.

"We were just catching up," Sean said awkwardly, clearly not having learned a thing about women in the last decade.

"This thing with the murders," I interjected. "The police have been questioning us. We were just going over it, trying to see what we might know that could help. Any connections to Ruthi and all."

That shut her up. No one wanted to talk about Ruthi. Tabby's glossy pink mouth looked conflicted as to whether to compassionately frown or smile nonchalantly. *Oh, you're just talking about your dead sister with your ex-girlfriend? Oh how funny! I totally get it!*

"Oh. Yes. It's really horrible, isn't it? Those poor girls. Sean," she stepped to him and put her arms around his shoulders. "This must be so hard on you."

Sean stiffened and pulled away slightly. "Yeah." Was all he said.

Tension hung in the air for a few prolonged, painful moments. I shifted uncomfortably on my barstool. Tabby unwrapped her arms from Sean and stood a little straighter.

"I guess I'll leave you guys alone, then," Tabby said with little conviction. "You're still coming over for dinner tonight, right?"

It was directed at Sean, but Tabby's eyes flicked to me.

"Yeah, sure. Of course. I'll call you a bit later, okay?" Sean said, taking her hand. She nodded. He kissed her cheek—a little chastely in my humble opinion.

"Um, hey," I said as she turned. "I'm sorry about the other night. I drank way too much, and I was upset about some things. I was a total bitch."

Her lips flitted with a smile and her eyes softened. "Thank you. I appreciate that. We all make mistakes. It was nice to see you, Clara," Tabby smiled—but it looked like more of a grimace.

"You too," I said. She lingered an awkward moment longer before turning to go.

Sean and I stood in silence for a few moments after Tabby had left.

"Sorry about that," Sean said.

"Nothing to apologize for. I should go," I said.

Sean looked hesitant, but he nodded. "Yeah, okay."

I picked up my purse and fingered the leather, so many things unsaid weighing me down, holding me in place.

"I'll let you know if I find anything else," I said.

"Let's talk tomorrow."

I nodded and left without saying anything else.

My head was spinning as I left the bar. If I had to be in the center of a murder investigation, did it have to be in my dreaded hometown with my ex-boyfriend? I couldn't maybe be trapped in some exotic foreign hotel with a twinkly-eyed, tanned pool boy? I needed...I didn't know what I needed. I walked past Patsy's Beachside Café. Food, I could use food.

I was lost in thought as I bumped into a man walking past. His coffee splashed over, landing on my forearm.

"Gah!" I jumped back.

"Oh dang, so sorry," he said. Recognizing the voice, I snapped up to see Nigel, our friendly neighborhood pharmacist.

"Oh, hi Nigel. No worries, I wasn't paying attention. My bad."

He pulled a paper napkin from his pocket and wiped the coffee from my arm.

"These murders have the whole town on edge, I suppose," Nigel said. "Glad to run into you. How's Ginger? She taking her meds?"

I shifted uneasily. I forgot how personal small towns could be.

"Oh, yeah, she's fine thanks."

"So you'll be headed back to Austin soon?"

I tensed. Had I mentioned Austin to him? Maybe mom had.

"I'm...not sure really. Still have some things going on here."

His thin lips stretched across his freckled face. "Right. Okay then. I've gotta run. Good to see you."

He nodded to me and went off down the sidewalk, leaving me deadpanned. God, this town was making my head spin. I was too open here. Too transparent.

I perched at a little sidewalk table in the sun, hoping the rays would melt away my confusion.

"Good afternoon, welcome to Patsy's," a chipper little bird voice said. A spritely teen girl with two black Princess Lea buns in a pleated mini skirt and high-top Converse stood with her pink notepad and pen. Her chipper voice didn't match her heavy eyeliner or bright lips. Her name tag read Thalia. I smiled, instantly liking her style. We might have been friends, Thalia, I thought warmly. That thought led me down a darker path. I had a friend who looked like you. She ended up face down in a shallow grave. I felt sudden fear for Thalia. There's a killer on the loose after girls just like you.

"What can I start you off with?" Thalia said.

"Wine. Red. Biggest one you have," I said half joking.

Thalia looked confused. "A bottle?"

I seriously debated it. "No, just a glass, please. Whatever your house is."

Thalia smiled and nodded.

Soon after, she set down a rustic balloon of thin red wine.

"Thanks," I looked up at her and studied her for a moment. She looked about sixteen or seventeen. "You go to St. Thomas?" I asked.

The corner of her mouth turned up in a grimace. "Yeah, unfortunately."

I smiled. "I did, too. Guess it hasn't gotten any better?"

"They have crotchety old nuns in your day?" she asked.

I laughed. "The crotchetiest."

"You gonna ask me about Hannah?"

My ears went back, metaphorically speaking. "What?"

"All anyone wants to talk about. People keep asking me if I knew her."

"Did you?"

Thalia shrugged. "Yeah, a little. You pretty much know everyone here, right? Weren't really friends though. Same with that Kate girl. Still, so sad, you know? Crazy to know someone your own age who's died."

I pressed my lips together and nodded. "I do know."

"My mom is like totally freaked out to even let me come to work," Thalia said.

"I bet."

Thalia shrugged. "So anything else?"

Fifteen minutes later, I was finishing off my wine and making a dent in a bowl of thick and creamy seafood chowder when a shadow obstructed my sun.

"Clara," a chilling female voice said. I looked up. Kendra Killarney stood in a high-necked blouse and long A-line skirt, her red hair chic and cropped—looking like an out-of-place Lucille Ball. Her face was still handsome, but it was thin and worn with years of strain peeking through. She wore too much makeup, a gaudy gold cross around her neck and pantyhose--time-warped back to a time and place even before Ruthi's death.

Sean had told me his mother had fallen into crippling depression after Ruthi and I wondered what kind of long-term toll it had taken on her psyche. Kendra had never been my biggest fan—that was no secret—but at that moment she looked utterly affronted to be in my presence. She stared down at me with hard, foggy eyes, like pale pond water.

"Oh, hi, Mrs. Killarney." I wasn't sure whether to stand, so I just extended my hand awkwardly. She glanced down as if to inspect it, then gently, without any real effort, set hers in mine and gave it a pitiful shake.

"It's good to see you," I kept on.

"Wish I could say the same."

It would seem her opinion of me had not improved with time.

"I'm sorry to hear that," I said. "Is everything all right?"

She pursed her thinning pink lips.

"I don't need you coming back around here stirring up trouble." Her penciled-in brow arched ever so subtly in the same way Sean's did.

"I don't know what you mean," I said, meeting her hard stare directly. A task I was unable to do, even as the rebellious teen I was. But if a mob of masked rioters in Madrid hadn't scared the wits out of me, Kendra Killarney certainly wasn't going to kick out my knees.

"I think you've put my family through enough grief. You being back here does nothing but stir a hornet's nest. One that's been dormant for many years now."

"I hate to break it to you, Kendra," I saw her mouth purse at the informality of her first name. The Killarneys were staunch, old-fashioned Catholics. "But you don't own this town. I have every right to be back here. My family lives here, just as you do."

"That's never seemed to matter to you before."

I heaved a heavy sigh, not wanting to duke it out with her on the sidewalk. I despised the woman, but her being my elder and Sean and Ruthi's mom had always earned her a level of respect in my book.

"I'm sorry my being here is so upsetting to you. But I have reasons that are keeping me here."

She studied me like I was an insect she intended to squash.

"Then I at least will hope you'll stay away from my son while you take care of your business."

I laughed, in disbelief. "Kendra, if you couldn't keep us apart when we were kids, what makes you think you'll have any more luck now? Sean's a grown man. He can make his own decisions." I drank the rest of my wine, almost defiantly, wondering if she was still a teetotaler. She didn't react —I guess her son did own a bar now.

"He has a nice life now. A nice girlfriend. Very nice. One with morals who can keep his head on straight in ways you never could. Don't you dare mess that up for him."

The words shot right through me, rippling through the wall of self-denial about the girl I really was underneath.

I bit back venom and forced a snarky smile. "Not a problem. Have a nice day, Mrs. Killarney." I turned back to my soup, staring into the milky broth until she'd clattered off.

24

L ater that day I was sitting at the kitchen table going through work emails on my phone when Aunt Jo came through the kitchen side door in a flurry of grocery bags. She huffed in, thrust the bags onto the counter, then stopped short when she saw me sitting there. Mr. Muffins jumped from my lap and ran to circle around Jo's feet with the expectation of treats.

"Clara," Jo said dryly. She had an eerily distant tone-- miles from the warm jubilance she'd shown me the previous week.

"Hey, Jo," I said, trying to warm up the room.

She remained silent for a few moments, her eyes holding back something. Her auburn hair was pulled back into a severe twist, stretching the sides of her plump face tightly across her cheekbones.

"Everything okay?" I went on. She pursed magenta lips together, turned and began unloading the groceries onto the counter.

"Just doing some errands for your mom. She needs a bit of help, as you may have noticed."

I didn't miss the bitter bite in her tone.

"I'm here if she needs me," I said, getting defensive.

Jo exhaled a high pitched, "Hmm," and proceeded to place items into the refrigerator and cupboards.

"Is there something you'd like to say?" I said.

Jo stopped what she was doing, took a deep breath and turned to face me.

"Clara. You're my niece, and I love you. But you better start remembering that you are a grown woman, not some irresponsible teenager."

"What is that supposed to mean?"

"Grown women can't just be going out getting three sheets drunk and showing up on the arm of some boy, blacked out."

I winced. She apparently hadn't been to Dirty Sixth Street, Austin.

"You think Ginger needs that kinda stress? You're here to take care of her, not the other way around."

I fought back my anger and took a few calming breaths.

"I'm sorry about that. And I'm sorry she told you," I half muttered. "I'm under a bit of stress too, if you didn't know."

"For being a smart girl, Clara, your emotional intelligence is lacking."

"Thanks, Jo. Noted." I turned back to my phone.

Jo grunted like a pissed off mare. "Think you're the only girl who had it rough growing up in a small town?"

I was taken aback. "No. I never said I was."

"Then stop acting like just because you got bullied by some uptight tarts in your time you get to remain in stunted adolescence for the rest of your life."

My jaw dropped.

"Pardon my rudeness, Jo, when I say, you don't know the first fucking thing about it."

"Watch that tongue."

"No, you watch yours. You said yourself I'm a grown ass woman. I'm allowed to have a voice. Don't pretend like you were here for me any more than she was," I pointed to mom's bedroom.

"Getting picked on was the least of my worries back then. Let's see, in addition, there was," I began to count on my fingers. "Dad being an abusive drunk, mom's affair with a married man, oh, and then my best friend being slaughtered and me finding the body. And now I'm a murder suspect. Any of that warrant a few drinks?"

"Clara—"

I shoved myself up from the table, making a racket of the chair sliding across the floor. "You want to judge me, feel free to take a number and get in line. But I don't give a shit."

I picked up my phone and went down the hall to my bedroom, slamming the door after me. I could be an insolent child all right. Just watch me.

25

The Drunken Mermaid was starting to feel like a second home. I didn't really want Sean at my house, with my mom asking questions and making accusations, and I wasn't brave enough to be alone in his. Or perhaps just not strong enough. So we kept meeting at his bar.

As in our youth, Sean was always a text away when shit hit the fan at home.

"I think we should talk to the parents," I said, not able to take my eyes from the printouts of the disturbing photographs of the poor departed girls spread out on the bar top. I couldn't believe the paper actually ran such gruesome images. We lived in salacious times.

"Clara, I don't know what good that's going to do. They're grieving."

"I know, but maybe they would be able to tell us something that they couldn't tell the police."

"Why wouldn't they be able to tell the police?"

"What I mean is, maybe they'll find it easier to open up to us because of our, you know, shared experience. There might be something they don't realize they know because police questioning makes people nervous. They have a way of twisting up your mind until you're not even sure what they're asking you. Don't you remember how intimidating they were?"

"Hard to forget."

"So maybe we can appeal to them."

"What is it exactly that you're hoping to find out?"

I shrugged. "Just something that could give us a clue to who might want to hurt those girls and blame it on me."

"Have you ever met them?"

"The parents? No, you?"

"Not really. I've seen them at church, and I think they've popped into the Mermaid once or twice, but that's about it."

I raised my brow. "Church?"

"I go on occasion with mom," he said, shrugging. "And Tabby."

"Hmm. Interesting. Sean the pious," I said.

"Don't look at me like that. I'm still bad to the bone, I promise."

"Yes, terrifying," I grinned.

"All right, we'll go see them. But if they're reluctant to talk, we're not pushing them. I know what they're going through and what it did to my parents back then. I don't want to make it any harder on them."

"Of course not. I do have a conscience, you know."

"Since when?"

I glared at him.

HANNAH MARCH'S PARENTS LIVED IN ONE OF THE NEWER developments on the south side of town. A cluster of miniature faux Victorians posed with well-manicured lawns and some planted trees—a complete juxtaposition from the sleepy, weather-worn bungalows that characterized most of Point Redwood.

Sean pulled the truck up to the sidewalk, and we gave each other here-goes-nothing looks.

The reporters circled like vultures outside the March's—quiet, stalking and patiently awaiting the kill. We took deep breaths and stepped from the truck. Like dogs awaiting bones, they looked up and came alive, rushing toward us.

Flashbacks from those days following Ruthi's death invaded. The barrage of flashing bulbs and the cacophony of shouted questions. The juicy possibility that we might have had something to do with it wasn't lost on any of them. Twisted accusations flew from their mouths.

Was Sean secretly in love with her, so you killed her? Did you do it together?

Was Sean having sex with his sister?

I can still hear the crack of Sean's fist against the reporter's jaw, the camera crashing to the ground, the bulb shattering.

HEADLINE: UNSTABLE TEEN JUMPY AT INCEST ACCUSATIONS.

Sick fucks. How would they expect him to react?

"Well, you know, they were AWFULLY close. Bizarre little threesome they had there," said concerned neighbor Mrs. Gates. "That Clara was always a little disturbed. Dysfunctional family, you know."

Gossip is currency in this town.

"Sean! Clara! What brings you here? Do you think this case is related to your sister's murder?" A young reporter with an iPhone snapping rushed over.

A barrage of similar, same old, questions came at us.

Sean stopped walking and stood tall and wide, bracing himself for battle. His steely blue gaze ensnared the intruders in his line of vision. He raised his hand assertively as the reporters rushed closer.

"I will say this one time before I kick your teeth in. Leave us the fuck alone."

The three reporters' eyes widened into wary saucers. Then like snails in salt, they shrunk away.

I looked at Sean in disbelief.

"Isn't making violent threats against another human a crime?"

"Did you hear a threat? I didn't hear a threat. Just a polite request."

I grunted and shook my head.

A WOMAN WITH HEAVY EYES BEGGING FOR THE RESPITE OF A peaceful night's sleep opened the door to the March's house. She wore loose jeans and a baggy tee shirt over a small frame. Her dark hair was in a messy knot, and her face was blotchy. Underneath the haggardness were traces of a pretty woman, but her grief had taken over.

"Yes," she said, glancing out warily to the lingering reporters outside. They didn't jump at her appearance. Likely they'd been warned.

"Mrs. March?" Sean asked, already putting on the charm. He was always the one to do the talking when we were looking for answers or needed out of a sticky situation.

"Yes, I'm Jessica," she said. Her voice was ethereal and distant.

"My name is Sean Killarney."

Mrs. March's eyes registered the name.

"Yes, hello. I...I know your mother from church."

"This is Clara Kendrick. She grew up here, too. Her mom is Ginger Kendrick."

I winced, not sure mentioning my mom was the best toll for entry. But Jessica didn't seem to know or care about mom's local homewrecker reputation.

"We were wondering if you had a few moments to talk. I know this is a tough time for you, but we both understand what it is you're going through, and we have some questions," Sean said.

Jessica hesitated and shifted in the doorway uncomfortably.

"I don't know," she said. "I don't see what good that would do."

Sean took a breath.

"I understand. But you see, we're a bit involved in your daughter's case, given the similarities to my sister's murder. You know that my sister was killed eight years ago?"

Her eyes wavered, but her chin bobbed in slight acknowledgment.

"Yes, of course."

"We believe that the cases are connected. And for both my sister and for Hannah, we want to stop this bastard."

Sean's declaration of revenge seemed to touch something in Jessica. Her forlorn eyes narrowed into something more menacing, something determined. She stood a little straighter.

"All right. Come in."

She opened the door fully and escorted us both inside. She led us through the front hall and into the living room. The home was tidy and Pottery Barn chic— catalog displays of table settings and hanging wrought iron wall frames with smiling family snapshots. But it looked unlived in—a layer of dust had settled on everything including the remote controls on the wooden coffee table. Something suffocating and heavy hung in the air. Despair? Ghosts? I knew that feeling. It was exactly how Sean's house had felt. I hadn't been able to stand it.

"Please, sit," she motioned for us to take a place on the leather living room sofa.

"Thank you, Mrs. March," Sean said.

"Jessica, please."

He nodded. "I know you will have talked to Detective Lindsey about every detail you can imagine, so I don't want to rehash those things. We were wondering if you knew anything about my sister's case."

Jessica shifted, folding and unfolding her hands. "Well, I do know that she...she was handled the same way as my Hannah. That the circumstances are nearly identical."

Sean nodded. "But they didn't know each other by chance?"

"No. We only moved here mid last year. Long after..." she splayed her hand awkwardly and didn't finish the sentence.

"And was Hannah interested in my sister's case by any chance?"

"What?" Jessica asked, surprised.

"Sometimes kids can get into local crimes."

"I don't imagine so. Honestly, I don't know if she knew all that much about it. Of course, everyone at church and the PTA knew that Kendra lost her daughter tragically. But we didn't talk about it much, and Kendra never spoke of her."

I shot Sean a glance. Wasn't that strange? Kendra never mentioned Ruthi to anyone? He likely registered the thought in my eyes but didn't react.

"Jessica, have the police given you any indication of a lead?" I said, deciding just to dive in.

"Not really, no. They've mentioned they have some possible leads, but they said they don't want to get my hopes up about anything until they know more. I just can't imagine anyone wanting to hurt my sweet girl. She was... she barely even spoke to anyone, she was so shy. She was reflective and thoughtful. The kind of girl who cared about animals and loved solitary endeavors, like sketching."

Just like Ruthi. My stomach turned.

"My sister was a lot like that, too. It's hard to think someone in this town could be capable," Sean said.

"Was Hannah doing ok at St. Thomas? Getting along with everyone?" I asked.

Jessica's eyes darted about the room. "I think the whole Catholic school thing was a bit of an adjustment. We're not exactly a religious family. I've tried to get involved with the church because it seems that's just what people do here. But Hannah wasn't having it. I told her just to think of it as a unique education. To be honest, she didn't have a lot of friends in town, but she never mentioned trouble with anyone."

Jessica's vacant eyes turned to me. Her glassy stare was unsettling as if she was looking right through you into the recesses of your soul.

"You were her friend?" she said.

"Ruthi's? Yes, she was my best friend, other than Sean. The three of us were inseparable. Frankly, she was my only friend. I was a bit introverted myself, Jessica."

"Hannah had a friend like that."

I perked up. "She does? Did? Who?"

"Her name's Vicki. Vicki Gates."

My heart lurched, and I froze. I looked sharply to Sean.

Sean's eyes were perplexed. "Veronica Gates?"

"Yes," Jessica said. "Lovely girl. She's been a help through this whole endeavor."

"That's Tabitha Gates' younger sister, right?" I said, trying to sound light. I had no clue Tabby had a teenage sister.

"Actually, it's her niece. Tabitha's father has an older daughter from his first wife who passed away," Jessica said.

I looked at Sean, trying to hide the freak out in my eyes. Did he know about this?

"Oh, isn't it a small world?" I said, pressing my lips into a smile so that I wouldn't scream profanities.

"I'm sure it's been hard on Vicki as well," Sean said, his voice smooth and comforting as honey.

Jessica's eyes glazed over, going to someplace else. A memory of the two girls, perhaps? She snapped back and smiled thinly. "Is there anything else you need to know?"

AFTER WE LEFT, I WAITED UNTIL THE TRUCK HAD TURNED THE corner before I swatted Sean in the arm.

"Ouch!" he laughed. "What the hell?"

"Were you going to tell me your girlfriend knew Hannah?"

"I didn't know! I barely know her older sister and have only met the niece once or twice. Tabby and Megan aren't close."

I shook my head, confused and overwhelmed.

"God, it's all just so weird. What about Kate Gordon?"

"What about her?" Sean said.

"Are we going to find some personal connection to her, too? Is she like Tabby's secret illegitimate first cousin or something?"

"I don't know, maybe. Small town for you. Really shouldn't be surprising if we do. Half this place is related."

"I guess I forgot that." I looked out the window, watching the evergreen trees and mountains roll past as we drove. A light spattering of summer rain started down. How could such a beautiful place be so rotten at its core?

"We need to speak to Kate's parents, too," I said.

"To what end? We didn't get anything from Jessica March."

"What? Of course we did. We found out tons about who she was and who she knew."

"It doesn't change anything, Clara. It just makes it more personal."

"What?"

"Tabby knowing her. Having a connection to this place. She's no longer just a foreign face in the paper. That's what's bothering you. Now she's a girl from this town. A girl who had friends, who knew your mother from church."

I chewed my lip. He was right. She was even more like Ruthi now. And I didn't know how to process that.

A VISIT TO KATE'S GRIEVING PARENTS YIELDED MUCH OF THE same information. Kate was a quiet girl, inoffensive and introverted. Who would want to hurt such a harmless thing? Her mother asked us through cascading tears. While Jessica March was vacant of emotion, Beverly Gordon was still drowning in the tidal waves of early grief.

The Gordons were also relatively new in town. Again, I had to ask myself why anyone would just up and move here. For them, it was because Tom Gordon was writing a book.

He wanted a peaceful place in nature, free from the distractions and noise of San Francisco.

Yes, Kate knew Hannah, but Beverly didn't think they were close friends. Kate didn't really have a lot of close friends. No, they weren't Catholic but St. Thomas seemed to be a good school.

"She was so pretty, and the boys were always hanging around her," Beverly sobbed. "Tom didn't trust any of them, but Katie didn't seem all that interested in boys anyway. She was a quiet girl, liked to read. Frankly, she was a bit anxious and nervous much of the time."

A lot like Ruthi. She had an ethereal beauty about her too—fair skin and dark hair, haunting eyes. Guys at St. Thomas were always testing the waters with Ruthi, but she couldn't care less about any of them. The idea of dating sent her into a panic.

"I appreciate that you must be looking for some closure of your own, but I'm really not up for this," Beverly said, standing from the couch.

Sean and I both nodded.

"Of course. We're sorry to have intruded. Please, if there's anything my mother or I can do, please let us know," Sean said.

"Same here," I offered, although I'm certain I meant it less.

WE THANKED BEVERLY AND TOM AND LEFT. I WAS NOW MORE confused than ever. All I was hearing was fewer and fewer reasons why anyone would be targeting them. But knowing the pattern and the similarities to Ruthi, it was clear there *was* a pattern. A fucking serial murderer. In Point Redwood. My head was spinning.

We cruised along in his truck in silence for a while. My phone buzzed, and I jumped.

"A little on edge?" Sean teased.

I breathed and checked it. A text from G.

Georgina: Hey! Jim and I were thinking of the Mermaid in a couple hours. Want to come down?

I laughed and showed the text to Sean.

"Hey, I know that place," he said with a smirk. "How about it?"

"I could do. But first, we have someone else we need to talk to."

Vicki Gates was a hard-eyed, pensive thing. She wasn't one to speak before thinking--that much was clear from the calculating look in her dark eyes. She sat on her front porch opposite us, a can of Sprite in her hand. Her St. Thomas uniform was unbuttoned one button too far, a lacy pink bra peeking out. She wore one black and one white knee sock. Long, straight hair obviously dyed black. This girl was trouble in the making.

"I was wondering when you'd come by," Vicki said to Sean, her tone brassy. She pressed her lips to her Sprite can, leaving a glossy pink ring.

"Why's that?" Sean asked.

Vicki shrugged. "To ask about Hannah. I know the police questioned you."

"How'd you know that?" Sean asked.

"I heard mom talking about it to aunt Tabby the other day."

I shot Sean a look. Tabby and Megan aren't close, huh?

"Are you and your aunt close?" I asked, unable to resist the probe.

Vicki shot Sean a hesitant glance and shrugged. "Um, not really. I mean, I like her of course. But she's kinda...she's kinda religious and uptight. She gets on my case about everything. Like once she *thought* she saw me smoking and told my mom."

I raised my eyebrow at Sean and struggled to hold back a laugh.

"I'm sure she's just looking out for you," Sean said.

"Whatever. Anyway, they're all so stupid," Vicki went on.

"Who, your mom and aunt?" I asked.

"Yeah. But also the police. I told them she had a boyfriend, but they didn't listen."

My heart sped up. "A boyfriend? Hannah did?"

Vicki ran her thumb along the tips of her purple nails.

"Yeah. Older guy. I honestly don't know who he was, but I know she was seeing someone. Someone she wasn't supposed to. I caught some texts over her shoulder."

"What kind of texts?" I asked.

"You know like secret meet up stuff. Kissy emojis. Thinking about you. See you tonight."

"Who'd you tell?" I asked.

"The cute cop."

"Rhodes?"

Sean glared at my suggestion that Rhodes was the cute cop. I shrugged, shooting him a *well, a spade's a spade,* look.

Vicki nodded. "Yeah, he asked how I knew and when I said it was just a hunch, and just I got the feeling he said they'd need more than that, but they'd keep it in mind."

Vicki shrugged it off. "I tried."

She pulled a pack of cigarettes from her skirt pocket and lit one up.

～

MY HEAD WAS SPINNING AS WE DROVE BACK TO THE MERMAID.

"Why wouldn't the police look into that?" I asked.

"Guess they didn't think Vicki was reliable. She is a little shifty looking."

I dropped my head to the side dubiously. "Isn't it their job to pursue all angles? Even the shifty ones?"

"Oh, c'mon, Clara. You remember how these yahoos operate. The only reason Rhodes wants this case solved is because it interferes with his drinking time." I snorted with amusement. "And Lindsey's okay, I guess, but I get the impression he's not part of Mendocino's A-team."

I sighed, unsure of what it all meant, or where to turn.

"I suppose. So what do we do now?"

The truck pulled up behind the bar. Sean turned off the ignition, then looked at me.

"Nothing. We do nothing. Let cops do what they do. If they don't want to follow a lead, that's their business."

I chewed my lip, getting red lip gloss on my teeth, which I mindlessly licked off.

"Vicki could be totally off on the older boyfriend thing. Or she could be flat-out lying," Sean said.

"Why would she lie?"

He shot me an incredulous glance. "Do teen girls need a reason to do anything they do? They're all little sociopaths."

I rolled my eyes. I wasn't so quick to discredit the one person in town who actually seemed to know something about Hannah's personal life.

MUCH LIKE MYSELF, SEAN HADN'T BEEN MUCH ON FRIENDS growing up. We were natural introverts, finding solace in solitude. Ruthi, Sean and I had always been thick as thieves. So it was strange to see Sean the Man consorting with other grown men in a normal American way— talking football and drinking beer. Maybe sharing a knowing glance over a busty blonde. Whatever normal men did.

Georgina's husband was suburban chic in jeans and a light blue polo, polished brown shoes. Styled sandy hair. A funny contrast to our workaday hometown boys hardened by sea salt and dirt roads leading to nowhere.

"Clara, this is Jim," Georgina said with a glimmer of happiness in her eyes. Was that love? How quaint.

I shook Jim's hand as he smiled a bright, million-dollar smile back at me.

"Heard all about you. Nice to finally meet you," Jim said.

I winced a little. And what rumor mill did Jim subscribe to?

"Nice to me you too. G says you met at Long Beach? Where you from?" I said.

"Yeah, we had one of our general requirement science classes together. I'm from down there. A shitty suburb of LA."

Georgina rolled her eyes. "When he says shitty he means there isn't a Neiman Marcus within walking distance."

"What's a NEE-MAN MAR-COS?" Sean said in a low dopey drawl, scratching his head.

I laughed. "Better get that boy some proper boots, G, if you're going to stick around."

"Never," Jim said with mock seriousness, pointing a finger at me.

It was official. Georgina and Jim Martin were stinkin' cute.

"Hey, Clara." I heard a voice next to me and turned to see Nigel walking past our table. He still wore his pharmacist's coat and nametag, looking completely out of place in the Mermaid.

"Oh, hi Nigel," I said, smiling awkwardly. The others offered up strained greetings as well.

Nigel stared at me for a long moment—long enough to unnerve me. "Um, what's up?" I asked, waiting for him to say something.

"Just wanted to say hi. But you're busy it seems. I'll talk to you another time," Nigel said. He lingered a moment longer, then turned without saying anything else.

"That guy gives me the creeps," Georgina said as Nigel walked away. My thoughts exactly.

"He's harmless," Sean said. "Just awkward. He always was, even in school."

"Not everyone could be as cool as you, Killarney," I said, trying to lighten the moment. Something about the ginger-haired pharmacist did set my teeth on edge though, I had to admit.

"Will you hurry up and get those people drunk already?" Olivia said dryly from behind the bar. She slammed a Jameson bottle on the counter. Her dark eyes were fixed into a glare, but her lips played with a little smile.

"Yes, ma'am," Sean saluted and filled up a row of low balls.

"It's nice having you back in town," Georgina said to me, a hazy smile on her face.

I furrowed my brow mid-sip. "Why? We never even hung out!"

She shrugged. "I know. But this town is really boring. And you, my dear Clara, are anything but. Adds a little flare to life to have you back in town."

"Thank you?" I laughed. I suppose there were worse compliments.

27

That night, I lay in bed struggling to keep my head above the sea of emotional turmoil threatening to pull me under. My mind raced with a million thoughts. Was mom going to be okay? What did Sean think of me now? Why did I care what Sean thought of me now? Who killed Hannah and Kate? Who killed Ruthi—I dared to venture into dark places as the clock ticked past.

As a kid, I spent many nights drifting into dreams to the lull of the lapping waves against the rocky shoreline outside. Their swaying cadence soothed my rattled adolescent mind like a lullaby I imagined other parents sang to their little ones. The ocean is bold and vast and constant. When I felt small and adrift in a vast sea of darkness, the wide embrace of the Pacific was my comfort. As I lay in my old bed, grasping for sleep, its lapping tickle enveloped me in that familiar memory.

As the pull of dreams finally wrapped around my agitated mind, I was shaken awake by an ominous DONG! I shot up, pulling my covers to my chin. I exhaled when I recognized it was from the ancient grandfather clock that was the bane of my childhood. I took a few steadying breaths and relaxed my body, making a mental note to disable the annoying thing in the morning. I lay my head back down on the fluffy pillow. A thump in the distant darkness pulled me up again. My heart accelerated to a rapid staccato as that pestering feeling of monsters-in-the-closet tugged at me. It thumped again. Then, a shuffle. My heart caught in my throat as the doorbell rang. I glanced at my phone: 3:15 a.m. My belly flopped. Nothing good ever happens at 3 a.m.

I slipped from bed, shivering from the ocean air breathing through the cracked window. I pulled on a hoodie over my tank and gingerly moved toward the living room to investigate. Shadows danced across the living room, sashaying in and out of wavering moonlight. I took slow, vigilant steps into the room and toward the front door, opening my ears for any uninvited sounds. The curtains rustled in the ocean breeze, and the echoes of languid waves trickled in, but all else was silent. The beach is a dauntingly quiet slice of nature at night.

Mom hadn't woken up, and I assumed she'd knocked herself out with a sleeping pill. Using my phone flashlight, I made my way through and clicked on a small table lamp, sending a reassuring honey glow across the room. As I neared the front door, I attempted to swallow the lump in my throat, reminding myself that I didn't believe in ghosts and other things that go bump in the night. But I very much believed in serial killers in remote beach towns. My veins crackled with ice as my fingers brushed the frigid brass doorknob. *Don't be such a girl*, a young Sean's cocky voice said in my ear. I smiled a little and turned the knob.

I thrust the door open to collide with icy air and vast darkness, but nothing else. An inky sky dotted with a scattering of diamond lights stretched out over the quiet, rustic road. I sighed. Drunken teens or a wandering vagrant, perhaps. Nothing more. I laughed a little and dropped my gaze.

And saw the severed head of Mr. Muffins at my feet.

28

I don't remember the sound of my shrieks. I don't remember my vision blurring to black. I don't remember falling. The next thing I knew, a bathrobed mom was clutching me from behind. I heaved into her, regaining my consciousness. I glanced down again at the mangled furry corpse in the doorway. I nearly fainted again. I pulled from mom's embrace, then threw up in the sink.

Mom wrapped me in a blanket, made coffee and phoned the police.

"Can you think of someone who would want to do something like this?" Detective Lindsey asked, jotting down notes on a little pad while a few other local officers poked about the scene.

"You mean, do I know any sick fucks who like butchering innocent animals? No one comes to mind." I shivered and clutched my coffee with both hands. My head was throbbing and spinning at the same time, inducing constant waves of nausea.

Mom was surprisingly calm, considering she'd been in Mr. Muffins' company for nearly two decades. Poor fucking cat. Who would do such a thing? I tried not to envision it, but the image was branded into the matter of my brain.

Lindsey sighed and looked as though there was something pressing he needed to get out but was forbidden from saying anything.

"It's pretty obvious by now that these killings are connected to you, Clara. How, we can't be sure, but someone is sending you a message," Lindsey said.

"Guess they've never heard of text," I said.

"I understand your need for humor right now, Clara, but please be serious," Lindsey said.

"You don't understand shit!" I yelled. "You have no idea what this is like. Do you know how long I spent trying to forget this place and the horrible things that happened here?"

"Calm down, honey," Mom set her hand on my shoulder. "Everyone wants to get to the bottom of this. We have to work together."

"How are you so fucking calm, mom?"

"Please mind your mouth, Clara," Mom said. "Would everyone like more coffee?"

"Thank you, ma'am," Lindsey said, nodding. "Going forward, we're going to place a patrol outside your house."

"To keep an eye on me?" I said.

"To protect you."

"Waste of county funds, if you ask me."

"Not asking."

I was always a little distrustful of cops. It's not that I found them corrupt or inherently out to get certain people. It's just that I found them incredibly useless. They were always harassing me for things I never did when the real criminals hid unseen behind picket fences, in pretty little houses, beating their wives.

"Thank you, detective," Mom said, refreshing everyone's coffee. Mom used to share my skepticism, but I guess she'd come around now that she no longer lived in fear. Dad had a new wife to beat now.

The sounds of running footsteps echoed up the front porch. The door swung open, and Sean ran in, breathing heavily, blue eyes wide and worried.

"Shit, glad you're okay," he said.

"What are you doing here?" I asked.

"I heard what happened."

"How?" I glared at Lindsey.

"We called Sean to see if anything suspicious had occurred at his residence tonight," Lindsey said.

"Anything?" I asked. Sean shook his head. He walked over to me, a little too close, then took a step back. He sat down at the kitchen table, and mom set a mug of coffee next to him.

"Thanks, Ginger." He smiled up at her. Where Sean's mother despised me, my mother always had a soft spot for Sean. I think she knew how much I'd leaned on him all those years when she was otherwise occupied.

"So what are we supposed to do now?" Sean turned angrily toward Lindsey. "Just sit around until it's a human head next time?"

"Morbid, Sean," I muttered.

"If the situation calls," he said, shrugging.

"We're posting security outside the house. I think it's best if you didn't go out at night for the time being," Detective Lindsey said.

"You mean house arrest? Fuck that," I said.

"Then how about just don't be out alone. In all cases, the victims were alone when abducted."

I shuddered, thinking about the fear those poor girls must have faced.

"I think I'm a little old for his tastes," I said.

"Let's not take chances, Clara," Lindsey said.

"He's not really abducting them though, is he?" Sean asked. We all came to attention. My gut turned.

"Excuse me?" Lindsey said.

"Well, at least he's not really holding them long. It's more of a straight killing than a kidnapping."

Lindsey looked as uncomfortable as I felt.

"Yes, both girls were found less than twenty-four hours after they'd gone missing. In the case of Hannah March, the parents didn't even know she was missing."

"How is that possible?" Mom said, horrified as if she would have even noticed if I'd been missing for a week at that age.

I'd love to think back on my youth and remember my daddy on the front porch, arms crossed and some kind of menacing mustache covering a puckered mouth. My mother tugging at his shirtsleeve begging him to understand and remember what it was like to be 16. But no. If Dad was home at all, he would be six fingers of scotch deep, fist itching to punch something. Mom would have been locked in the bedroom, loading up on Xanax, or at the top of the hill, loading up on Bill Connolly. A mother would have been nice, but maybe I don't blame her. Maybe anyone would react that way. Instinct kicks in, and it's fight or flight. She chose flight.

"She'd been out with a friend, drinking," Lindsey said. "The friend said Hannah just disappeared. She didn't want to tell anyone because she thought she'd get in trouble for drinking. Or because they thought maybe she'd run off with a guy."

Poor stupid teenagers.

"And my sister. She was never abducted. She was just flat-out killed," Sean said.

My heart lurched, and I placed both palms on the kitchen table to keep from falling from my chair.

"Yes," Lindsey said as if we needed confirmation. As if Sean and I would ever be able to forget.

"So that should help, right? I mean with the psychology? Like he's not torturing them or playing out some sicko fantasy," Sean said.

"It would appear not," Lindsey said.

"Silver linings," I muttered.

"Look, we're investigating every possible angle here, but we don't have enough to make any conclusions about the why. If you think of anything else, please call us right away. But other than that, try to get some rest and try not to go out alone. Just because you're not a dark-haired teenager, doesn't mean there isn't an unpredictable killer out there. We don't know what he'll do next. Clearly."

"Yeah, okay," I muttered, not intending for one moment to sit in a corner and cower.

Lindsey nodded and stood.

"I'm sorry this happened to you. Try to get some rest." Lindsey and the other officers cleared out, leaving us to wallow in our thoughts.

"You going to be all right?" Sean said as I walked him to the door about twenty minutes later after mom had taken a sleeping pill and gone back to bed.

I shrugged. "I guess. I don't know. No, probably not."

He laughed slightly. "Stay tough. Whoever this bastard is, we're going to find him."

Our eyes met for a moment—things unsaid dancing between us. I wanted to pull him into me, pull him to bed and hold each other like we used to. I wanted to feel his mouth on mine and his hands on my body and feel him press into me, erasing all doubt, all fear. But we weren't those people anymore.

His lips formed a mournful smile. Then he nodded and left, driving his truck off into the breaking dawn.

29

I desperately wanted to crawl back in bed and fall into sleep for the rest of the day. Or even the rest of the year. But both my nerves and the coffee had me wired. I went to my computer and resumed my Google search to try to find connections. This time, I narrowed it to Point Redwood. What were the secrets hiding beneath the surface? Who was this person who was terrorizing this place, who had potentially followed me to Austin and God knows where else? I thought about my path since I'd left Point Redwood. I'd gone straight to Bangkok, fluttered around there for the better part of a year, then on to conquer every hostel in Europe. It would be impossible to find any kind of pattern there. And how would someone have been able to follow me? I was barely in the same place for a few days at a time.

But I didn't go straight to Thailand, did I? There'd been a couple weeks of misadventures in New Orleans. Crime was rampant in NOLA though. If there was a murder that coincided with my time there...how would we even link it?

Didn't mean anything. I didn't believe my own arguments. I began my parameters.

Teen girl murder.

Water.

Body washed up.

Bingo.

A tumble of dark hair, milky skin, pale distant eyes. I closed my eyes and tried not to be sick. It was a coincidence. Only a coincidence. Wasn't it?

I reached for my phone and texted Sean.

Me: *I can't be alone right now. Can you come?*

Sean: *Of course. I'll meet you down at the beach. Our spot.*

I PACED THE EMPTY BEACH COVE WHERE SEAN AND I SPENT many an evening cuddled up together, kneading my fingers into my tangled waves of wind-blown hair as my bare feet shuffled through the damp grains of sand.

"Clara, sit down. You're making me nervous," Sean said from where he sat on a large flat rock.

I laughed incredulously. "Oh, I'm sorry. Have I upset you? My apologies for FREAKING THE FUCK OUT RIGHT NOW!"

He reached out and grabbed my wrist and pulled me close, my chest at his face level. My heart did a little flutter.

"This is going to be fine. We'll figure out what's going on."

"Sean, I don't know if you realize that my cat's fucking head was left on my porch. Mr. Muffins." A wave of sadness for the poor little creature finally came over me, and I started to tear up.

"That cat has—had—been around almost as long as I have," I sniffed, then heaved, choking back swelling sobs.

"Shh, hey, I know." He stood and pulled me into his chest. Subtle alarms went off all over my body. I wanted to tell him at that moment how much I needed his touch. He reached around and pulled a pint of whiskey from his back pocket and unscrewed the cap. "Drink," he commanded.

"It's a little early," I said.

"It's afternoon in Europe."

"Can't argue that then." I took a calming breath and a long sip. "Thanks. Sean, I can't stay here."

"You don't have a choice. The police said we both have to stay in town. Especially now."

"They think I had something to do with this. I know they do. What the hell am I going to do?"

"Nothing. You didn't do anything, so you have nothing to worry about. Maybe we should ask them about the other murder on the Lost Coast."

"You don't think they've already looked into cold cases statewide?"

"You might be giving PR's finest a little too much credit. I'm not saying they're idiots, but these guys are used to one meth head killing another over ten bucks. Not some calculated, premeditated serial killer."

I chewed my lip and racked my brain for answers. Why would someone want to target me? Or mom? Suddenly mom popped into my head.

"Sean..." I started, an eerie feeling creeping over me. "Do you think...any chance mom's stroke was intentional?"

"Like she did it on purpose?"

"No. Like someone induced it somehow? On purpose?"

His blue eyes went wide. "That might be going a little far."

"This whole thing is a little too far. As far as I'm concerned, this town has gone batshit crazy."

I groaned and leaned against the tall rock wall. I pressed the small bottle to my lips and swallowed again.

"Hit me," Sean said. I extended the bottle to him with a half-hearted smile.

He grimaced but didn't say anything. Something in his eyes glinted with the sheen of memory. Did he go back there like I did? Back to brisk summer nights in the back of a Chevy truck, plaid skirt raised, a teenage dream. Cheap hops lingering on our ragged, desperate breath. Classic twangs humming in the background. The buzz of summer mosquitos.

"Do you ever think about what life could have been like for us? Had...had it not happened that way?" Sean finally said.

"No," I said curtly. Sean looked taken aback, as if he expected a gushy romantic sentiment. For all his tattoos and scars, Sean had a poet's soul. And for all the years passed, he'd forgotten I didn't.

I sighed. "Sure. I think about it. But it's not like you and I would have stayed together. Let's be realistic. First loves don't last. You would have gotten drunk and fucked some Alpha whatever coed traipsing around on holiday. Or I would have foolishly fallen for my married English professor with outrageous notions."

"Why do you get the professor and I get the bimbo?"

"Because I'm smarter than your dick."

"You know I was in Iraq, right? Not a lot of coeds on careless holiday."

"You came back on leave," I grinned.

His blue diamond eyes twinkled the way they did once

upon a time on a salty beach with the bitter wind whipping against our huddled bodies.

"I don't allow myself the luxuries of 'what ifs', Sean. It's just...too hard."

"Yeah. I know. I don't either. I just thought maybe if you did, you could cheer me up. It would be nice to have some good memories again."

I laughed, and he took my hand. My laughter froze mid exhale and my body tensed. I ripped my hand away—I don't know why. The feel of him against me shot heat and adrenaline and dopamine through every extremity. It was like a sweet drug you'd been denied for so long. I closed my eyes against the tidal wave of memory his touch invoked so that I wouldn't have to see them replaying in his eyes in front of me.

Eyes still closed, I felt his hand brush against my cheek.

I could smell the salt and seaweed in the air. I could smell him—smoky whiskey and spice tangoing with rugged masculinity. My hips instinctively tilted toward him. I slowly opened my eyes, half-lidded, and I saw the desire flare in his dilated pupils. Come away with me, those eyes said. Like they did a decade ago. Let me take you to the edge of the world and the center of the Earth. Let me take you to oblivion. His fingers brushed down my cheek and traced my jaw, slowly and carefully. His body was close to mine now as my back pressed against the sharp rocks.

"Sean," I whispered. I don't know what I meant with his name on my lips. Please stop? Please don't stop?

"I know," he said, not breaking his gaze on me. He leaned a little closer, and every part of me melted into the air. I couldn't feel my limbs or my lips or my breath.

Our lips found each other's in that moment of lowered defenses and fear. Warm and sharp with the burn of liquor and the desperation of distress. I pressed back, gnashing, burning, tasting. We fell into each other in a tangle. He wrapped his arms around my waist and hoisted me up, back pushing into stone, not breaking his lips from mine.

I pressed my hand to his chest and pushed, ripping our lips apart. My hips dropped.

"Stop," I said, barely breathing. His blue eyes were wide with uncertainty.

"Why?"

I saw his blood, purple and inflamed against his pale canvas, pounding beneath his skin—coursing with desire.

"It's just...won't Tabby be wondering where you are?" I said, averting my eyes to the sandy floor. He breathed deeply.

"I get it." He pulled away from my embrace. I let him go though I desperately wanted to pull him back. Press him to my body and never part.

"No," I said with regret. "You don't. We should go."

If I didn't force myself to leave immediately, I was going to do something I'd regret.

"Clara," he started.

"Let's just keep this friendly, okay?" I said with as little inflection as possible.

"Yeah, okay, sure." His tone was sour. "Wouldn't want to upset your boyfriend back in Austin."

I snapped around and glared at him. "Excuse me?"

He looked like he was about to say more, but he held it back. He stared at me with heavy eyes as I turned and headed up the beach.

≈

Sean was only half listening to whatever Tabby was

rambling on about while she chopped vegetables for dinner —something about a church fundraiser and back to school. Thoughts of Clara were consuming him, and not all of them good. Anger wrestled with longing—that deep, soul stroking longing of seeing the thing your body craves most and not being able to touch it. He was crazy for entertaining the idea. He was crazy for having let his mouth find hers. But fuck, if it didn't feel good. Like a cigarette and a shot of whiskey after a battle.

"...And we'll need your truck for a good part of the day. Sean. Sean! Are you listening to me?"

He snapped up to meet Tabby's direct, disapproving stare. She had one hand on her hip and the other clutching the chef's knife. Her blonde curls were pulled up in a ponytail, and she had a silly checked apron on over her tee shirt and jeans.

"Huh? Yeah, sure. Whatever you need," Sean said.

"Did you even hear what I said?"

"You need my truck. No problem." For what, he hadn't a clue, but he knew better than to let on. Disappointed Tabby lectures were as bad as the nuns.

"What's with you tonight anyway?"

"Just a lot going on, sorry."

Tabby sighed and set down the knife. "What happened last night?"

"There was just an incident at Ginger's. A kind of... vandalism." That's putting it grotesquely mild, he thought.

"Ginger's? You mean Clara's?" Tabby said, crossing her arms.

"Ok, yes, Clara's."

"So, what? You're their protector now?"

"Tabby, will you relax? That Lindsey guy wanted to know if anything had happened here. There are a lot of strange connections to my sister's case. And like it or not, both Clara and I are in the middle of it."

Tabby's expression fell into understanding sympathy, and she walked over to where he sat on the couch.

"Sean, I'm sorry. I know this is all so terrible. I can't even imagine. I just don't like the idea of you hanging around Clara. Not only is she your ex, she's a mess. And she clearly has no respect for me."

Sean's stomach tossed about as he thought about the taste of Clara's lips mingled with the salt air and whiskey. He looked back up at Tabby. She was pretty. Peaches and cream skin and bright eyes. Always put together and charming. What the hell was he doing fucking it up with some long-lost flame? He took Tabby's hand.

"I know, I'm sorry. I'll try to keep my distance during this whole thing," Sean said.

Tabby smiled warmly and sat on his lap. She wrapped her small arms around him and nuzzled close.

"Thank you. I love you terribly, Sean Killarney. I hate the idea of ever losing you to someone else."

I love you too would have been the natural response, but Sean only pulled her close and replaced words with a detached kiss.

30

W hy the hell did I let myself go there with Sean? How could I have NOT gone there with Sean? Because, Clara, he has a girlfriend, remember? A girlfriend who doesn't remind him of his dead sister and a life that doesn't involve you. You're just going to get hurt when he realizes he can't deal with your shit anymore. Sean might have been the only person left capable of hurting me at all.

I clicked on my laptop. I scrolled through a few work emails. Concern for my safety. Wondering when I'll be back. Nothing too heartfelt but it was nice to know my life was waiting for me when I finally managed to leave this town. Although *when* was starting to feel like *if.* I half feared my personal leave was going to turn into medical leave due to my mental breakdown.

My phone buzzed with a text from Lola.

Hey girl, how's it going there? What the hell is happening in that weird world of yours?

My fingers stroked the screen, and I debated a response. I sighed and tossed the phone to the side. How could I even begin to explain? Despite my deep affection for the girl, Lola was in a world a million miles from my current reality.

I pulled up my Google search again for teen girl murders. Something just felt...connected. I could feel it somewhere deep within in me where intuition lays dormant, waiting for someone to rouse it.

I did a mental assessment. Who hated me enough to want to terrorize me? Lots of people had disliked me back in the day, for a lot of different reasons. Point Redwood was conservative, overzealously Catholic, old-fashioned and small minded. I'd heard it all: I was trouble, misguided, rebellious, the daughter of such a *sinful woman.* I had tried so hard not to care what anyone thought. In fact, I'd found a certain amount of pride and freedom in my labels. When there were no expectations thrust upon you, you had the freedom to be the person you wanted to be. But even the toughest elements will break with enough pressure.

Let's see, Sean's mother had always disliked me. Most of my teachers. The virginal pep-squad student council types with their perfect attendance and seemingly genuine dedication to Jesus didn't look too fondly on me. Especially the ones who tried relentlessly to seduce Sean away from me—I wasn't buying their virgin claims. But I had mostly kept to our inner circle of Sean and Ruthi and stayed out of everyone's way. I didn't get into fights or pick on anyone. I'd ignored their jabs and attempts to goad me into an altercation. Despite my strong desire to put a few people in their places, I was far from being a bully myself.

Back then, we thought Ruthi's death had been a random act. No one could find a shred of evidence that pointed to any motive. They'd even suggested it could have been manslaughter rather than homicide—maybe whoever killed her did it by drunken accident. It was a party, after all, they said. She'd gone off with some guy. She was tiny. It was dark, and the rocks were sharp.

I didn't buy it. They didn't know Ruthi. She didn't sneak away with random boys into the inky darkness of night.

I pulled up a new search browser. Without thinking, I typed in Tabitha Gates.

A private Facebook profile revealed little more than a couple of profile photos and basic information. Instagram was much more telling with a series of public photos wide open for the world to see. I never understood why people wanted to expose themselves like that. Be the star of their own little show. Completely open to the world, no privacy.

No thanks. I didn't even like that you could Google my address.

Filtered snapshots of foamy cappuccinos. Bubbly faced Tabby making kissy faces to her rat dog. A selfie of her and Sean at the beach. I lingered on that one, letting the jealousy simmer. A shot from some kind of charity function. A smiling Tabby, sweet green A-line dress and kitten heels, blonde curls from another decade, standing with her arms around two young girls.

The caption linked to an article in a local paper about her heading up the Catholic Charities board last Christmas. *Tabitha Lynn Gates, graduate of St. Thomas High School in Point Redwood, California on the Mendocino Coast. Tabby, as her friends call her, earned her nursing degree at Ukiah Junior College and returned to Point Redwood to give back to the community that has always supported her dreams.* (Gag).

So Tabby was a nurse. I hadn't even thought to ask Sean that. Not that I cared, but I guess I couldn't help but be curious. Nurses and school teachers--the ideal female professions to coddle and care for others. *The reward is that you're helping others,* I could hear her saying in a high pitch coo, hand over her heart. I imagined after she popped out a few ankle biters she'd be selling Krispy treats at the little league games and church fundraisers, going on about the plight of the poor she never helped.

I closed the browser, removing Tabby's giddy smile from my sight. I leaned back and sighed. I was getting nowhere. What was the connection here? What was I missing?

My phone rang. Lindsey's number lit up my screen. My heart skipped, and I sucked in a breath in Pavlovian response. Who died this time?

I took a breath and answered.

"Clara, hi. Good time?"

"Does it matter?"

"Ray of sunshine as always, I see."

"What do you want, Lindsey?"

He cleared his throat.

"I heard a little rumor around town that you've been talking to the victim's parents."

"So?"

"Care to tell me why?"

"Not really."

"Clara, I thought we had your cooperation on this."

"I told you I'll help if I can, but that doesn't mean every move I make is your business."

"I consider everything about this town my business at the moment," Lindsey said.

"Is it a crime to visit your fellow townspeople?"

"You've made it pretty clear these aren't your people anymore."

"You don't know very much about small towns, do you, Lindsey?"

There was a tense pause.

"Look, Sean and I just wanted to extend our condolences. We know a little something about what they're going through after all," I said.

"Right. Sure," Lindsey said, sounding utterly unconvinced. "I hate to have to say this, but I'm going to ask you to stay away from the victims' families."

"Restraining orders are tricky in a five square mile town."

"Clara. I'm asking you to cooperate. The town is already on edge, and I don't need you and Sean getting the families riled up. Don't give me reasons here, okay? Just don't."

I hung up without responding.

31

The next day my resolve crumbled. I shifted my phone back and forth between my palms, and before I could talk myself out of it, I typed a message to Sean.

I think they're hiding something.

Sean wrote back: *Meet me at the bar in 10.*

"Don't you think you're getting a little paranoid, Clara?" Sean asked, filling up two beers from the taps. He set down one in front of me where I sat at the far end of the bar.

I took a long sip, swishing the hops around in my mouth, then shook my head.

"No, I don't. I know it sounds a little crazy, but it's not like the police would be willing to just share all their evidence with us, right? No matter how much they say they 'want our help.' I call stinky bullshit."

Sean ran his finger around the mouth of the glass absentmindedly.

"So, if you had to guess, what are they hiding?"

"Evidence against me."

Sean's brow went up. "Why would you think that?"

"Gut feeling. I don't know...I hear it in Lindsey's voice. Suspicion, accusatory. It's like he thinks I had something to do with Ruthi too."

"That's insane. How could they think you would ever hurt Ruthi?"

I bit back the sting of salt to my eyes. "I don't know. I don't know how *anyone* could have hurt her, but I would have rather died."

He took my hand from across the bar, calming me.

"I know that, Clara. They're idiots if they can't see that."

I pulled my hand away and focused on my beer. Focused on the swirling dark malts. Anything to not meet Sean's icy gaze. Anything not to think about his lips on mine--salt and saliva and whiskey intermingling.

"Who the hell is doing this?" Sean asked.

"I'll assume that's rhetorical. I haven't the slightest idea. This town has some serious weirdos, but a crazed killer?" I shook my head.

"What do you want to do about it, then?"

"I want to know what they have on me—what they *think* they have on me."

Sean laughed a little dubiously. "Okay, and how do we get that?"

"Break into the police station, I guess."

Sean blinked, his expression warring between shock and incredulity. "Look, Nancy Drew, let's take a step back from that. That's a pretty serious crime."

"Wouldn't be the first time we've bent a few rules," I grinned.

"That's not a bend, that's a solid break. As in breaking and entering."

"Oh, when did you get so self-righteous? Tabby have you walking the pin-point straight and narrow?"

I regretted the words instantly. He lowered his eyes and didn't answer.

"Sorry," I said.

"It's fine. But yeah, she's pretty up and up. I'm not a reckless teenager anymore, Clara. And you shouldn't be, either. We can't just break into places."

I sighed. "Know any computer geniuses that could hack in?"

We both laughed at that.

"It's not like we're going to steal anything," I went on. "Just take a peek. How else are we going to know what we're up against here?"

"Clara—"

"There is a madman out there, targeting young girls, terrorizing me, and the police think I'm involved."

"You don't know—"

"Yes, I do. I know it. Let us not forget Mr. Muffins. And it's going to get worse. We have no idea what this guy is after or what his endgame is. And if the police are focusing on me, then that means he's free to do his worst. I'm not going to sit around waiting for it to be on me."

Sean exhaled long and hard. He rubbed his shadowed chin and gave me a hard look.

"You'll be the death of me," he said.

32

Sean and I waited until the wee hours of night. We both knew the main station well—having had a brush or two with the law in our youth. Normally after ten, there'd only be night security on patrol. Not counting a couple of recent teen murders, Point Redwood was usually as safe as they come. Active duty officers would be at home, bellies full of chicken and light beer, safe in their beds, spooning their wives, ringers on in case duty called. But I had no idea what to expect tonight. The town was on red alert since Hannah's body had washed up.

The night had an iridescent glow as the moon climbed toward full. Around midnight, we parked Sean's truck a few blocks from the station. Dressed in all black, my hair pulled up under a beanie, we snuck down the road. I giggled at our clandestine operations.

"We're like a couple of cat burglars," I whispered.

He rolled his eyes at me, the blue catching in the moonlight. "This was your idea."

"And it's a good idea. Well, it's the right idea, anyway. Good is relative."

We perched twenty yards out or so from the front of the station to monitor activity for a bit. The portly night guard was making his rounds, flashlight scanning the surrounding area.

"Is that still Peter?" I whispered.

"Shh," Sean snapped. "And yes, it is. He may not be alone."

Sure enough, another guard, much younger and thinner, stepped around from the back and walked over to Peter. They exchanged a few muffled words, nodded and then Peter went back inside the station while the younger guard stayed on watch outside.

"You up for this?" Sean asked as if it wasn't my idea.

"Typical Tuesday," I grinned.

"All right. Now I think you'll have ten minutes or so. Be fast. But be fucking quiet."

"Yes, I know. Okay, go," I gave him a little shove.

It was pretty straightforward heist material. Sean would tell the young guard that his truck broke down and his cell was dead. Can he use the phone to call AAA? Once inside, he'll chat up Old Peter for a few, then make a fake call. Ask to charge his phone. Meanwhile, I jimmy the back window and sneak on in (one of the many talents my younger self learned). I'd also learned about the back window sneaking *out* of the police station one fine fall afternoon in my middle school years. I feared it was too simple to be realistic, but I'd learned never to underestimate the naivety of small towns.

Once Sean was off, I crept as quietly as I could around to the back. I held my breath so tightly I nearly fell over from dizziness. Calm, Clara. Keep it together. Just like the old days. Except that your life and freedom are on the line. No worries.

I slipped around the back of the building and fell against

the brick, pressing my body into its cool comfort. I took a few calming breaths, then silently I made my move.

I *quietly* slid an old crate under the window. Praying it wouldn't collapse under the weight of me, I eased one foot up and then the other. The wood creaked slightly, but I found my balance and held my breath. When it felt as though it would hold, I pulled out the letter opener I'd snagged from mom's desk and slid it into the window. It wouldn't budge, damn it. I jiggled, and the opener stuck in where I couldn't pull it out. My heart picked up its pace. I heard the rustle of something, and I threw myself against the wall and held my breath. A cat scuttled by and I exhaled. I counted to three and turned back to the task at hand. I put slow pressure on the little opener and bit my lips until I tasted metal. Finally, a tiny *click* and I felt it give. I slowly pushed the window in.

I was barely conscious of my movements over the next few heart-pounding moments. I grabbed onto the sill and hoisted myself up—never in my life so thankful for pull-up training.

I slid through the opening and slowly dropped myself down into the dark back room where I knew they kept case files. I pulled out my phone and using the little flashlight, began my search. I spotted the file cabinet, locked naturally, and quickly looked around for something to pick it. I opened the desk drawer and—low and behold—a file key. I nearly laughed. Small towns really are trusting.

In a larger precinct, our half-ass Hardy Boy antics might not have stood a chance, but there wasn't much going on in Point Redwood other than these murders, so exactly what I needed was sitting nice and neat in the top file.

Open Case: Hannah March and Kate Gordon.

And right below it.

Cold Case: Ruthi Killarney.

My heartbeat escalated as my fingers grazed the yellow envelope. I knew every intimate detail of what had happened, but...what if I didn't? What if there was some missing piece that still lingered in between those pages? First things first, though. I opened the current case file and thumbed through the notes. Details about each death. Blunt force trauma to the head and strangulation, just like Ruthi. Knocked out, strangled then forcibly drowned? Wait, no. Hannah and Kate had no water in their lungs. Death by strangulation. But Ruthi did. Meaning...Ruthi was forcibly drowned? Taken for dead and thrown into the water still alive? I was going to be sick. Both Hannah and Kate showed signs of possible sexual assault. Just like Ruthi. Although they hadn't concluded it was assault with Ruthi. They'd insisted we were being naïve; that she likely had a sexual partner. As if I wouldn't know that very intimate detail of my best friend's life.

I flipped through the haunting photographs and medical reports and found Detective Lindsey's notes.

M.O. same as Killarney cold case. Connection seems evident.

Suspect, Clara Kendrick. Victims don't seem to personally know Kendrick, but she was exceptionally close to Killarney girl. Romantically involved with victim's older brother. Discovered body. Alibi weak.

Lost Coast cold case matches M.O. and suspect's location.

I caught my breath. Suspect's location? I racked my brain. Was I up there at the time of the girl's death? I rechecked the date. Lindsey suspected me and was leading me on, just as I'd expected.

No motive evident for Kendrick but connection undeniable. Gut says she's involved. Investigating the brother as possible accomplice but connection is weak. Kendrick cooperating for now.

I wanted to throw up. I was expecting the information but the reality that they thought I could brutally murder three innocent girls was unimaginable. And if they were sexually assaulted...I shuddered. This wasn't the time for contemplation. I took a snapshot of the notes with my phone. I checked the time. Shit, time's up. I heard the rustle of footsteps, and I froze. Low voices resonated off the walls. Was that Sean? It was getting closer. Dammnit.

I closed the folders and meticulously set them back in place. I locked the file, replaced the key and scurried to the window. Holy fuck, it was too far up to reach. Why the hell didn't I think about that? I glanced around the room frantically, heart racing and palms dripping in my leather gloves. There was a desk chair, but if I moved it to the window, someone would know there'd been an unwelcome guest. My breath sped up. I felt panic swelling. If I was caught in here, not only would I be trespassing on police property, I'd be tampering with evidence, and likely look red-handed guilty of three murders. No, no, no. I reached up to the window. I could get my palms just barely over the sill, but there was nothing I could stand on. The voices and steps grew louder, closer. I had no choice.

I took a step back, reached for the sill, digging my fingers into the concrete, put one foot on the wall and *pulled*. My shoulders burned, and I bit down to keep from grunting with exertion. Pull, pull and my body rose up the wall. My forearms and shoulders wobbled and smoldered, but I fought through. Mind over matter, my boxing coach always told me. Your mind controls what your body can endure. Tap the adrenaline. Finally, I felt the edge of the sill under my belly, and I collapsed onto its support. Something ripped into my abdomen, and I bit down hard to keep from squealing. I breathed in and pushed myself through the window, tumbling out the other side into the cold air. I landed onto the dirt with such a loud thud I knew someone would have heard. I took a split moment to catch my breath, then I pushed myself to standing. And bumped into a shrouded figure.

I shrieked, and a hand came over my mouth.

"Jesus, are you okay?" Sean asked, steadying me.

I struggled for breath, clutching my side.

"Dammit, yes. But you scared the shit out of me. Fuck, Sean, I was right. They think I did it." I could barely choke out the words. His eyes went wide. Something rustled in the leaves.

"C'mon, let's get the hell out of here," he said.

"The window." I hopped back up on the crate and quickly shut the window, then moved the crate back. "Ok, let's scram."

Sean took my hand, and like the little criminals we were, we crept silently through the cloak of night and down the road where we'd left his truck. I held my breath until we were buzzing down the backroads.

We drove in near silence, the hum of nerves dancing around the truck cab. I didn't ask where we were going, but Sean seemed to be on autopilot. As we climbed up Mountain House Road, I sensed without asking we were headed to his place. The truck curved along the narrow road, fog seeping in and masking the vision. But he knew these roads by heart. We all did.

We pulled up to a little bungalow surrounded by arching redwoods. Eerie fog danced around the trees. Sean's house was a fixed-up wood-paneled cabin with breathtaking views over the coastline, nestled back into the crisp redwood backdrop of the mountains.

"This place is incredible," I said as I stepped from the truck and glanced around the peaceful scene. I breathed in the pine and chilly air.

"Thanks. It was one of the rental properties Gramps owned for years. I bought it off dad after Gramps died. It needed a ton of work, so it didn't appraise for much."

"You just lucked out all over town."

"Must be smart," he grinned. "C'mon, let's get warm inside."

We walked into the little house and instantly the warm scents of leather and lingering fire washed over me. It was strange being in a place that was entirely Sean. Not his bedroom in his family's two-story home on the edge of town. No scents of his mother's home cooking or the constant yapping of the family dog. It was masculine and safe—leather and craft beer and the intertwining dance of sea air and pine trees. Serenity and shelter.

He clicked on a few dim lights, revealing a cozy space with floor to ceiling windows. Etched crown molding above dark wooden panels. Elegance spliced with masculinity.

"Wow, Sean, this is incredible. How much work did you put in?"

"The structure was durable and intact. Old homes have stronger bones. It just needed some love. Surprisingly, it didn't take all that much."

"I'm happy for you," I blurted out, not knowing where it came from.

He looked at me curiously.

"Thanks," he said with a little doubt in his inflection.

He glanced down at where I was subconsciously clutching my side.

"Are you hurt?"

The pain suddenly broke through the adrenaline.

"Huh? Oh, shit, yes. God dammit. I cut myself on something climbing out that window."

"Here, let me look."

"Get an M.D. in the past eight years, too?" I teased.

"I happened to have patched up more than my share of wounds worse than this in Iraq."

He lifted my black tee shirt and tossed his head back and forth, non-committal like. A small pool of blood had coagulated over a shallow slash.

"Is it bad?" I asked.

"Nah, just a scrape. I should clean it though, so it doesn't get infected."

He left the room for a moment and returned with a bottle of alcohol and a cotton ball.

I held my shirt up as he pressed the soaked swap to my abdomen. I winced slightly, as much from the sting as from the shock of his fingers gently brushing my skin.

"All better," he said sweetly.

"Thanks," I said, lowering my shirt back down. A thought suddenly dawned on me. "Shit, Sean. I left blood on the sill. DNA."

His black eyebrows went up as if he wasn't sure whether to agree with my assessment or reassure me.

"I...I wouldn't worry, Clara. What are the chances they're going to randomly swab the window sill for blood samples?"

"But they might if they discover someone was in there."

"And why would they? Did you leave a trace?"

I thought about it, then shook my head slowly. "No, I put everything back exactly as it was."

"Then I wouldn't worry. Our little break in will forever go unnoticed."

I chewed my lower lip, grasping for the same confidence.

"Hey, want a drink?" he asked after a moment of awkward silence.

"Absofuckinglutely."

I took a seat on the rustic modern brown leather sofa and Sean went to fetch a bottle of wine and two glasses.

"Look at you, so bachelor chic," I said as he handed me an elegant balloon glass of red wine.

"Expecting a mason jar?" He asked, taking a seat on the opposite end of the sofa. He turned toward me.

"I wouldn't be surprised. Most men don't own a proper set of wine glasses until they find the right woman."

He smiled faintly, and I suddenly wondered if he had found the right woman and these were the byproducts. I tried not to imagine Tabby sitting in my place, John Mayer crooning in the background.

"I'd hate to drink a perfect Dry Creek Zinfandel out of just any old thing," he said.

"The Italians do it. And the Spanish. The French too, I think," I said, overly exaggerating my thoughtful expression. "And I'm pretty sure the Hungarians take it straight from the bottle."

He laughed. "I suppose you would know, then. You've been everywhere."

"Not where you've been."

"Be thankful for that."

"But you've seen things. Things that make this world," I said.

"I'd rather have been in a sidewalk cafe debating the merits of wine balloons to tumblers."

"I'd rather be there now," I muttered, taking a hearty sip. He raised a brow.

"I don't mean *now,* now. Just...I'd rather not be dealing with all this."

"Yeah, I know." He looked pensively into his wine.

"This is good," I offered. "Hard to get really good California wines in Texas. Sure, we have the big-name stuff but not the quality local stuff you find here."

I was babbling. His eyes were distant, clearly not registering my onslaught of musings.

"So are you going to tell me what you saw or do you need another hour of small talk about proper cheese knives?" he finally asked with a faint smile at the corner of his mouth.

I breathed. Right. That whole thing. I took another long sip and licked my lips.

"I saw the case files. The ones for Hannah and Kate, and..." I chewed the words. "And the one for Ruthi. Lindsey's notes—he thinks I...he thinks I killed them, Sean. All of them."

Sean was dead silent for a moment.

"That's insane," he finally said. "It has to be something—"

"I know what I saw."

"Are you sure?"

"Yes, he knows about the other murder on the Lost Coast too. According to his notes, he can't find a motive yet, or substantial evidence, but his gut is telling him that it's all me."

"I guess that's why you haven't been arrested yet. Anything on me?"

"They have eyes on you but aren't convinced you're as depraved as me. God, Sean, what the fuck? What am I supposed to do?" Tears pressed at my eyes and my voice quivered.

"Hey, calm down." He reached for my hand. His touch sent an instant calm over my trembling body. "They have nothing on you. Because there *isn't* anything on you. So Lindsey has a suspicion. It means shit. They always have to focus on someone, and you're just the most convenient target they have at the moment. The town wants answers, and they don't know what else to do."

"I need to leave, right? Get out of Point Redwood. Not back to Austin. I have to go somewhere the killer won't find me."

"Clara," his hands went up to grab my face. "Calm. Down. You're being crazy. You're not going anywhere. Don't you think that would only ignite their suspicions? Stay here, help Lindsey anyway you can. Go to him with what you found about the other murders."

"But he already knows about them!"

"But he doesn't know *you* know he knows."

We both suddenly laughed at the ridiculousness of the statement.

"My head is spinning," I said.

He tipped the bottle into my glass.

"I know, Clara. Mine, too. I may not be public enemy number one in their books, but it doesn't make any of this easier on me."

This whole thing had to be eating away at Sean just as much as me. Kicking the hornets' nest of razor-sharp memories. I suddenly wondered, did Tabby know about any of this? The question threatened to come out, but I bit it back. I didn't want to know what Tabby knew or didn't. I didn't want to think about Tabby at all.

"I don't know my next move, Sean. And I hate that. I hate feeling out of control."

He took my hand in his. Tiny jolts of electricity buzzed up my skin. It prickled with gooseflesh.

"We'll figure it out. We have each other."

The words were like a punch straight to my gut. No, we didn't. Not anymore. I wanted to pull my hand away, but I let it linger in his warm embrace for a few moments, savoring the sensation of his calloused skin on mine. I finally mustered the nerve to extract it.

"That's a thoughtful sentiment, Sean, but it's not like it used to be."

He didn't respond to that.

"C'mere," he finally said. "Let's look at something beautiful to distract us from all this ugly."

He held out his hand. I took it. He led me to the expansive floor-to-ceiling windows in the living room. Outside, the mountainous coastline stretched in winding peaks and valleys of evergreen and rock. Twinkling lights from far-off sleepy towns littered the navy blanket. Point Redwood lay fast sleep in the cradle below.

"This is breathtaking," I said, feeling my heart lighten at the sight. The view boasted freedom to fly and safety from all that could find you. The famous Point Redwood lighthouse shone like a faint beacon of nostalgic hope directly in front of us. My heart sank a little to see it so clearly. How could he look at that every day?

"It doesn't upset me," Sean said, reading my thoughts.

"How could it not?"

"There are far more good memories in that tower than

bad ones. Nothing we did in that lighthouse that night was evil. It wasn't our fault."

I pressed back tears and wished I could feel the same.

I turned and looked at him earnestly. "Yes, it was. She'd be alive had we stayed with her. Had we not gone up there."

"We don't know that. We can't possibly know anything about the killer's motives. And we can't live our lives based on what ifs. Life happens. We can't even remotely guess every turn it's going to take."

His hand found the curve of my cheek—flushed from nerves and wine—and traced a small moon arc. I closed my eyes and breathed in my surroundings. Cinnamon and leather and musk. Dark nights and whiskey. Salty air and pine. All things Sean.

I opened my eyes and saw him staring at me with that azure gaze that could cut through glass.

"Sean," I whispered but couldn't find the words. "I shouldn't be here." I turned my regard back to the window, transfixing on the glittering panorama below.

"No? And why not? Were you fibbing about being otherwise attached?" A thick black brow arched just slightly, and he pressed his glass to his lips.

I flopped my head back to him and gave him an incredulous look.

"No. But you still are."

He gave a small, quiet laugh.

"Yeah, you're right. It's easy to forget that with you. It's easy to forget a lot of things with you. It always was."

"Like good judgment?" I teased.

"Something like that." He took my glass and moved to refill it along with his own.

I took the glass back and sipped, perfect velvet dancing across my tongue. Then I brought my eyes back to his.

"Sean, even without your commitment to Tabby, I shouldn't be here because we're damaged people. We're haunted by poltergeists too dangerous to ever bring about anything good. And this investigation is just bringing to the surface a plethora of demons I'm not ready to face."

His hand came to my left arm then, tenderly stroking the intricate art peeking out from my tee shirt. I shivered at his touch.

"I suppose some would call us damaged," he said softly. "I think we're just interesting."

I laughed. Sean could always calm my fears, no matter how irrational. Did Tabby have a slew of insecurities he needed to quiet? God, I wished I could stop thinking about her.

His eyes and fingers traced the expanse of tattoos down my arm. He pushed up my shirt sleeve and examined my shoulder.

"I like them," he said.

"Really?" I asked dubiously.

"Of course, I do. Tells me the girl I used to love is still alive in there, causing trouble. Making her own rules."

I blushed. "Decorating skin is hardly trouble to anyone but myself."

"You've got some serious pain tolerance, Kendrick."

His hands went to the anchor at the peak of my arm. Crude design and faded, but constant.

"And I will always be your anchor," he recited gently, under his breath.

"Do you still have it?" I asked. I could sometimes still feel the bitter sting of that first needle ebbing in and out of my tender skin. It didn't matter that it was in good company now, the first ink felt as raw to me now as it had ten summers ago in a Point Redwood basement, clutching a bottle of Jameson in one hand and Sean's hand in the other.

A subtle smile tickled his lips as if the phantom needles still grated his arm as well. He rolled up his sleeve to reveal the juvenile ink. A mermaid, long hair covering breasts, drunken eyes in faded blue ink. Warmth flooded my extremities to see it there. A permanent record of what we once were.

"And you'll forever be my siren's call," he said.

My cheeks flushed, and the words promised so many years ago echoed in the recesses of my mind.

"I picked up a couple more in the army. But you never forget your first, right?" he said, rolling his sleeves back down.

So many firsts with Sean I could never forget.

"I loved you then," I said. The words came up from my gut in an unexpected bubble.

"Oh yeah?" Sean said, a twinge of incredulity present.

"You don't believe that?"

"We were young, Clara. What did we know of anything? Besides, how can you abandon something you love?"

"You don't know very much about love, do you, Killarney?"

"And what do you know of it, Clara McKendrick?"

I laughed and shook my head. "Still calling me that I see."

Sean shrugged. "I maintain that your name should have had a Mc."

"That would make me Irish, not Scottish."

"I know," he smiled, icy blue eyes twinkling against his smooth, marble complexion.

I pulled myself from the snare of his stare and focused

on the room. I noticed the old piano in the corner. I walked over and I ran my hand along the espresso wood.

"Do you still play?" I asked, tilting my head. I thought back on the years of lessons Kendra had insisted upon him as a child. But he'd stuck with it, long past the time most parents give up, polishing his skills through high school until he was pretty damn good. Sean's lips curved a little.

"A bit. Makes for a good stress release."

"I bet the ladies love that," I said, teasing.

Sean *hmphed*.

I grazed the wood with my touch.

"Play me something?" I said.

"I...I don't know. I'm kinda tired."

"Please?"

He smiled. "All right. What do you want to hear?"

"Something to make me forget."

He went to the piano. He ran his hand along the wood of the closed cover. He lifted it slowly and slid his fingers down the ivory keys, coaxing out tiny, faint notes. He took a seat on the wooden bench and flexed his fingers. I leaned against the sofa and relaxed my eyes.

The piano sonata filled the room—each note dancing in and out of the streaks of moonlight shining from the window overlooking the foggy coastline. I sipped my wine and let the music comfort my soul. The broad expanse of his shoulders rose and fell with concentrated breath as his nimble fingers caressed each key. It wasn't a perfect tune, but it was raw and alive with the vitality of his passion. As the melody sped up, the energy inflated the room. My heart swelled along with it as each note renewed me. It stirred something within me—something dark and warm and intoxicating that I couldn't identify, but I could feel in every nerve ending. As the song reached crescendo, I set down my glass and stood from the sofa. I moved toward the music and let my body find his in the moonlight.

I stepped behind where he sat on the piano bench. I ran my hands along his shoulders, then traced each muscle of his back, then up the cool skin of his neck. The melody slowed, and his skin prickled at my touch. He leaned back into me. I brought my lips to his pulsing neck, then ran a trail up to his ear until he shuddered. He exhaled a faint moan. The music stopped. He turned and looked up at me, eyes lidded and glazed. His hands reached behind my hips and slowly pulled me closer. Our eyes locked for a few suspended moments. Then his hands touched my cheeks, pulling my lips down to his. I fell into his kiss with desperation warmed by the lingering ghost of his sonata and Zinfandel. His hands gripped my hips and pulled me onto his lap. I let one leg fall to each side of his hips. In an instant, we were a burning mass of kisses and hands desperately grasping at each other.

"Clara," he breathed into my mouth.

"Yes," I said.

In silence, we stood, and he took my hand. I followed him through the shadows of the living room and down the hall. We stepped into his bedroom, shards of moonlight penetrating the half-closed blinds. He pulled me into him and led me down onto soft pillows that smelled like him.

Our bodies danced in moonlight luminescence. In the darkness, our souls spoke to one another. Whispers that need no words. I pressed my lips to the hot skin of his abdomen and worked my way down the trail of coarse, dark hair. I always reveled in the scent of him—salt and sweat and leather. I could still taste that first kiss so many years ago—warm lips that fit perfectly into mine. I could still feel his hands pressing into my lower back, sending jolts of electricity to every extremity. I had believed back then with every fiber of myself that Sean was the only thing my soul would every need to be whole. That his would be the only lips I'd ever taste in the darkness. The naivety of youth is a cruel beast.

My lips pressed on despite the flood of memories assaulting my senses—shaking my composure by ripping me back to forgotten places. The trail of his stomach dipped down to a playfield of black hair and warmth. My mouth found him in the darkness as if it had never left this place. As if there hadn't been others beside me in the many lonely nights.

As I moved, he moaned and writhed, and I was tempted to abandon control and bring him over the edge. But I'd waited eight years to feel him inside me again. I realized now how desperately I had needed that piece of my soul back. Sean turned me over, and I saw the desire in his icy gaze as it caressed over my figure in the darkness. His lips touched mine again, then my breasts and neck. His hand dexterously slid into the bed stand drawer. With dexterous ease and the faint smell of latex, he pushed inside me, hard and raw with abandon, and I whimpered at the force of it.

"Am I hurting you?" he whispered, guttural and grating against the pulsing skin of my neck.

"Yes," I whispered through choked breath.

Sean stiffened, and his body pulled ever so slightly away. I tightened my arms around his back and pulled him closer, thrusting him harder, farther into me.

"Don't you dare stop," I said.

I had imagined him so many times as I lay in lonely darkness, wondering if he ever imagined me beside him. In the beginning, right after I left, thoughts of Sean had still been my salvation in dark places.

I'd blindly walked through these past years, tracing the labyrinths of my mind, its dingy mazes, all leading to stumped ends. But with one breath of his on my skin, one touch of his lips to mine, the world exploded into luminescence, guiding me back toward hope. In the tender moment of our embrace, I could almost believe that the dark days were over now. What we did —lying there in darkness, entwined around each other, soul and body—that was all that mattered now. I wiped a tear from my eye and rolled into him.

The morning fog intermingled with the breaking daylight, sending a stream of sunshine across the room, swathing us both in a golden glow. I stretched my arms out and assessed where I was. I was waking up beside Sean, in his very own house, after eight years apart. My cheeks broke into a warm smile, my body alive and balmy with a thin layer of sweat. In that moment between dreams and reality, I thought just maybe we were right for each other. Just maybe we could leave the memories in the dark places and go forward in a life far from here.

Sean rolled over and opened his eyes. He smiled at me through the hangover of sleep. I stroked his stubbled jaw, then his lips. He kissed the tips of my fingers lightly.

"Hey you. You're really here," he said.

"I'm really here." I smiled back. "Did you think I'd disappear in the night?"

"Never know with you."

"I can't believe I'm waking up to you again."

"We never did a whole lot of waking up next to each

other, considering we were teenagers. A lot more of sneaking in past curfew," I said.

"True, I suppose," he said, smiling.

He stroked my shoulder gently.

"I almost didn't recognize you with that tan," he said with a strong dose of mirth. "No longer the fair Scottish lass."

I smirked at his romantic description of my pale teen self.

"Three hundred days a year of sunshine in Austin," I said, examining the warm honey hue of my forearms.

"Not like this frigged outpost, I guess."

"Misconception about California. People think the entire state is like San Diego. Had to break it to them down in Texas that I barely saw the sun those eighteen years."

Sean laughed. "It's good for the blood."

I ran my fingers up his chest and around his shoulder. I traced the Celtic cross tattooed there.

"So, you still consider yourself a Catholic boy then?" I said half in jest.

He touched a finger to my lower lip.

"I'm not sure."

"And what kind of man can't remember if he's a Catholic or not?"

"Any man looking at you. I think you're enough to make any man forget his religion." He nibbled at my shoulder.

"Sean Killarney, you have a way of making a girl blush," I whispered.

He leaned over and kissed me, his hands running the smooth expanse of my back, pulling me into him.

We made love again, hard and fast and raw. Making love. It was not a term I even thought in my own mind, let alone said out loud. It was a notion of long forgotten times, of mystical British poetry and faded romanticized ideas. I didn't make love to men—we fucked after too much tequila or at best we just plain old had disconnected sex, climaxing in mediocre orgasms that came and went like a slight tickle. But this was so much more than that. It always had been.

We laid there for a moment afterward, heavy breaths but no words. He finally pulled from my embrace.

"Maybe some coffee?" he said.

He pushed himself up, letting the covers fall around his waist. Then I saw in the break of day what the glow of moonlight had hidden. The raised white line traversing his tight abdomen relayed a thousand memories words could never justify.

"What happened?" I barely breathed out. I gently traced the puckered scar with a fingertip. His stomach muscles clenched at the touch and he took a shaky breath.

"Stab wound," he said curtly. He took my hand and pulled it away. My breath caught.

"What?" Horrifying mental images of what those words entailed danced through my vision. "Iraq?"

He nodded.

"How?"

"It's a long story, Kendrick. One better just forgotten."

My heart protested, wanting to know every detail of that moment that had forever marked his psyche, marked his body. But he didn't need to speak the words to tell me. The sadness in his eyes revealed the shadow cast across his soul. Attempted explanations of the unexplainable wouldn't make it any more real to me. No words would ever bring me fully into his darkness.

I conceded and moved my hands up from the scar along his chest. I brought my eyes to his.

"I'm glad you came back alive," I said.

"Alive but not the same." He grimaced slightly.

"None of us are the same as yesterday."

He stroked my cheek, brushing rogue blonde strands from the sweaty skin. I leaned into him.

"What was it like?" I said.

"What?"

"Over there. The fighting."

Sean pulled me close and sighed into my hair. I could feel the sordid memories coursing through his body.

"Dark." He paused. I waited patiently for him to continue, not forcing the thoughts to the surface. "Have you ever been to a place void of all humanity? It will drain your soul."

"Like a dementor," I said softly, smiling. He sighed, and I feared for a moment I'd mis-stepped with humor. Sarcasm was my defense. But Sean gave a tiny laugh and squeezed me a little tighter.

"Like dementors. If an entire country was made of a dementor."

"I'm sorry you had to go through that," I said.

"There's no point in regrets. Who knows what would have come of me had I simply stayed here with my grief. At least the army distracted me. Put my grief into perspective."

"Perspective?"

"Everyone suffers loss. And as shitty as losing my sister was—and losing you at the same time—there were people over there who'd lost everything they'd ever known. Every*one* they'd ever known. Entire communities razed, leaving innocent people to despair on the streets. Families living in garbage bins."

"I hate to think that just because some have it worse, it minimizes what we went through."

"That's not what I said. I just said it gave me perspective.

I don't know—I guess being around so much despair and loss helped me deal. I could grieve alongside them. I don't know if I could have gone on with a normal life where everyone was just going about their days. Moving on."

"I do understand that," I said, the ink on my arm burning.

We rose from bed, sipped coffee on the balcony swathed in the brisk morning and pretended as though the last eight years had never come to pass. We were once again the only two people in the world.

"Are you all right?" he finally said.

"Hmm? Why wouldn't I be?"

"I thought you might have been crying last night. Afterward."

I gazed into my coffee. I would not unburden that moment of weakness on him. Not now in this perfection.

"Oh? No, I wasn't. Maybe I was sleep talking. Everything is perfect." I smiled. He took my hand and nodded.

"It is. At least for now."

36

Night fell like a thick blanket around us, presenting a spectacular display of diamond patterns illuminated by the darkness of the beach. Occasionally the breeze picked up and nipped at our skin, but soon enough the liquor would numb that sensation.

The drone of laughter and a soft guitar melody faded into the deep ocean beyond as I watched the waves gently lick their way up the shore. I let myself fall into their cadence and dream of the future to come. A future far away from Point Redwood.

The first drink led to the third, and the third soon turned into at least six. Somewhere between the serenity of the coastal night, the crackling of the bonfire and the dancing waves, I lost myself. I lost track of time, of my senses, of my surroundings. Sean nuzzled my neck from where he sat behind me on the beach.

"Let's go for a walk," Sean whispered in my ear with breath no heavier than a wispy summer breeze.

I scanned the beach to find Ruthi. She was sitting by the bonfire, swaying to the soft guitar music.

"She'll be fine," Sean said, reading my mind.

"I promised I wouldn't leave her," I said.

Sean pressed his lips to my throat and heat exploded down my spine.

"Just for a few minutes. She'll be fine. She's talking to Jerry. He'll talk her ear off all night," Sean said.

I glanced to my friend again. She did look happy enough, laughing softly at whatever Jerry was saying. She could survive a few minutes without us maybe...

"Let's sneak into the lighthouse," Sean said.

I laughed through my haze. "Why the lighthouse?"

Sean nibbled my ear, and I saw spots. "We've never done it in a lighthouse. Why not?"

His hands found their way under my shirt and up to tease my breasts. I could barely think.

"Just for a few minutes," I agreed.

SHE WENT DOWN SO EASILY. SUCH A WEAK THING—PALE AND *timid and fragile. Didn't even see it coming. She was a waste. In the way. Everything will be better now that she's gone. I did what had to be done. Off the rocks, into the shallow water below.*

Now the other one must go too.

37

Post-shower, Sean stared into the bathroom mirror and contemplated his treacherous mistake.

He did wrong. No other way to shape it. He'd done a bad thing. God dammit, a really bad thing. And the worst part was he didn't regret it. Not that he didn't feel guilty about it—but fuck, he was Catholic after all. He felt damn guilty about everything. But he'd do it all again. Every heart-pounding second of it.

What was it about Clara that turned him into a hormone-rattled, reckless teenager again? He'd always been willing to throw every caution to the wind if she asked. Willing to risk anything. Hadn't he learned anything about reckless abandon? Fucking hell.

Now what? Did he tell Tabby? Common decency would dictate yes. But what good would that accomplish? Break her heart to alleviate his own guilt? Didn't seem fair. But he couldn't very well stay with her as if nothing had gone on, could he? C'mon, Sean, do you even want to stay with Tabby after this? How would he go back to that mundane now?

She was a sweet girl. Fuck it, a really sweet girl. She'd been so good to him these past years, and they could build a solid life together. And he owed her, after the things she'd given up for him. Solid, good, sweet. Clara was none of those things.

38

I got home that morning with my head spinning from wine and sex and memories roused. Whatever we did last night, did not quell my fears about what was to come.

Mom was sitting in the living room when I stepped in. The house was deathly silent, and a strange tension hung in the air. I held my breath, knowing I smelled of sex and guilt.

"Mom?"

"Clara. You're home." Her voice was cold.

"Everything okay? You sound weird."

"Where have you been?" she snapped, her accusatory tone knocking me off my guard.

"Just out. With friends."

"You didn't call."

"I—sorry, mom. I'm not used to having to check in. Honest slip."

"Were you with Sean?"

I didn't answer.

She didn't turn to me. She clutched what looked like

photographs in one hand. I stepped closer. Finally, she turned to me, her eyes like glass.

"What's going on, mom? What are those?" She didn't respond so I carefully reached for the photographs. My stomach fell. Pictures of mom and Bill Connolly in a lover's embrace. Taken from the outside, looking into his bedroom through a window. The pictures must have been fifteen years old. There was a youthfulness to mom's eyes and smile. The beautiful woman she once was radiated happiness through the lens.

I looked up, alarmed. "Where did these come from?"

"An envelope on the front steps this morning."

"What? Why? Who are they from?"

"I don't know the answer to any of that. Do you?" Her tone was level and flat, cold.

"Me? What would I know about it?"

"I don't know, Clara. But you've been gone for nearly a decade, and life has gone on just fine. Then all of a sudden there are dead girls and headless cats and incriminating photographs." Her voice crackled with anger.

I deadpanned, speechless and taken aback.

"I didn't have anything to do with this!" I shouted, flinging the pictures at her. I felt like a child again, when word first got out around town about her and Bill. Knowing it was my fault but not understanding why.

Who did you tell, Clara?! Why would you do this to me?

I didn't know, mama!

As if it were an eleven-year old's responsibility to keep her mother's affair a secret.

"Why would someone send these?" Mom asked. "Is it a threat?"

Good question. Why would someone blackmail her over an affair long dead for a decade?

"It's not like it was a secret, Mom."

She glared at me in a way that pissed me off. *And whose fault is that?* Those eyes said.

"Don't look at me like that. I'm just being honest. This," I pointed to the scattered pictures, "was your mistake. Don't blame me when shit comes back to bite you in the ass."

Her angry expression fell.

"I know. Back then—" she said meekly, her voice cracking.

I held up a hand to stop her. I used to blame my mom for finding happiness. Blame her because I thought she was abandoning me to the darkness. Catholic communities aren't very forgiving of women who commit cardinal sins. And I wore the scarlet letter by proxy. Not like Bill ever felt the backlash of any of it.

"It's okay, mom. I know what you were going through with Dad. I was there. And I don't blame you for it. But don't blame me, either. I was just a kid. I didn't understand then what was going on."

She didn't respond to that. As a kid, people often mistook my self-sufficiency for maturity. The two are not mutually inclusive.

Mom reached down and picked up the photographs. "It doesn't make any sense. Why bother blackmailing me after so many years? And for something that isn't a secret? Your father's long gone, and Bill and his wife have since separated."

"Was there any kind of note?" I asked.

She shook her head. She ran her finger over the memory captured in faded color. She handed me the manila envelope.

"No. Just this."

CORINTHIANS 6:18 was written in bold red letters across the front.

I thought hard on the scripture. *"Flee from sexual immorality..."* My stomach slowly rolled over.

"I don't think someone's trying to blackmail you, mom. I think someone's just trying to scare you. I think...I think they just want you to know that they know things about us. That they've been watching for a long time. That they were able to get that close to your secret life without you knowing."

Mom looked up at me, her eyes glassy and worried.

"Does this have something to do with the murders?" She asked.

I fought down a swelling panic in my throat.

"I don't know mom. I really don't. But I don't think it's a coincidence."

Whoever was trying to get at me, was prepared to go through those I loved.

39

I texted Sean immediately to tell him about the photographs. He knew all about mom and Bill, of course, everyone did, but the unidentified voyeur was as much a mystery to him as to me.

Come by the bar tonight. After 7. He wrote back.

I readied myself to head to the Drunken Mermaid around eight. Things felt different than they had only twenty-four hours ago. It was like being fifteen all over again, finally crossing that threshold from friendship to more. But so much more complicated now.

I pulled on my trusted skinny jeans and boots, and a fitted V-neck tank that offered a peek at the goods, but just a peek. I took a little extra time with my makeup and gave my waves a little primping. Was I pretty? I don't know, I sort of thought so. *If you're into that kinda look,* I remembered a drunk guy in Austin telling me once.

When I asked what he meant, he'd said, "You know, the girl who's been around kind of look."

I nearly punched him, but then thought, what's so wrong with that? I *had* been around. Around the world, around pain, around perseverance. I'll wear those scars, proudly.

With a swab of lip gloss, I grabbed my purse, mom's keys and headed out.

The bar was mildly full, patrons scattered about, creating a low hum of noise. Folky rock highlighted the background mood.

Sean was working behind the bar wearing a blue flannel. Sleeves rolled up to his elbows. I bit my lip as I thought about his lean torso moving on top of mine. He spotted me and came over. His eyes twinkled with memory as he looked at me.

"Glad you could come. Just give me a couple of minutes to wrap something up, then Liv can take over for the night. Have a seat. Watcha drinking?"

"Oh, um, maybe just a beer."

He nodded and complied.

I sat, sipping a hoppy ale and observed the goings on of a small coastal town bar.

Salty old fishermen who'd likely frequented the original Pirate's Cove sat clutching tall pints, going on in low grumbles about the weather, the latest catch, the damned tourists. That was the thing about the old-timers. They loathed the tourism the summer months brought in but failed to see that without that burst of income, we'd be all but desolate in the winter months—lone candy bars on barren store shelves and three-day-old news on the rack. Hand scratched out menu items and duct taped chair legs. Local fishing commerce didn't sustain a town like ours anymore.

A group of younger kids—I'd barely put them at legal age only because Sean was smart enough not to admit minors—tossed darts and laughed by the fireplace in the back corner. What would that be like, to have never left this town? To have your formative years be nothing but this isolated workaday life? I suppose I get why people return to their roots, why someone like Georgina would find comfort in the simplicity of a small town to raise her family. But how can you ever form a real opinion on something if you have no comparison? Or was it better to embrace your community and never be the wiser?

A mellow pop song swayed in the background, and an older couple saw fit to take a turn in each other's arms. The Millers? Had she been a school teacher? Yes, maybe. The fire crackled in the corner, and a gentle breeze snuck in every time the front doors opened to the salty air to let in a new patron, who would undoubtedly be greeted with smiles by all. A home like this would be nice, I supposed. A community, familial support. But it would never be for me.

Finally, Sean came over, wiping his hands on a bar towel then tossing it into a sanitation bucket at the foot of the bar.

"Are those actually clean?" I asked, glancing dubiously at the murky water in the red plastic bucket. My one experience with service was a brief stint at a hostel bar in Chiang Mai where sanitation buckets were non-existent.

Sean gave me a little snicker but didn't answer.

"Come with me," he said.

I followed him as we walked through the bar and exited out the back door into the alleyway. I glanced about nervously—feeling prying eyes reach into my brain to sort through the sordid details of last night.

"What's this about?" I asked.

"Just follow me."

Sean led me into a little storage shed behind the bar and, for a moment, kinky thoughts popped into my mind. Leading me into naughty clandestine, are you, Sean? Was there a blanket laid out with candlelight and an aged scotch? Alas, no. He flicked on the one-bulb overhead light to reveal just a dumpy storage unit with crates of booze and cardboard boxes marked "Wet-naps" and "Sterilized white towels."

"You finally going to do me in, then? I always wondered how I'd go," I said, smiling.

"Not today, Kendrick. I want to give you something."

Again, my mind snuck back to the previous night--warm bodies pressed together in desperation for deliverance.

"Not like that," Sean said, noting my expression. I pursed my lips and tried to wipe all emotion from my face.

He shifted some boxes around and pulled out a tattered old trunk. He opened it, rummaged through, then pulled out a .38 pistol.

I gasped and took a step back. He stood and cradled the gun in his palm, staring down at it.

"Here," he said, extending it to me. When I hesitated, he wiggled it at me. I gingerly opened my grasp to take it, and Sean pressed the cold metal into my palm. Distant memories of broken curfews and ringing beer cans flooded my mind.

"You remember how to use this?" he asked.

I wrapped my fingers gingerly around the butt of the .38.

"Aim and pull?" I said with a wry smile.

Sean's lips twitched with amusement, spliced with fear.

"That's the general idea. Try to keep your eyes open when you do."

"Sean," I said with protest. "Why are you giving me a gun?"

He pressed his hand to mine holding the gun.

"It's just a precaution, Clara. You know me. Always paranoid."

"About what? You think I need protection?"

Sean rubbed the back of his neck.

"We don't know what we're dealing with here. I'd feel better if you had a little backup plan in case...I don't know. In case anything goes awry."

My heart fluttered. A boy giving me a gun to keep me safe? How romantic. My lips twitched at the notion, but I couldn't deny the way the gesture warmed me.

"Thank you," I said, checking the safety and setting it down.

"Just carry it with you, okay?"

"I can't carry a concealed weapon, Sean," I laughed.

"Who's gonna know? And who's gonna care around here? Police Chief Montgomery? C'mon, he likely thinks it's actually legal to carry."

"God, he's still Chief? He's got to be a hundred." I laughed.

"About right."

"All right. I'll keep it handy. The serial number isn't tied to a triple homicide or anything, right?"

Sean wiggled his eyebrows but didn't confirm or deny.

I slipped the pistol into my purse.

"This suddenly makes this whole thing feel so real," I said, shuddering.

Sean put a hand on my shoulder. "This is very real, Clara. Don't kid yourself otherwise."

"How did we get here?"

He shook his head.

"Fuck if I know. I thought I'd closed the door on this nightmare forever."

"That's the thing about real nightmares, isn't it? They never really go away because they live in the recesses of our minds. Lingering in the shadows. Quietly waiting to reappear at our most vulnerable moments."

"Be safe, okay? Just be safe whatever you do, wherever you go."

"I never thought I'd have to fear anything but judgment in this town," I said.

"That's the thing about small towns. The real dangers are waiting quietly in the shadows."

"With our nightmares."

"One and the same."

I shifted my bag, the worn leather feeling twice as heavy with the weight of its contents hiding inside.

"Thanks for looking out for me," I said.

"You know that the thing with your mom isn't your fault."

I gave him a doubtful look.

"You weren't the one who had the affair," Sean continued.

"But I'm the one who told."

"It's not your fault some crotchety nun overheard you. You were a kid, Clara. Why should the burden of those secrets be on you?"

I bit my lip and tried not to quiver. If only I'd kept my mouth shut all those years ago. It would have made both our lives so much easier.

"She was just looking for a bit of solace. A respite from dad," I shook my head. "I ruined that. I took it all away."

Sean took my arm and pulled me close to him.

"Clara, listen to me. You are not responsible for any of that. Not for your dad being an abusive prick, not your mom having an affair. Not for the small-mindedness of a bunch of uptight Catholic crones."

I started to tear up and bit down on my lip to stop it. His

lips came to my forehead, and a fingertip brushed under my eye. I hated feeling weak. I hated *being* weak.

Over the years I'd wondered if I subconsciously did it on purpose. If I wanted her to wake up and feel the reality of life. During the terrible years with dad, I never understand how mom could still be happy some days. What could she possibly have left to smile about? Dad wasn't home as often, but when he was, the fury was on overdrive. Drunken fists flew with abandon. But mom would still hum and smile and put on lipstick. Then I found out about Bill, and it shattered the already fragile existence I'd managed to tight-walk. What right did she have to be happy? What did Bill think of the bruises and the fractures? What kind of a man sleeps with a battered woman?

"It wasn't fair the way everyone turned on her," Sean reassured as if I didn't already know.

I shrugged. "Life isn't fair."

"She was so unhappy. People had to see that," Sean said.

"It doesn't matter if you're unhappy. You suffer through it because that's duty. Our little community doesn't allow for divergence."

"Like some Victorian novel."

"And what do you know about Victorian novels?" I snorted.

He toyed with a cheeky grin. "I took a class or two."

"On Victorian literature?"

"Well, British lit anyhow."

"When did you take classes? After the army?"

"No, during. I was thinking about a degree. Before I deployed anyway. After that...I just lost motivation."

"But British lit?" I laughed.

His smile faded into a sullen grimace. He shrugged.

"Literature is calming. And it reminded me of you."

A QUIVERING FIST WRAPPED AROUND MY HEART AND squeezed. My chest heaved. Sean stepped into me then, slid his arm around my waist and pulled me to him.

"This is a terrible idea," I whispered to the night.

"I like terrible ideas."

He lifted my chin and kissed me. Slow and tender, then hard, wanting. My lips parted, and we stood, tasting and pulling each other closer. His kiss deepened, and in a moment we were lost in each other. My body flooded with the need for him, pulsing against the surface of my skin. We fell back against the wall of the shed. His hands grasped at every part of me. My heart raced, and my breath came in short blips.

I grasped at his jeans, tugging, yanking. He groaned deep in his throat and pressed his body harder into mine. He wrapped his arms around my waist and hoisted me up onto a low chest of drawers. We tugged at each other until there was no fabric standing between us. He pressed into me, and I moaned against his mouth. The brisk night, the smell of wood, the feel of salt on the air—it all melted into a numbing wave of euphoria.

40

I was sitting at Patsy's, reflecting and jotting down memories in my notebook, trying to unravel my jumbled mind on the page, when a shadow crept into my sunshine.

"Clara."

I looked up into the face of Detective Lindsey...standing next to Ryan Rhodes.

"Holy shit." I laughed, giving Rhodes the once over. "If it isn't Officer Rookie Rhodes."

He towered over Lindsey by a good few inches, broad shoulders and Pop-eye arms protruding from a tight black tee-shirt. He still had his strong jaw and boyishly handsome face.

"Detective Rhodes now. Didn't think we'd ever see you back here, Kendrick," Rhodes said.

"Makes two of us," I said, leaning back in my chair.

Rhodes studied me for a few moments, his mouth toying with a faint smile. His hazel irises flicked just slightly down my frame then up again. Yeah, yeah, Rhodes, I got your number.

"Is there something I can help you with?" I finally asked.

"Actually, you might be able to. Are you free to come by the station later today?" Lindsey asked.

I remained impassive, but I wanted to scream.

"No, I'm not."

"Clara, c'mon. For old times," Rhodes said, charm on overdrive.

"Two girls are dead, Clara. Strangled, beaten, thrown out like trash. Don't you care?" Lindsey asked. I rolled my eyes.

"Look, you want to talk? Pull up a chair. I have time right now. But it's all you're getting," I said.

Lindsey and Rhodes exchanged wary looks then Rhodes shrugged.

"Have it your way," he said.

The two detectives snagged chairs from another table and took their place across from me. I closed my notebook and sat up straight.

"All right. How may I assist Point Redwood's finest?"

"So this town is pretty Catholic?" Lindsey started.

I snorted. "Rhodes could have told you that. He grew up here too. Made a damn cute choir boy."

I bat my eyes at Rhodes.

Lindsey pursed his lips.

"Right. What I'm getting at is, growing up, did you and your friends—how do I put it—buy into it?"

The question caught me completely off guard.

"Buy into it? I...I suppose for a little bit. I mean, we all believe what our parents tell us for a while, right? I don't know. I guess it depends on who you ask."

"I'm asking you."

"Personally, I found the whole thing pretty damn hypocritical, but what does this have to do with anything?"

"When Ruthi was killed, they ruled out sexual assault definitively," Lindsey said.

My stomach tightened, and I curled my fists reflexively at the memories.

"Yeah. They were wrong," I said curtly.

"And how do you know that so conclusively?"

"You can read it in the report."

"Clara, c'mon," Rhodes pushed.

I sighed. "I know it because she was my best friend, my sister. My God damn bosom buddy—however you want to say it, we were closer than anyone."

"Except for Sean," Lindsey said.

"Entirely different."

Lindsey raised an eyebrow at me skeptically.

"If Ruthi had had sex with anyone—fuck, if she had so much as thought someone was mildly attractive—she would have told me. She was raped. And if you want to deny it, then that's your stupid fucking problem," I said.

"Glad to see you still have the same dirty mouth, Kendrick," Rhodes said, full lips curling at the side.

I glared hard.

"Why are you asking me this?" I said.

"As you know, these new cases match Ruthi's very closely, and we're trying to make a judgment call," Lindsey said.

My heart did a little tap dance in my chest.

"Were..." I choked on the words, and I took a breath. "Were Hannah and Kate raped, too? For sure?"

Lindsey looked uncertain, his mustached mouth twisting. His gray eyes flicked to the papers in his hands, and I knew the answer.

"I can't discuss all the details with you."

"You want my help? I want honest facts."

He nodded slowly. "It's difficult to say. About the assault, I mean."

"What? Isn't that your job?" I said, incredulous.

"Both showed signs of recent sexual activity, but not necessarily trauma. It could have come from a normal sexual encounter, although the friends we've interviewed said both girls claimed to be virgins." He shrugged.

I chewed my lip. It was inconclusive. Catholic girls had been known to lie even to their friends about sex. This is one God damn judgmental town, and no one wanted to be found out. *He without sin* did not apply.

The same thing had happened with Ruthi. Sexual activity evident, but rape kit inconclusive. No semen, no obvious trauma other than the tearing that comes with normal first-timers. Sean and I knew better, but we'd had little luck proving that to anyone other than his parents. They certainly didn't want to believe their daughter had been slutting around pre-maritally. They'd rather picture their daughter raped than willing. Fuck this town. No, seriously fuck it.

"Can't you like check their Instagrams or something? Find out if they had boyfriends?" I asked.

Lindsey shot me a look that said, *yeah didn't think of that one, Clara.*

I leaned back in my chair and folded my arms over my chest.

"So what you're asking is, were these really good little Catholic girls or were they covering up their sinful ways to everyone they knew?

"Something like that."

"Wouldn't be the first good girls to veer off the path," Rhodes added suggestively.

"I don't know what to tell you guys," I said, ignoring

Rhode's inappropriate insinuations. Glad to see he hadn't changed much. "I can speak to Ruthi, but I didn't know anything about Hannah or Kate. Didn't even know they existed until I got here."

"Hmm," Lindsey said as if he didn't believe a word out of my mouth.

"You want my advice, Lindsey? Ask yourself what's more plausible. That three girls were lying to everyone they know about having a boyfriend, or that the sick fuck who murdered them also raped them. Why didn't you ask me about Samantha Bellows?" I blurted it out before I realized it. Shit.

Lindsey considered me or a moment.

"How do you know about her?" he asked.

"I read it on the Internet. That Web is everywhere these days." I prayed my sarcasm masked my trembling nerves.

"Do you know anything about Samantha's death?" Lindsey asked pointedly.

"No. Just that the M.O. is similar."

"We're still looking into things. We're not sure they're related," Lindsey said.

"Why didn't they know about it back when Ruthi was killed?" I asked.

"From what I can tell, the departments didn't have great lines of communications back then. The murder fell into Humboldt jurisdiction. Owing to oversight or incompetence, the connection between the two was never made." Lindsey glanced to Rhodes for confirmation.

"There was a wave of drug killings up there that year. Samantha's case got lost in the chaos, I guess. Wouldn't be the first time," Rhodes said.

I pushed myself from my chair, grabbing up my notebook.

"Well, maybe now she'll actually get some justice. I don't have time to help you do your jobs. Bother someone else."

I slipped a twenty under my plate and left.

41

The next night, I joined Georgina for dinner at her quaint house on the ridge overlooking the town. I handled the little pistol as I prepared to head out, the cold metal feeling ten times its weight in my grasp. I slipped it into my purse, then took it out again. I couldn't just start carrying a gun every time I left the house. And I wasn't going to dinner with a suburbanite mother packing.

I drove up the road, avoiding looking at the glowing lighthouse on the horizon, and headed up the ridge. They'd built up the little ridge with new construction, creating a tranquil suburban slice in our little town, miles away from anything that could remotely be considered urban. I parked mom's car outside a mini faux Victorian with a manicured lawn. There were even a little white fence and a mailbox with wooden animal designs. How very quaint.

I had dreams of a similar life once. Dreams about family and kids and little houses in quiet neighborhoods. It was strange to see what life could be like when it was uncomplicated by past demons. A cozy living room littered with a toddler's toys. Smiling family portraits lining the hallways.

A real dining table with matching flatware and cloth napkins. I guess I was meant to dance a darker tango than this. Not for Sunday BBQs.

Georgina's husband was out for the night with friends, so we had a good old-fashioned girls' night, complete with giggles and wine—a foreign concept to me. Even in Austin I wasn't one for a lot of female friends, other than Lola. But I wasn't complaining. It was nice to think about something other than the investigation or Sean. Having what she deemed a "small life," Georgina wanted to know all about my adventures over the past eight years. I gave her a high-level version of my travels, throwing in a few juicy details about my escapades with sexy foreigners, and watched her little face light up with amusement.

Then she asked about Sean, and I quickly diverted. I couldn't even process Sean in my own mind, let alone explain the thing between us to someone else. It was every-thing terrible and everything perfect at the same time. Try reconciling that with your heart.

Jim arrived back around ten, and that was my cue to leave the happy little family to their domestic bliss.

When I was halfway down the hillside road, the dash-board lights suddenly started flashing. Startled, I swerved the car. I regained control and tried to figure out what was going on. Check Engine light. Beeping. Shit. I pulled over to the side of the road, well aware of my creepy-as-fuck surroundings. I double checked the locks on the door, then pulled out my phone to call mom and see what the deal was. No service. Of course not. I sighed and slammed my head against the seat. I'd just have to risk the car blowing up in the next two miles.

I turned the key. Nothing. Wouldn't even turn over.

Just fucking great.

Despite my alternating curses and prayers, the engine wouldn't turn over.

I peered out the window and tried to figure out exactly where I was. It was difficult to tell in the dark, but I thought I was only a couple of blocks off of Main Street. It turned woodsy quickly as you got toward the water, but it wasn't that far to town. Pre-driving, we trudged all around this area on bikes and by foot after all. I had no choice but to hoof it home. Or at least into town where I could get service to call for a ride.

I pulled on my leather jacket—silently cursing that I needed a jacket at all in the dead of summer here—and took a breath before stepping out into the brisk night.

The silence of the wood engulfed me, pulling me into sensory deprivation. It's hard to imagine a place can be so quiet. Living in downtown Austin, I'm used to the constant hum of city life—a chaotic lullaby. But tonight was static, calm.

Then my ears picked up the subtle low purr of the night dancing about—rustling leaves, the soft song of crickets, the lap of the ocean over the bend. I've always found comfort in the call of the sea. A reminder of where I am, so close to the edge of the world. A beacon toward home. I shivered and set out down the desolate road.

Every sound is echoed in the country. Every step on pavement and every slight tickle of a pine tree needle. It's calming, but it can be uncanny if you're not used to it. I walked down the road, breathing in the fresh air, trying to calm my racing mind. Trying not to think about the serial killer lurking in the woods. After a few minutes of walking, I came upon the Point Redwood cemetery, which sat on the edge of town on the little road that led to the beach. I've always found eerie beauty in a graveyard. In the South, especially New Orleans, their graveyards are works of macabre art. Soulful mourners silently stroll the grounds, placing brilliant bouquets for their loved ones. Gothic revival mausoleums guard over the departed. Unmarked graves honor unidentified hurricane victims. The Point Redwood cemetery was a bit more Stephen King than Anne Rice, but it still held a quiet loveliness.

The evening was cool, a light breeze rustling summer leaves. I ran my hand along the iron fence, remembering those days when Sean, Ruthi and I would sneak in here with stolen wine. No one would bother finding us in here as our little small-town Catholics were wary to step where angels fear to tread.

In the distance, I saw the lighthouse on the hill. A shimmering beacon of hope from a lost time, now a tourist attraction for the Mendocino explorer. How many nights had it served as our secret place in the shadows? Until that last night. That lighthouse only meant death to me now. A chill crept through me, and I pulled my coat tighter.

I decided to take the small path that ran the perimeter of the cemetery—a little shortcut. I needed to be inside ASAP. I hustled along the path, wary of every shadow and sound.

I heard footsteps. I stopped, heart pounding. I rotated my head hesitantly to each side. I took a breath and flipped around. Nothing. You're fucking paranoid, Clara. I kept moving. My boots echoed eerily off the path in the silent night. The air smelled of salt and sand, and a slight sea breeze danced around me. The footsteps grew louder. I swallowed hard. It wasn't real. Just the wind. Or a raccoon. Or a serial killer.

In books it's said that the fear chills you to the bone. But it doesn't start like that. It starts with a slow creep up your arms, then reaches around to tickle your spine. Tendrils ascend each vertebrate, with slow precision, plucking each nerve like a harpsichord. Only then does fear begin its descent toward your bones.

I sped up, and the footsteps picked up. I could outrun whoever it was. I knew this graveyard like my own home. But there's no one there, Clara, remember? You're imagining things. Prove it, self. I stopped suddenly and turned around.

And I screamed.

42

A shrouded figure was a hundred yards behind. No face, only a dark shadow. Fucking Hell. It stood, watching. I froze, staring into its nothingness. I thought of the gun Sean had given me, and I cursed myself for not having put it in my purse.

I took a step backward, and it took one forward in turn like a shadowy mirror. I was freezing and pouring sweat at the same time. My head was spinning, my heart pounding. No way this guy was taking me too. I'm not a weak little girl, mother fucker. Bring it. If I was certain he didn't have a weapon, I would have stayed and faced him down.

I turned and bolted into the cemetery. The footsteps hurried after. I didn't dare turn to look. My legs burned as I ran, turning corners around headstones and tombs. Was it keeping up with me? I couldn't look. I ran and ran, heaving, cold salty air stinging my lungs. I missed a low headstone and smashed right into it, tumbling forward. I landed on my wrist, twisting it awkwardly. I let out a low groan but couldn't take the time to wallow. I jumped back up, spinning slightly as I did to catch a glimpse of the shadow chasing me. But he was no longer chasing me. He was right there beside me.

He grabbed my right wrist, and I screamed. I twisted and turned, trying to break free of his grip. Instinctually, I twisted my body, bending his arm back in the process. The figure let out a growl as his arm twisted back unnaturally. His body contorted and I dropped down, pulling the figure down with me. He loosened his grip just enough for me to gain momentum. I revved back my leg and let my knee plow into his gut. The figure grunted and dropped his grip on my arm enough for me to pull free.

I turned again and ran. Ran faster than I'd ever done in any training. My legs burned, but I pushed through. The footsteps faded into the night, but I didn't look back. I ran until the landscape of the cemetery opened up to white sand. I ran toward it, not knowing what awaited me. My foot sank into the first step of sand, and I crashed into someone. I screamed but a hand went over my mouth.

43

"Shh, shh, Clara, it's me," Sean said. I shuddered and collapsed into his chest.

"Fuck, Sean, Oh my God."

"Hey, hey, what's wrong? What happened?"

"There was a man...a man chased me. Through the cemetery. All black." I choked out.

"Wait, what? Slow down, Clara. Where?" Sean looked behind me.

"He was behind me and then I ran, and he chased me here."

"Why were you in the cemetery?"

"My...mom's car...it broke down, and my phone didn't have service, and so I was taking that shortcut path, and he was just there." I rambled through shaky breath.

"Hey, hey, it's ok." He pulled me closer.

I heaved against his chest, collecting my composure. I pulled away from Sean and something registered.

"What are you doing out here?" I asked. Why was Sean out on the beach alone in the middle of the night?

"I was out for a walk. It's a nice night."

He was too quick to answer.

I looked him over. Black jacket, dark jeans—nearly black. An icy shudder went up my spine. I stepped away from him, a terrible feeling filling me.

"What's wrong, Clara?"

I shook my head slowly to the side.

"Were you...were you following me?"

He laughed. "What? No, of course not."

I tried to picture the figure. A shadow. But it could have been Sean. I stepped backward.

"I need to go."

"Clara, wait. Where are you going to go? I'll drive you home."

"No," I backed away. "Just leave me alone." My head was spinning. It couldn't be—but my instincts were on fire.

"Clara—"

"No!"

I turned and ran, stumbling in the sand. Sean followed.

"Don't follow me!" I screamed.

"Clara, stop! What the hell is wrong?"

He gained on me quickly, sand and panic weighing me down. He grabbed my arm.

"Clara, stop!" His fingers dug into my bicep. Instinct took over, and my right hook came around. My fist connected with his jaw and he went down. I stumbled, found my balance and ran as fast as I could down the beach. Sean's calls faded into the laps of the ocean.

CHUCK'S OIL, GAS AND MINI MART WAS STILL OPEN WHEN I stumbled in, huffing and spinning and ready to pass out. The pimply teen boy behind the counter reading a magazine looked up disinterested for a few moments, then turned back to his comic.

I grabbed a bottle of water from the cooler and slammed in on the counter, wiping sweat from my brow.

He looked at me and blinked, confused.

"Rough night or something?" he asked in some kind of male version of upspeak.

I glared and threw down a dollar.

I pulled out my phone and was relieved to have service.

"Hey, is there a tow company in town?"

He looked at me like I'd asked him to name every capital city in Africa.

"Never mind," I shook my head and pulled up my search browser.

A HALF HOUR LATER, BRIAN MCMILLANS (METH HEAD DADDY, mom was a bartender, brother went to prison) was hitching mom's SUV to the back of his tow rig after a failed jump attempt indicated we were looking at more than a dead battery. We dropped the car off at the shop, and then he was kind enough to take me back home.

As I assumed, mom was fast asleep, and the house was pitch black inside except for eerily moonlit shadows. My skin felt like it was peeling off and my mind raced a million miles per hour. I either needed a drink or to punch something. Or both.

I poured some red wine into a tumbler and went to the garage. I rotated sipping and letting my fists pummel into canvas for a while before my body finally collapsed with exhaustion.

My phone buzzed.

Sean: *Are you okay? What was that all about anyway?*

I closed the screen. I was being crazy. I had to be. A terrifying thought of the things Sean might be capable of crossed my mind. How well did I really know him anymore? The man had been to war, suffered loss and pain. Maybe he'd snapped. Maybe he was never who you thought, Clara. Maybe that night eight years ago...No. That was absurd. Sean was with you when Ruthi was killed. He didn't hurt her. And Sean wasn't chasing me through a graveyard.

But somebody was. I wasn't crazy about that. Someone was out to get me. To what end, I had no clue. Terrorizing me? Framing me? Killing me? One way or another, I had to get to the bottom of this before it was too late.

My phone buzzed again.

Sean: *Please talk to me. I don't know what you think I did, but I would never hurt you. How do you not know that?*

My thumb circled the screen keyboard. I typed a few words, then deleted. Then typed again.

Me: *I'm sorry. I freaked out. My mind feels fractured, and for a moment I didn't know what was real.*

Sean: *I'm real.*

Me: *I know.*

Sean: *Want me to come over?*

Me: *No. I just want to sleep. Let's talk tomorrow.*

44

S ean and I stumbled through the cool sand, fingers tightly interlocked like unbreakable chains in the wake of our clandestine encounter in the old Point Redwood lighthouse. The moon raised high in the indigo sky lit a glimmer of path along the rocky shoreline as unruly waves crashed into the abandoned night with intemperance. My eyes—half-lidded with the veil of satisfied lust and warm whiskey—scanned the deserted beach for Ruthi. My desire to share my current state of jubilance with my best friend gushed over with sloppy rapture.

I called for her, my voice hoarse and laughing and lost on the winds of breaking dawn. Sean swayed and fell into me, his arms shielding me from the attack of Pacific Ocean wind. I called into the gray expanse of mist and fog for Ruthi, but the beach responded with an eerie emptiness.

I was suddenly cold—frigid to my bones despite the blanket of booze around my nerves. *We shouldn't have left her alone*, the swelling guilt whispered in my ear. She was delicate, fragile, easily spooked.

She was fine, I contended to my conscience. These were

our friends. And it was high school graduation night. She would forgive me this indulgence.

But, no, she would have no occasion to do so.

In a spotlight of moon glow, Ruthi lay in front of me, dark hair sprawled across the damp sand and frothy foam of the waning tide. Her pale eyes stared vacantly at the full moon above.

I ceased to breathe. I ceased to exist. No, no, no. But she was gone. And it was my fault.

45

The next morning, I sat at the sidewalk corner table at Patsy's and chewed my cuticles like they were the daily special. Horrific images, past and present, conspired in my mind to rip apart my composure. It was all too much. I had to get out of this hellhole before it devoured me alive. Explaining what had happened to mom had been a challenge. I kept the details high level, but she knew I wasn't telling her everything. They'd have the car another day or two, but Brian McMillans had been good enough to come give me a ride into town. No charge, he'd said with a wink. If I needed a loaner, they had a couple of used cars for sale on the lot. I was happy to use one for a few bucks a day. Small towns never do change. Sometimes, that's a good thing.

I'd go see Sean later, after ten more cups of coffee. I picked at my bagel with butter. I hadn't had these many non-alcoholic carbs in the past year.

I had to trust Sean. He was all I had right now. Sean wouldn't hurt me. Not like that, anyway.

God, I wanted a fucking cigarette.

"Clara," a high-pitched voice signaling something I did not want to deal with rang out.

I looked up from my coffee. Tabby Gates was standing in front of me, arms crossed. Her small mouth was pursed into a tight little pink bow. Her blonde curls lay over her slender shoulders, and I noted how her pink manicure was the exact same shade as both her lipstick and her satchel handbag.

"Hey, Tabby," I pretty much muttered. She breathed heavily, and I awaited the onslaught of insults.

"I need to talk to you," she said, practiced resolve in her tone.

"So talk." I had a decent suspicion what she needed to talk about, which set my nerves on edge.

She heaved, and I swear, her blonde curls were pulsing with her anger.

"I know about it," she said coolly.

"About what?" I tried to hold back the exasperation in my tone, but I had no capacity to deal with her.

"About you and Sean!" Her rosy cheeks flared an alarming shade of crimson and her doe eyes budged, cartoonish. I deadpanned.

"About our past? Of course you know that." I played it off.

"Don't be an idiot, Clara. The rumors always said you were smart. I'm inclined to believe them."

"What are you getting at?"

"The other night. I know you and Sean were together. You want to explain?"

"Maybe you should ask Sean."

"I'm asking you."

The determination in her tone set my teeth on edge. Hell hath no fury and all.

I sighed and tried to stay calm.

"Tabby, we're being investigated on these murders. Naturally, we're going to be spending some time together. But there's nothing between us. He's all yours, cupcake."

My flippancy clearly ignited her rage even more.

"Don't lie to me!" She squealed, garnishing the attention of neighboring tables.

"Jesus, Tabby. Can you not make a scene? Calm down."

"Me make a scene? Your being back in Point Redwood makes a scene. You don't get to show up after all these years and ruin a good thing. Sean is mine."

Something in her declaration lit a match in me. Mine? Yours? Right, girlie. Dream on. Sean was always mine.

"You're being paranoid," I said.

"So you're going to try to tell me that you didn't stay the night at his place?"

My stomach lurched, and I clenched my muscles to keep from reacting. How did she know? A woman always knows. Cheaters be warned.

"Can you please just go? I have a lot on my mind, and I don't have time for this." I did my best to show I couldn't be bothered with her schoolgirl antics, but secretly, my guilt was festering.

"I was about to say the same thing to you. I think it's time you go back to wherever it is you've been hiding out."

Stupid little bitch, I will use you as a cocktail garnish.

Breathe, Clara.

I sat up straight, crossed my arms and looked her dead on.

"I don't get a lot of say in the matter. Believe me, I'm on that highway and as far away from this shithole as I can be the moment they say go."

Tabby's brown eyes narrowed, and I could tell she was trying to intimidate me. As much as anyone who was once head of the virgin club could possibly intimidate anyone. I gave her credit for trying, though.

I sighed. She was poking my mean side, and I didn't feel like tearing into her.

"Look, Tabby. I don't have a fight with you, okay? There's nothing going on between Sean and me. I'm not trying to get in between you. If you make him happy, then I'm happy for you."

She twisted her mouth and studied me. I knew that look. Calculating her next move, next word.

"I'm not stupid, Clara," Tabby said calmly. "I love Sean. I won't let you ruin that."

I nodded but didn't respond. Sean was the type that a girl would fight for and I couldn't blame her. But he wasn't mine to fight for anymore.

Tabby gave me one last look before she turned on her heel and walked away. I studied her as she got into her little SUV. Her eyes followed me down the street as she drove off.

46

I sat on the beach that late afternoon, watching the waves ebb and flow and reach futile crescendo against the rocks. The sun was sinking into its distant cradle, yawning across the horizon before it relented to the night.

I shouldn't let Tabby get to me, but how could I not? I deserved everything she'd said.

"Hey you."

I turned. Sean was heading down the beach path, hands in his Levi pockets. The coastal wind teased his shaggy dark hair, and his fair cheeks were flushed from the sting of salty air.

"Hi. What are you doing out here?" I said.

"Just out for a walk. Can I join you?"

I shrugged and nodded. He took a seat next to me in the sand. His cheek had a faint bruise.

"Sorry about your face," I said. He snickered.

"Remind me not to get on your bad side. One hell of a hook."

He reached his arm around me. I stiffened, suddenly a jumble of nerves and embarrassment. We hesitated in time for a moment and then before I realized it, he'd pulled me into his chest and pressed his lips to my forehead. My stomach did a backflip, and I couldn't tell if I was over-whelmed with affection or fear. His hands ran down the length of my back tenderly.

I stiffened and pulled from his embrace.

"Sean, don't."

He looked down at me curiously with those bright diamond eyes.

"Are you still freaked out from last night? Shit, Clara, I'm sorry you got scared, but you have to know I—"

"No, I know," I interrupted. "Someone chased me through the cemetery. Someone was trying to scare me. I know it wasn't you. And I'm sorry for freaking out on you. I just, I don't know, I panicked. It just all seemed so perfectly timed. What were you doing out there, anyway?"

"I told you, I was just out walking. I do that sometimes, go for beach walks at night. It's soothing. You have to remember I work late. I'm a night person now."

I nodded. "Sounds reasonable enough."

Sean laughed. "I didn't think I had to have valid excuses for going on walks. What were you doing?"

"I'd been with Georgina. At her house. We had a little dinner and wine and just chatted."

"Do they know what happened to your car?"

I shook my head. "It wasn't a dead battery. It was like a full-on electric malfunction."

Sean ran his fingers through his hair absentmindedly.

"This is all getting out of control. What the fuck is going on, Clara?"

"Hell if I know. But someone is out to get me. Someone wants me to pay, to suffer."

"Did you call the police?"

"No."

"Why not?" he asked.

"Because I don't know who to trust, Sean." I pulled away.

"I think you're being a little film noir right now, Clara. When scary men chase you through cemeteries, you call the cops."

"Fine. I'll call Lindsey later."

"So what are *you* doing out here?" He asked a little smirk at his lips.

"Just thinking."

"About?"

"What a fucking disaster I am."

I was being serious, but he laughed nonetheless.

"A touch dramatic," he said.

"Sean, I think we need to talk about what's happening."

"What do you mean?"

"I mean what happened the other night. What's happening right now. Between us."

Sean nodded and pressed his lips together. "Ah. You regret it."

Did I?

"No. I just...I think we complicated an already complicated situation."

"You're probably right. But," he paused and looked around the tranquil setting for a moment, searching. "Having you back, even for those moments in a confusing night, it was surreal. The moment you came back—that first moment I saw you again—it was like life finally made sense again."

My heart clenched. I knew exactly what he meant. It was like finding home after years of running blind.

"Look, Clara, I know about your boyfriend in Austin," Sean finally said.

I snapped up to meet his eyes. "Sean, what are you talking about? I don't have a boyfriend."

He looked at me like I'd been caught sneaking out my window at night. "I...saw pictures."

"What? What kind of pictures?" My heart started to race.

Sean rubbed his jaw uncomfortably. "Someone, I don't know who—blocked number, texted me a...a sex pic. Of you and some long-haired guy."

My stomach twisted. Aiden...but who would do that? I suddenly remembered my hacked Cloud.

"Sean, I...I don't know what to say. I'm sorry. He's not my boyfriend. He's just...a guy. He doesn't mean anything to me. I don't know why anyone would send that to you."

"Scare me off, I guess."

We sat in silence for a few moments, trying to process yet another layer to this mess.

"Tabby had some words with me today," I said.

Sean's face fell.

"Yeah, Sean, remember your girlfriend? This isn't just about what feelings we may or may not have conjured up in a night of confusion and too much wine. You have someone in your life who seems to care a shit ton about you."

He stared into the sand for a moment, contemplating.

"What did she say to you?" he asked.

"She basically said she knew about the other night and warned me to stay away. Kind of threatened me, actually."

Sean chortled slightly. "She threatened you? I bet that was cute."

"Hey, it's what I would do."

"I think you'd have already poisoned her in her sleep."

"Sean, can you please not make jokes like that when I'm currently a triple murder suspect?"

"Sorry. I'm sorry she harassed you." He reached for me again, but I scooted back.

"I'm not," I admitted to my surprise. I turned and met his blue stare directly. "Sean, why are you even with her? The other night came so easily to us. You didn't protest or even raise an objection."

"It's complicated," Sean said. He ran a hand over his afternoon shadow.

"Oh? Enlighten me on its complications then," I said, growing frustrated.

He sighed and blew out air. "Tabby and I...ok, so you know how she's always been? Pretty religious, saving herself and all that?"

"An uptight virgin? Yeah, I recall."

He rolled his eyes at me. "Give her a break, just how she was raised. Have you ever met her mom? Makes Tabby look like a Burning Man devotee."

His gaze went out to the outstretched ocean. Then he continued.

"That summer. After Ruthi, after you left," he gulped in a breath. "We got together."

My stomach dropped.

"You had sex," I stated, the words settling like ash on my tongue.

He nodded. "Yes. And as you might imagine, it was her first time. So it was a big deal."

Eight years ago, Sean, the Sean that was still mine, had slept with Tabby.

"How long after me?" I whispered. My stomach turned and red rage burned at my cheeks. But I had no right. I had already left him.

"A few weeks after, I guess." He turned to face me. "I was a mess, Clara. My sister had just been murdered, and you were gone and all the shit the press was saying about it. She came to me and I...I just went there. Embraced the comfort."

I chewed my lip and forced down the swelling anxiety.

"Okay, so you took her virginity. Big deal. It happens to us all." I tried futilely to brush it off.

"Clara, it *was* a big deal. This is a girl who's planned on waiting for marriage her entire life. The thought of anything else never crossed her mind. So, yeah, giving that to me was a big deal."

"Oh, c'mon, you're acting as if she sold you her soul wrapped in gold. It's a fucking hymen."

"Can you please try to have a little tact here? When did you get so crude?"

I pressed my eyes closed for a moment to force out persistent images of Sean and Tabby.

"Sorry. So if it was such a big deal to her, why'd she do it?"

"I've asked that same question. She said she loved me. I was too much of a mess to care whether it was true."

"Okay, I understand. I can see why you think you owed her something. But that doesn't mean you're bound for life."

"There's more."

Fuck. My stomach churned.

"Okay."

"As you know, I left for Iraq right after. But, before that..." he breathed in. "She got pregnant."

I nearly fainted. My lungs tightened. Head throbbed.

"What?" I barely whispered. He nodded. "What happened to it? Did she...did she..."

"She lost it. Right after I left. Blamed it on the trauma of losing me."

I shook my head, confused. "I don't understand. Were you together? Like a couple?"

"No! We did it just the one time. Fucking odds, right? She wanted more from me. A lot more. Seemed to think we already had a lot more. But I'd already gotten my deployment orders. Plus, I didn't want Tabby back then. I didn't want anything but a one-way ticket to self-destruction."

"So she blames you," I said.

"I think she did. God, I was so relieved when she told me she'd lost it. I mean, shit, I was sorry for her pain, but I was nineteen and a disaster."

"I don't know how to process this, Sean." I stood, shaking out my hands. "What the Hell? Why didn't you tell me?"

He shrugged. "I didn't think it was something I needed to tell you. It was a long time ago."

"Is that why you came back here after the army? To be with her?"

"Not at all. When I got back home, I was still a mess, just for different reasons. She was there, was comforting. We reconnected. She'd grown up, matured. It was nice. She'd also come to realize that the loss was a blessing."

I leaned against a rock and sunk my head into my hands. My brain throbbed against my skull.

"Clara," Sean said, standing and coming toward me.

"No. Just don't, Sean. I need to process this." I looked up. "This changes things."

"Does it?"

"Are you that cold? Or just delusional? You broke her heart once, and you're doing it all over again. Has the world broken you that much that you don't even care?"

His head lowered and he nodded.

"I need to think about this, okay? I'll come by tomorrow," I said.

"Alright," he said. With a lamenting smile, he headed back up the beach.

47

I was at that point where I was going to break down or start punching random things I passed on the street. Before last night, I'd only ever hit another human in earnest once. And although I loathe the idea of ever hurting someone smaller and weaker than I am, I'll maintain that Bethany absolutely deserved it for tormenting some Muslim girl wearing a Hajib at a UT party.

Ooh, do you have a bomb in there? Or did your husband try to strangle you so you're hiding your neck? Bethany, an overly tanned plastic thing with bad highlights and ill-fitting spandex jeggings, sneered.

Maybe one of her sister wives cut off her hair in a jealous rage, another sniveling troll with too much lipstick said.

I mean, really, there are still bullies in college? And get your insulting polygamous rhetoric right, bitches.

It nearly got me expelled, but Bethany retracted the charges. Maybe I'm just that intimidating. I smiled at the thought. Bullies deserved to be bullied. Yeah, my therapist was a HUGE fan of my boxing classes.

That feeling was festering now as I walked down Main

Street the following afternoon. It wasn't exactly Tabby who was the crux of my frustration, rather just everything compounded.

I knew what blind jealousy could do to a person's psyche. Even with my hot and cold feelings about Aiden, every time I'd hear a rumor about who he might have been with last night after the show while I sat awake in bed, waiting for a text that would never come, it tore out a piece of me. Jealousy is a cruel emotion.

Whoever this killer was, they were ripping this town apart at its seams. Digging his claws into everyone's wounds. Was that his motivation? What did this town do to him that he wanted to see it burn?

"Clara?"

I spun on my heels, fists clenching. Georgina was standing there in workout clothes, clutching a yoga mat and a coffee.

"Oh, hey, G." I exhaled.

"You okay?"

"Yeah, fine. Why?"

"You look...perplexed. Troubled." Her big China doll eyes looked me over worriedly.

I did a self-examination and noted my hands were clenched at my chest, and my lip was bleeding from biting down on it. I untangled myself.

"Oh, just a lot on my mind."

"Is this about the murders?" she asked.

"How did you...what do you know about that?"

She shrugged. "Want to get some coffee?"

I hesitated. I just wanted to be alone and stew, maybe yell at Sean about something, anything, but Georgina's face was surprisingly difficult to reject.

"Yeah, okay."

We went into Patsy's Café and sunk into an isolated booth in a back corner. I ordered a cappuccino and a buttery pastry I was going to have to run off later. Stress and healthy diets don't play well together.

"So what's going on?" Georgina asked.

I picked at my pastry and contemplated what to say. How much could I tell her?

"These murders are...bringing up a lot of weird things for me," I started slowly. She nodded and waited for me to continue. I imagined she was that teacher all the kids came to with their owies and tears.

I took a breath.

"Police think I'm involved. They think I had something to do with killing those girls. Maybe even with killing Ruthi." I blurted it out, truth cascading from my lips before I could stop it.

Georgina's expression remained impassive. She nodded slowly, and I couldn't tell if anything about this was shocking or if she somehow already knew.

"And frankly, G, I don't know what to do about it."

"And what about Sean?" She asked.

"What about him?"

"Is he in the middle of this mess, too?"

"Yes. Although, he's not a suspect," I said.

"How do you know all this?" Georgina raised a thin brow.

"Don't ask." I shot her a glance, and she smiled.

"I see parts of you haven't changed," she laughed.

"Can I tell you something?"

"Of course. We're friends, right?"

"Are we?" I asked bluntly. She looked a little taken aback.

"I'd like to think so."

"Yeah," I said, surprising myself with my agreement. "Me too."

"So tell."

"I'm fucking scared. I'm never scared of things. I mean not really scared, you know? And right now, I'm freaked out about whoever is killing those girls and why they've dragged me into it."

A weight fluttered from my chest. There was something different about unloading to Gina over Sean. Something like a confession.

She didn't answer for a few moments. She sipped at her soy latte and studied me.

"Frankly, Clara, you're terrifying. Always were."

I nearly spit my cappuccino, laughing. Not the consoling response I was expecting.

"What?"

"I mean, you are a scary ass bitch. And I mean that in the most complimentary way possible."

"You're kidding?"

"Not at all. I mean, back in the old days you were intimidating because you always had this stone-cold look about you. Like you were thinking things that none of us could understand. That none of us would want to know about. Like you knew some dark secret about the world. And, well now, shit, look at you! You look like you could break me right in two." She nodded toward my biceps.

"Probably could, you peanut. Try lifting a weight."

"I lift a toddler all day, thank you very much. Dare you to try that."

"Now that's terrifying. Mothers are scary ass beasts. Wouldn't dream of messing with one." I laughed, shaking my head.

"I'll take the compliment," Georgina said, raising her mug in a toast.

"My point is, you're tough as hell, Clara. Inside and out. So whatever it is you're scared of, don't be. They don't stand a chance against you."

We sat silently for a few seconds, both pondering.

I mulled over her words. How was she so confident in someone she barely knew anymore? Someone she didn't know that well to begin with? What did she know about me that I didn't?

"Thank you. That makes me feel strangely better. Have to admit I never thought I'd be getting pep talks from a former ballerina."

"Do you know that I once went without food for seven days? Lemon water with honey only."

I raised my brow. "Huh?"

I was about ready for another pastry. My self-discipline was shit at the moment.

"There's this unspoken competitiveness in dancing. The thinner you are, the more beautiful, the more graceful. Everyone wants to be light as air."

"Sounds horrible," I half laughed. I thought about the people at my CrossFit gym who were always pushing themselves beyond healthy limits to be the biggest, the best, the strongest. I always thought they were so ridiculous. I guess it's not that different.

"I'd always heard that about ballerinas, but I never knew how much of it was true," I said.

Georgina shrugged. "I can't speak for every dancer out there, of course, but let's just say in my troupe we started drinking coffee at age eight because we heard it stunts your growth."

She raised a thin, plucked brow.

"Geez," I said.

"Yeah, not all sunshine in that sport. Part of the reason I left dance in college. Your body changes. Very few people can be ninety pounds forever."

"You're doing quite fine," I said, eyeing her teeny frame.

"I am a strong 105, I'll have you know." She said, flexing her twiggy arms endearingly. I just wanted to put her in my pocket and keep her forever. "Anyway, my babbling point is, I know about endurance and pressure and ridicule. You're not alone. And just because our experiences were different, doesn't mean that I don't understand."

My heart fluttered a little with an unfamiliar flicker of warmth.

48

I left Georgina feeling lighter, more in control. I went home and did a hard five-mile run through the woods by my house, my anger and guilt over Tabby and my fears about the murders melted into my endorphins, at least temporarily. As much as I rejected the idea, I had to go resolve things with Sean. Whatever this thing was we'd roused from the depths of its slumber, we needed to put it back down.

I showered, threw on a skirt and tee and finally worked up the guts up to make my way over to the Drunken Mermaid.

I stepped in. The bar hadn't opened for the night yet, and Sean was behind the bar top counting bottles, a little clipboard in hand as he checked things off. His sleeves were rolled to his elbows, and his faded Levis hung on slim hips. He had a little pencil behind his ear that made me smile at its cliché. He looked up.

"Hey," he said with a subtle smile.

"Hey," I said, shifting in my stance.

"Want a drink?"

Yes. "No, I don't think so."

He nodded and set down his clipboard, then poured himself a beer. We lingered in awkward silence for a moment before he finally spoke.

"So," he began.

"We did a bad thing, Sean," I blurted out. "I can't tell you what to do about Tabby. I don't know if you love her or if what you have together is a good thing or not. And frankly, I can't tell you whether we should pay attention to these feelings we've kicked up. But what I know is that I don't want to entertain any of those thoughts while you have someone else in your life. I'm not going to make a fool out of her. I know what that's like in a town like this. And I know what a broken heart feels like."

"Getting right to it, eh? So what are you saying then?" he said.

"I'm saying...I'm saying that we can't...we need to stay away from each other. You and I together is just toxic, okay? Bad shit happens when we're together. We're nothing but trouble."

"You used to like trouble." His lips twitched.

My belly did a little backflip, thinking back the cool summer nights under a mantle of diamond sky. A bottle of wine and a blanket. Two kids dreaming of tomorrow. Thinking back to a piano sonata on a moonlit night, two lost souls fusing in darkness.

As if sensing my backtrack, Sean's hand reached across the bar toward me. He stroked my palm.

"I can't lose you again, Clara. I know this is complicated and I'll let Tabby down easy. But please, don't just run away again. We owe it to each other to see what this is."

I stood. "I can't stay."

He came around the bar and took my hands in his.

"Please."

I met his eyes—icy blue like the hottest part of the flames.

"You always did love playing with fire. You'll get burned every time," I said.

He smiled. "I never seem to remember what it feels like."

"I'll remind you. It fucking hurts."

I started walking, got three steps, then turned back to him.

"Do you know what it was like to find myself after this place? I put those ghosts to rest, Sean. I can't wake them. For years, you and Ruthi were my identity. Losing you was like losing a piece of myself. Both at the same time? It was like my soul fractured and the pieces scattered to the ends of the earth."

His eyes narrowed.

"And do you think it was any easier for me? I think sometimes you forget that she was my sister. Her death ripped my family apart. She was MY responsibility, and I let her die."

I balked and blinked.

"You can't carry the guilt of life being cruel," I said as much to myself as to Sean.

"We don't get a choice what we feel guilty about."

"Maybe not."

"And the one person I needed for comfort through all that just vanished."

"What would you have done?" My voice climbed to a trembling shriek.

"I wouldn't have left you," Sean said.

"You were already away at Ft. Irwin! You already had a life that didn't include me."

"You know that I wanted you to come. Her death didn't change that," he said.

"How was I supposed to follow you to Iraq?"

"Don't pretend like you weren't checked out long before I was deployed."

"So I would have just lived on some base somewhere?" I asked.

"We could have worked it out. People can love across distances. People who care enough." He added the little jab.

My lips quivered.

"I didn't think you could handle staying with me after that night. A daily reminder of her. Every day you would have looked at me and seen her. Would have blamed me for my part. Her ghost would have been a vacant hole in our lives forever."

"So instead we got two vacant holes. Tell me, Clara, what have you been filling yours with? Booze, pain, sex? Is it working? Because nothing I seem to take in gets me any closer to fulfillment. How much of that ink is to make you forget?"

"They make me remember."

"Remember? What in hell would you want to remember?"

"What it's like to feel."

Sean reached around the bar counter and opened a drawer. He pulled out a faded pack of Marlboro Reds. He slid a slim cigarette from the pack and thrust it between his lips. I raised my brow.

"Isn't it illegal to smoke inside?" I said.

He glared. "I'll send myself a written warning."

"Since when do you still smoke, anyway?" A Marlboro always adorned my rogue in school, but I supposed just like the rest of us he got the memo about lung cancer and wrinkles and wised up.

"Since my sister's killer decided to make a reappearance," he said, lighting the cigarette. "And no, to answer the question in those brown eyes. I don't smoke anymore. I quit the day you left."

My heart clenched. The sting of the day I left was as raw and throbbing as a fresh wound. I could still taste the salt on my lips as intrepid tears consumed me. The coastal morning so weighed down with fog that tiny droplets took up residence on my lashes and cheeks. Fingers of breaking dawn pushed through the clouds in slivers of rose and clementine. My young heart cracked like glass in summer heat, and I raced to be as far from Point Redwood as I could before it shattered into oblivion. It was dreadful hard work keeping composure when your entire body wanted to collapse to the ground.

"Why?" I nearly whispered.

He took a drag, exhaling deliberate smoke rings. "Nicotine didn't taste the same without you as a chaser."

"Like you made it through the army without smoking," I deflected.

"Why the fuck are we talking about cigarettes?"

"What should we talk about, Sean?" I threw up my hands. "Should we talk about this sicko terrorizing us? Should we talk about how I might well be next on his list?"

"Don't say shit like that."

"Why not? Better to be prepared."

"If he wanted you dead, you'd be dead. He's playing with you." He set the smoldering Marlboro in a ramekin.

"Yeah, like a cat plays with a mouse before it rips it in two."

"Morbid, aren't you?"

"Severed cat heads on your porch tend to tilt you toward the macabre." I huffed, breathing in. Breathing out. "I need to go. I came to sort things out, but this isn't working," I said finally, pushing past him.

"Clara," he reached for me.

I stumbled, an unseen force holding me in place. I closed my eyes. I felt his pull on my arm—felt the invisible energy reeling me closer. I opened my eyes to his determined, steely gaze. He pulled me into him violently, pressing his mouth into mine. His tongue pressed into mine, his teeth gnashed at mine. He pushed into my body until I slammed back against the bar top. His hands roamed my waist, clutching at the dips and edges. They roamed up my shirt, sliding over my breasts, teasing my hardening nipples. I felt him pressing into me. His hands went up my skirt and roamed over the tender parts of me. I gasped and whimpered, my body burning up with an onslaught of sensation. But no, I couldn't do this. It didn't matter how much I wanted him—all of him—to take me away.

I pulled his hand from me and pushed him back.

"Stop."

"Why?" He breathed into my neck.

"Because…" Because why? I couldn't remember why. Not through the haze of need and desire swirling around me.

"Because…"

"Because you're scared?" he asked. His dilated pupils met mine.

I nodded.

"I fucking want you, Clara. I need you." His hands went back to work, gripping at my panties.

No. This couldn't happen anymore.

"Stop!" I snapped. His body tensed, and he pulled back.

"I'm sorry," he breathed. "I didn't mean—"

"It's fine," I said, catching my breath. "But we can't. I mean it. It's too difficult for me. This is too messy."

I pulled my skirt down and straightened myself. Everything shook and trembled, and my pulse was sprinting.

"Clara, don't be like this," Sean said, a little pleading in his voice.

"Just please leave me alone for now, okay? I think we need some space."

"Space," he repeated with an incredulous little smirk.

Space when you'd been apart for eight years? Yeah, I knew it sounded ridiculous.

"Look, I'll...I'll call you in a few days or something, and maybe we can talk it out. In the meantime, sort out your shit with Tabby," I said.

He nodded. "For the record, I regret nothing."

I didn't respond. I took him in for a moment longer, then left the bar.

I got into the car, and the tears erupted like a Texas thunderstorm.

As I headed down the main road, I saw Tabby in her little SUV, watching from the parking lot of the bar.

49

I returned home a tightly wound ball of panicked nerves. What the hell was I going to do about Sean? What was I going to do about Tabby? No doubt she was going to be furious after seeing me leave the bar. I shook my head. I didn't have time to deal with their relationship drama. I didn't have time for anyone else's bullshit when I was up my own metaphorical creek. I had to get out of this goddamn town before it destroyed me.

As I entered the house, something felt empty. The late afternoon was cold, even for Point Redwood, and the house was even chillier. I stopped in the entryway. It was too still. The air too heavy. It was that feeling you get when you know someone has been here—a foreign energy, a slight smell.

Once when I got into my car after leaving it parked during a long trip, I had the same feeling. After some investigation, all the signs indicated somebody had slept in my car—a muddy footprint, some random dog hair, a strange damp, musty smell. I've never forgotten that unsettling sensation--this peculiar feeling of violation, the feeling that someone has invaded your space.

I had that feeling now.

"Mom?" I called out softly. I was answered with silence.

So mom was out, no big deal. She was probably with Aunt Jo out shopping or doing whatever they did together. But still, something was strangely off. I shook away the sense. I just needed a hot shower, maybe a shot of whiskey. Maybe I needed to punch the bag for a while and shed some of these nerves. I hung my jacket in the front hall closet and headed down the hallway to my bedroom.

I flicked on the bedroom light, but nothing happened. Weird. I wiggled the switch a few times, but the bulb must have burnt out. Twilight had settled on Point Redwood, and my room was now basking in a faint silver glow from the fading light outside.

Something smelled weird. A faint metallic scent, like copper. Chills scuttled up my spine.

I pulled out my phone and switched on the flashlight to aid in the dim light. Everything looked in order. I was paranoid. But then I spotted something on the bed. Something that didn't belong.

I crept closer, hesitant as though it were an explosive. There was an envelope on top of the floral comforter. My name was on the front.

I swallowed hard and forced my fingers to pick up the envelope. I turned it over in my hands carefully. What the hell? More pictures? I took a breath, found my courage, and opened it. Sure enough, a small stack of photographs came out. They were slightly faded, old, poor quality. I looked down, and my heart nearly burst.

Ruthi.

Ruthi dead.

The eerie, spectral, images sucked air from my lungs. My skin prickled as a cold, clammy sweat pooled on my brow. I flipped through the pictures one by one, forcing myself to witness my best friend in her demise. The pictures were close up, masking the surroundings but highlighting the fright in her dead eyes. She had died terrified and alone. Where were you, Clara, as your best friend took her final gasping breaths? The friend you promised to look after, assured that everything would be ok? On a lighthouse floor. Selfish and oblivious.

I glanced down and noticed a small silver cross was sitting on the bedspread. I knew that cross. I had the same one. Delicate silver trinkets engraved with our initials that Mom had given to us on our 16th birthdays. We never found it and always assumed that the necklace had fallen off in the water when Ruthi drowned. But it didn't. Her killer had taken it. But why? A trophy?

I flipped to the last photograph in the pile, and I had to grasp the bedpost to keep from falling over. Scrawled in blood across Ruthi's lifeless body were the words YOUR FAULT.

I fought down bile. I carefully turned over the photograph. In the same cryptic smeared red, a note was scrawled:

Some people choose the wrong friends. Go away before anyone else dies.

50

I 'd turned over the photos and necklace to Lindsey. They'd questioned me, taken some photos of my room, slipped the evidence into little Ziploc bags and said they'd call me with any information. I wasn't holding my breath. By the incredulous look Lindsey gave me when I explained what happened, it seemed like he was chalking it up to fabricated evidence.

My head was a mess as I pulled up to St. Thomas. I couldn't erase the horrific images from my mind. I was a haphazard slop of emotions ranging from fear to anger to frustration, to the overwhelming need to be near Sean. But I was afraid to let Sean anywhere near me after last night. I couldn't let anyone else get hurt because of me.

When I was elementary school age, the public school finally shut down after years of struggling to maintain enrollment and funding. Our community, being generations-deep of Catholics, mostly attended St. Thomas preschool through high school anyway. Once the public school was no longer an option, parents either had to bus their kids to the next school over—about fifteen miles up a winding coastal road—or bite the bullet and send them to Saint T's. The parish, delighting in the idea of now controlling the entire educational system in our town, made every attempt to retain all students—reduced tuition, scholarships, and fundraising to make it free and easy. It worked. Every kid in Point Redwood was now enrolled.

I wasn't quite sure what I was doing there at St. Thomas, or what I hoped to accomplish. But at that moment, I was lost.

I hadn't been to confession in nearly a decade. I hadn't been to church in nearly a decade. I could still smell the incense and the hypocrisy.

"Forgive me, Father, for I have sinned. I finally fucked my boyfriend. No, we didn't use a condom and no, I'm not sorry."

No Hail Marys. Just detention. So much for priest-parishioner confidentiality.

St. Thomas was mostly abandoned when I stepped in, except for a few mournful pilgrims in the pews. I cleared my throat and walked down the aisle, feeling out of place without my plaid skirt and knee socks. I pulled my cardigan tighter around my chest. I walked to the gilded altar, lit a candle and knelt. I didn't know what to ask for, what to say in my mind. I wasn't even sure anyone was listening. The shuffle of robes and gentle steps came close.

"Clara, child. What a sight."

I glanced up from my place of supplication to see Father Richard's aged face. The years had added lines to his aspect, but somehow his eyes seemed softer. Then again, it was always the nuns ready to raise the ruler, not Father Richard. He was somber and strict but in a grandfatherly way. I was always jealous of those parishes with young, sexy priests. And the fact that I could find any priest sexy was yet another reason I hadn't been to church in eight years.

"Father," I stood and took his hand.

"It's good to see you, Clara. Your mother mentioned you'd been back in town for a bit."

I nodded and tried to smile.

"And it's good to see you in church. Should I expect you at Mass?"

"Maybe," I said. "Will you hear my confession?"

Father Richard's eyes narrowed cautiously, and he seemed taken aback. I would be too, I suppose, if the likes of me strolled in, looking for redemption. He looked me over as if searching for something, trying to solve something. Trying to identify my missing pieces, perhaps?

"Are you in earnest, Clara?"

I sighed. "Afraid so," I said, mouth turned up.

"Then of course. Remember how?" He said with a hint of jest.

"I've seen it on television."

He chuckled, then led me to the confessional.

I knelt in the wooden box and signed the cross over my heart.

"Forgive me father, for I have sinned," I began. The words caught in my throat.

"Go on, Clara. When was your last confession?" he said behind the wooden mesh that stood as a false sense of anonymity.

I took a breath. "It's been eight years since my last confession. Eight years and...some number of days, I don't remember."

I heard a little smirk. "Continue."

I didn't know exactly what I wanted to say. Did I even

know what qualified as a confession and what were just fearful ramblings?

"I'm responsible for the death of my best friend."

I felt his tension through the wooden mesh.

"Why do you think that?" Father Richard asked, his voice steady, but a hint of disturbance at its edge. I took a breath.

"Because I was off with my boyfriend at the time." My voice cracked. "And had we stayed with her she would still be alive."

"Off doing what?"

"You know. Getting busy." My cheeks flushed, saying it out loud to a man who could be my grandfather.

"Sexual intercourse?"

Ugh, I wanted to vomit.

"Yes. And look, Father, let's be frank. I'm not going to apologize for sex. I don't think it's a sin and all that. It's human nature."

"I can't forgive you for things you don't repent, Clara."

"I know. And I don't even know if I want forgiveness. I deserve to feel horrible for the rest of my life for what happened. But I think someone is trying to make me pay for it now. And it's not just me. They're going after my mom and Sean. I can't let other people get hurt because I fucked up. Sorry."

Father Richard took a deep, thoughtful breath.

"We are all flawed, Clara. We all make mistakes. God made us fallible."

"I don't think I can live with my mistakes."

"Are you confessing thoughts of suicide?"

"What? No! That's not what I meant. I just meant...I don't think I can be here, facing them. I don't know what's happening in this town, but I think the police are right. It has something to do with me. If I hadn't shown up, maybe those girls would be alive somehow."

"You're referring to Hannah March and Kate Gordon?"

"Yes," I nearly whispered, choking back tears. I pressed my eyes closed against the onslaught of their pale faces.

Father Richard sighed deeply and, for a moment, he was just a caring old man who'd watched me grow, watched me struggle through my adolescence. Watched me in detention.

"Clara. You cannot think like that. We don't know why God chooses to do some of the things he does. Or why he allows some evil to flourish. But it's not for us to decide, and it isn't for us to judge. You did *not* cause the death of your friend, nor the death of those two girls. Those were heinous acts, committed by some evil, not by two teenagers who failed to use good judgment."

For the first time likely in my history as his parishioner, the priest's words comforted me like a warm blanket. I didn't want to throw the book at him or run out screaming about his hypocrisy.

"Thank you," I said softly, holding back tears.

"Is there anything else you wish to confess?" he asked.

I slept with someone else's boyfriend, and I *really* enjoyed it. Am I blameless in that, too? No. I'd have to live with that sin. We couldn't blame our current bad judgment on the follies of youth.

"I still resent my mother," I said instead. "I'm happy I live far away from her. I often drink too much. I sometimes online shop during work hours."

At that last confession, Father Richard snickered.

"Shall we say three Hail Marys and some self-reflection as your penance, then?"

"Yes, father."

"Clara, think on this. Your past is what made you who

you are today, but your actions now determine who you can be tomorrow."

We sat in silence for a moment.

"Would you like to say a prayer of contrition?" he asked.

"Yes."

"Go on."

I took a breath, evoking long-forgotten words.

"God, I am sorry for my sins and the offense they caused you. I know I should love you above all things. Help me to do penance, to do better, and to avoid anything that might lead me to sin. In the name of the Father, and of the Son, and of the Holy Spirit, Amen."

I stayed silent for a few minutes, letting the words waltz around me in deliverance. I found breath and stood.

"Thank you, Father." I opened the confessional and stepped back into the light.

"And Clara?" Father Richard said behind me. "Watch your back. PR is a complicated place."

I snapped around. "What? Father, what did you say?"

But he was gone.

T he universal truth about small towns is that there will always be a 4th of July party and it's always a requirement to attend. The pier would showcase an impressive fireworks display, a little band would play, and the cheer squad would sell caramel apples.

It was the type of thing I'd typically avoid—I wasn't all that interested in seeing every face from my childhood in one setting—but Georgina had beseeched me with the bat of doll eyes and an irresistible plea. And there was something empoweringly defiant about the town carrying on as always despite the killings. Everyone was terrified to go out, to let their daughters out of their sight, but yet, they refused to be ruled by their fear. I had to give PR credit.

I'd been avoiding Sean the past couple of days. I knew there were things left unsaid and resolutions suspended in the air, but I couldn't bring myself to close that chapter just yet. I threw on my one dress and my stack-heeled boots, grabbed a denim jacket. Black lashes, glossy lips, and I headed out.

The usual summer fog had relented to a pleasant

evening bathed in the golden glow of twilight. I hopped into mom's repaired car. Electric malfunction, the mechanic had said. These things happen the moment the warranty goes out, he said. Uh huh, sure they do. I started it up and took a slow drive up the woodsy road to Main St.

Downtown had been decked out in Americana—red, white and blue streamers and balloons, homemade banners, pie booths, chili cook-off tent, beer tasting and a petting zoo consisting of farm animals. Classic cars lined the closed-off streets, and a local country rock band cranked out cover tunes to an enthusiastic crowd. I smiled at the nostalgia—the tableau that remained a static painting of my youth.

I spotted Georgina standing with her husband, Jim, and resting their young son on her hip. Clearly taking after 6'2 Jim, little Eli was comically large roosting on his mom's tiny frame.

"Hey buddy," I said, giving Eli's chubby little arm a gentle pinch.

His blue cotton candy-smeared face remained circumspect. "No!" he said, and buried his face in his mother's armpit, flinging the cotton candy cone outward, which Jim dexterously caught midair in a timed familial dance.

Georgina laughed and consoled the toddler with some easy hip bounces. "Don't take it personally. He's not quite socialized yet."

"That makes two of us, kid," I said to the little boy, smiling. He turned his head to me, and his tiny mouth offered just the ghost of a smile in response.

"Beer, Clara?" Jim asked, holding up a little red cooler.

"Yeah, thanks."

He handed me a light canned beer, ice cold.

"Seen Sean?" Jim asked.

Georgina shot her husband an annoyed look.

I paused mid-sip but didn't lower the beer. "Um. No. Why would I have? He's probably with Tabby."

I tried to hide the emotion in my voice, but my tone cracked just slightly. Jim's eyes looked instantly uncomfortable. I imagined he was excellent at putting his large foot in his mouth at dinner parties.

"Jim, it's okay," I finally said when he looked to Georgina for a life vest. "Sean and I are friends. Nothing wrong said."

He visibly relaxed, and I tried my best warm smile. Then I tipped my beer to my lips and drained it. The band picked up behind us with a rockabilly tune, drowning out the awkward.

I envisioned techie Jim as one of those "cool" dads. The kind that would wear a baseball cap backward and knew how to play Mario Kart—even the secret mirror levels. All the little boys in the neighborhood would beg to play at Eli's house, only for the chance to experience The Jim-meister.

Eli would grow up a happy kid, likely. Two young, energetic parents to dote on him. A cozy house on a hill. A safe little town to call home. I arrested that thought. Point Redwood wasn't safe any longer.

A THREESOME OF WOMEN WITH YOUNG CHILDREN AT THEIR skirts moseyed up to our circle.

"Georgina!" A woman with cropped auburn hair waved gleefully as she walked up, a pearly cheeked ginger little girl at her side.

"Hi Bess," Georgina said, going in for a friendly hug. Bess turned and greeted Jim in turn with a platonic Euro cheek kiss.

"Hi, Anna," Georgina crouched down to the little girl. "How are your dance classes?"

"Um, pwetty good," the little girl said, twirling shyly in her red polka dotted dress.

Georgina smiled and stood.

"She's the first one in her class to master fourth position. Aren't you sweetie?" Bess cooed at her daughter in an unnaturally high octave.

"She's getting big," Georgina said, dreamy-eyed. I could picture her with a little daughter in tow, teaching her to plié.

"Where have you been hiding?" Bess said. "Haven't seen you at Pilates in weeks."

"Oh, yeah, just busy with summer school. I took on an extra class."

Bess, tall and willowy with sharp green eyes glanced to me.

"Clara, right?" Bess said with accusation.

"Guilty," I said, forcing a smile. I extended my hand. "Nice to meet you."

"Oh, we've met," Bess said. I waited for a follow up that didn't come.

"Oh? I'm sorry, my memory's a little cloudy."

"Elizabeth   Jordan,   nee   Williams.   Two   grades below you."

"Oh," I smiled and nodded with recognition, although I had no clue who she was. "Good to see you again."

"Hmm. I'm sure." She said with an air. "You've come back with quite a splash then, haven't you?" She grinned, but it was lightyears from friendly.

"You know me. Always making headlines," I said dryly, my defenses hastening to attention. I pressed my second beer to my lips and let a hearty serving slide down my throat.

Georgina tittered uncomfortably.

"Anywhoo," Bess said. "We were heading over to the petting zoo with the kiddos. Did you want to come?"

The question was definitively posed to Georgina and not me.

"Oh, thanks, but we're right in the middle of something," Georgina said.

"Mmm," Bess said eyeing me again. "Well, then. See you all later. Enjoy the festivities."

"Remember the Mama Mafia?" Georgina said as Bess strolled off.

"They came to see the freak show," I said, dryly.

Georgina tilted her head to the side. "Oh, don't be so sensitive, Clara. Who cares what they think?"

"Seriously, Clara, this town is more like a Venus fly trap than I could have ever imagined," Jim said, shaking his head. "It lures you in with the beautiful landscape and the quiet siren's song of the enticing ocean. Then as soon as you get close, as soon as your guard is down, SNAP! You're done for. Never even saw it coming."

"Oh, Jim, I could have told you that," I said, grinning. "But glad you're a quick learner."

I excused myself to the bathroom. I took in the ambiance as I strolled the makeshift midway of festivities. Salty sea air mingled with crackling meats and BBQ, laughter and carnival game noises rang out, and I almost forgot I was in a town I despised. I was angry that I had to hate it. Angry that what could have been fond memories of an idyllic small-town upbringing had been stolen from me by cruelty and tragedy.

Standing in front of the Main St. public bathroom mirror, I tossed my hair a few times and reapplied lip gloss. Coming to this thing was definitely an exercise in mind over matter. Amazing these biddies didn't have anything better to do than gossip about me.

I saw something in the mirror behind me. I gasped and started, then realized it was just Maryanne Danson and another platinum blonde woman. Right on cue, I mentally sighed.

I turned, lip gloss still in hand. Both were in high-necked sundresses and tall, flat, ill-fitting boots. My eyes narrowed in on the blonde, and I recognized her as Tabby's friend from the Mermaid—Tina, I thought. They stopped short when they recognized me. Maryanne crossed her arms over her chest. I gave them a quizzical look, but they just stared at me, faces impassive.

"Well, Clara, we meet again," Maryanne said.

"Yeah, hi," I said. They held their stance.

"Did you need something?" I finally said.

"I supposed we could be asking the same thing of you," Maryanne said, her thin pink lips pursed into a tight smile.

"Excuse me?" I instinctively straightened my spine.

"Little birdies are singing about you and Sean," Tina said.

My stomach did a little backflip, but I kept my face impassive.

"Not sure what they're singing, but there's nothing to tell. Sean and I are old friends."

"I don't know what you have to do with those dead girls, but you can't just come back here and stir up trouble with people. People who have happy lives. Don't bring your misery here."

My emotions waged between fury and guilt. She had a point, but I wasn't going to concede to it.

"Still harassing people in bathrooms I see, Maryanne. You all can think whatever you want. I learned to ignore gossip a long time ago. Some of us are grownups now."

Maryanne took an aggressive step toward me. I was sure I could flick away anything she threw at me, but she did have an imposing figure.

"Tabby's too trusting and sweet to ever suspect anything, but I know people better than that. I know what your mom did to Sara Connolly."

"You know, she didn't hold Bill's dick captive," I snapped, so damn sick of hearing about my mother's trespasses and never once about Bill's.

Maryanne ignored my outburst.

"Tabby and Sean have a life together. Stay away from him," she said.

My chest heaved as the fingers of fury spread through my extremities.

"Maybe you should take it up with Sean. He's the one with the commitments, after all."

"Are we clear?" Maryanne said piggy nose raised high.

I took a calming breath.

"Yeah. Crystal." I shoved my lip gloss back in my handbag and slung it over my shoulder. "We done here?"

Maryanne and Tina both gave me haughty—and snotty—looks before nodding.

I groaned and shoved past them. I was ready to throw in the towel on this stupid event.

I walked out of the bathroom and headed to where Georgina, Jim, and Eli were standing near a booth.

"Clara, too!" Eli shouted as he spotted me walking over. His little pudgy face was scrunched up like a bulldog puppy.

"Clara doesn't want face paint, Eli. It's for little boys and girls, not grown up girls," Georgina said, looking exacerbated by his antics.

"CLA-RA, TOO," he insisted.

Little Eli was in need of a bit o' discipline.

"He skipped his nap," she mouthed to me. I nodded in understanding.

Eli began to stomp his little cowboy boot in the dirt.

Georgina looked to me with a raised brow, looking like a little cartoon character with her wide eyes and long lashes.

I laughed and looked down at the kid, whose indignant frown had been replaced with wide-eyed pleading.

"Of course I want face paint," I said, trying to contain my laughter. "You do a sea star?"

The soccer mom behind the booth shrugged. "At your service."

"What about you, little man?" I asked Eli.

"I want a lion!" Eli squealed with delight as he scrambled up on the chair. My man Eli and I were not about to let some pack of bitches ruin our fun.

With my chic new nautical makeup, we strolled Main St., Eli now clinging to my hand.

"You've made a friend," Jim laughed. "He doesn't warm to a lot of people. Consider yourself lucky."

I smirked but gave his tiny hand a little squeeze. Despite his earlier near meltdown, I got why people had kids. There was something cleansing about a child's affections. Blind appreciation and willingness. Just give them some love back, and they'll love you forever. Or at least for about eleven years.

"So, *have* you spoken to Sean?" Georgina asked once Jim and Eli were in stride a few yards behind us.

I sighed. "No. We left things in such a weird place, G."

"I gotta ask," she said, her meaning crystal clear.

"Don't."

"Okay, fine. But I'm sure I already know. Be careful with that. That's a messy situation."

"There is no situation. I'm going back to Austin soon, and I'll likely never see Sean again."

"Famous last words," she laughed. "And, speak of the devil."

My eyes shifted up, knowing Sean would be walking toward us somewhere. He was scruffy with a few days' growth, wearing a dark denim button-up over weathered Levis. My arms ached to wrap themselves around him, pull his warmth into me. It wasn't purely desire. It was so much deeper than that. A gravitational pull. I flicked my eyes away, out to the quaint revelry surrounding us; focusing on the mingling smoke and grease in the air, the melodic sound-track of childhood laughter and poorly amplified steel guitar.

"Hey," Sean's low, smooth voice resonated on the air. I swallowed.

"Hi," I said, not meeting his eyes.

"Nice face paint."

"Thanks."

"Can we talk?"

"Now's not really a good time," I said with little conviction.

"Hey, we're gonna go get Eli a snack," Georgina said. "Um, we'll catch up in a bit."

I shot G a, *seriously?!* look. She gave a small shrug and scurried away with her little family.

I sighed and turned back to Sean. His gaze was fixed pensively at the surrounding revelry.

"I'm not sure what there is to talk about, Sean," I began.

"No? Seems to me there's a lot left unsaid."

"I don't know what to say. We took a sledgehammer to Pandora's Box, and now I don't know how to put it all back."

"Why does it all need to go back? Maybe those things needed to come out."

"To what end?"

"I don't love Tabby. I know that now."

"Hell, Sean. Even I know that. But it's not just about Tabby. It's everything. I have a life in Austin. You have a life here. Not just a girlfriend, but a business and a family and friends."

His expression was pensive. "All that seems changed now, doesn't it? The reality I've built these past years is just a façade for the things that really matter to me."

"Things like what?"

"Things like you, Clara. You matter to me." He reached for my hand.

"Sean, stop it." I pulled my hand away. "Someone will see you. This town is toxic to me. It doesn't matter what we might think we have, you living here overrules it."

I half expected him to protest that he would leave everything behind for me. Sell it all, forsake his family. But that was the teenage boy I knew, not the man who'd survived war and death and found pragmatism along the way. People didn't just shed their existence for the potential of emotional fulfillment. Because we all know that even the happiest of times are short-lived.

"Do you regret coming back here?" he asked.

I contemplated. "That's a complicated question."

"Try."

I blinked a few times, pressing back a swell of unwanted emotions.

"I didn't have much of a choice. So regrets are futile."

He nodded slowly, contemplatively. "For the record, I'm ending things with Tabby anyway."

"That's good."

"I owe her that, at least."

"Yes. But you owe yourself as well. Don't stay with someone that doesn't make you happy because of guilt. Life's too short. So fucking short. I need to go."

"I'll see you around?" he said.

"Sure."

He turned and hesitantly walked away down the Main St. midway, fading into the lingering festivities.

I SAT ON A STONE BENCH WHILE I WAITED FOR GEORGINA AND family to return, mindlessly listening to the band on stage.

"Clara," a meek voice tickled my ear over the hum of the country rock melody. Tabby stood beside me, demure and humbled in the moonlight. I hesitated before responding. She was the last person I wanted to deal with.

"Hi," I said curtly.

Her eyes flickered to the side and the ground, then to me, uncertainty dancing in her pupils.

"I'm not here to pick a fight. Actually, I wanted to apologize," she said.

I started back. Apologize? She owed me nothing.

"What for?" I asked.

"For overreacting the other day. For getting in your face

about Sean. I was out of line, and I know you're old friends and you've been thrown for a loop with these murders. I can only imagine what it's been like for you both. And I understand why you need each other. I was just...well, embarrassed to say, just plain jealous. I mean, you're Clara. You're the one who got away."

My jaw dropped a little, and I quickly snapped it shut.

Sean's words resonated in my mind. *I'm ending things with Tabby. I don't love her.*

"Oh...that's okay. I would have reacted that way, too." What else could I say? That she wasn't being crazy at all? That I had, in fact, slept with her boyfriend and I felt bad about it? Although not nearly as bad as I should?

Tabby smiled at me.

"I don't want to stand in the way of you two being able to support each other through this. Maryanne told me she said something to you and, well, I don't want things to go back to how they used to be in high school." Tabby shifted uncomfortably, her eyes darting about. "If I could just ask... remember that I do have feelings."

My heart sank to the very pit of my stomach then churned about until the tickle of bile crept up my throat. Holy Hell, Tabby Gates is a nice, understanding girl.

"Yeah, of course," I managed to choke out. "Look, I'll be gone soon and then you and Sean can sort out...whatever it is that needs sorting. I'm sorry if I got in the way of anything."

I prayed for her to nod and go, but she lingered, toying with a wheat blonde curl.

I heard voices and sighed with relief to see Georgina headed our way. Tabby glanced warily to them, then back to me, then back to Georgina with a maple syrup smile.

"Hi Georgina," Tabby said, her voice going up an octave.

"Hi," Georgina said with uncertainty. She flicked her wide eyes to me. I gave her a *tell you later* look.

"Hey little man," Tabby said in a baby voice, crouching down to Eli. "Getting so BIG."

Eli blushed and hid his face.

"Aww, don't be shy," Tabby said.

Eli looked around nervously, then pivoted and ran straight toward me. He barreled into my lap and threw his arms around my neck.

"Clara!" he said with giggles.

Tabby's eyes narrowed with something like contempt, but she rebounded well.

"Kids do love the new, don't they?" She stood and straightened herself. "Can't wait for my own. Hopefully a little Killarney," she winked at Georgina and smiled.

Georgina laughed uncomfortably and avoided looking at me. My stomach lurched at the memories Sean had confessed.

"I was just about to head home. See you guys around. Pilates on Sunday? Oh, and don't forget to sign up for the Back to School pageant. We have a lot of planning to do," Tabby said.

"Yeah, sure thing. See you, Tabby," Georgina said.

"Well that was damn awkward," Georgina said once Tabby's curls had swished into the distance.

"You could say that. No offense, G, but I am so ready to be out of here," I said.

"I understand." She glanced to Eli in my arms, whose eyes were drooping with the weight of exhaustion. "And I think someone else needs to get out of here, too."

"Here, I'll take him," Jim said, walking up behind us. "The car seat is in my car."

"Thanks. I'll meet you back at the house?" Georgina said, handing over the fading toddler.

"Yeah, take your time. See you later, Clara." Jim kissed Georgina's cheek and left with Eli slung over his shoulder.

"He's a good guy," I said, nodding in approval. Georgina's pearly cheeks beamed.

"Yeah, he really is." She blushed like a little school girl with a crush. I humbly succumbed to my envy.

52

Georgina walked back to her SUV, giddiness streaming through her warmed blood. She swayed a little in the dirt, and her head bobbed to each side. She probably shouldn't have had the third beer since they'd taken two cars—didn't have the tolerance these days. Oh well. Fun night! Was there anything better than a warm summer night, good food and good friends? Funny that she considered Clara a good friend after so much time had passed. But she was—one of those connections forged on some other universal plane. She giggled.

She reached her car and stuck her hand into her bag to find her keys. A rustle behind her startled her. She yelped and dropped her keys into the dirt. She spun around. Nothing. She took a breath. Control yourself, G. It's not like you've never had a couple of beers. She laughed, nervous and uncertain. Admittedly, the entire town was a little jumpy right now, but she had nothing to worry about. She wasn't a teenage girl—even if she did look like one a little.

Another rustle.

The hair on her neck stood, and her skin prickled. She

froze, shivering as a chilly breeze crept past. She gingerly reached down to retrieve her keys, forcing slow exhales, as her hands skimmed the dirt below, searching. She fingered the cold metal and stood, fumbling to unlock the car and reaching for her cell simultaneously.

A shadow stepped up in the window behind her. She opened her mouth to scream, but the world went dark.

53

*S*tupid bitch. Never learns. Self-righteous. Doesn't know when to quit. I'll remind her.

    Shh, pretty, my pretty. Don't say a word.

54

After Georgina left, I strolled the main street for a bit, taking in the enduring scents of summer and small-town revelry. The night had whittled the crowd to a few lingering teenagers and chatting women. The vendors and entertainment had packed up, leaving downtown a shell of sticky memories kicking around in the light breeze.

I turned the corner and stopped short. Sean was standing there, arms crossed, eyes narrowed. I pressed myself back against the building. Ugh, I couldn't face him right then. Not yet. A female voice was whimpering.

"I'm sorry, Tabs," Sean said, his voice bleeding concern.

"Sorry?" Tabby's voice quivered. "It's because of her. I was right all along."

"No. It's not. Look, I care about you, I do, but I just don't think this is right."

"All of a sudden?"

"I don't know—maybe—I guess I've felt that way for a while. And I don't want to lead you on if I don't see a future.

You deserve to be happy. To be with someone who can make you happy."

"*You* make me happy, Sean!" She was crying now, her tone cracking on the air.

Sean sighed. "You only think that because we're content."

"Is contentment not happiness?"

Valid question, Tabby. I'd asked myself the same thing countless times in a self-deprecating whiskey haze.

"No, it's not. Contentment is uncomplicated and pleasant. But it's not real. It's not love." Sean said.

"But I do love you. With all my heart," Tabby said through tears.

My heart went out to Tabby in that moment. Sean was doing her a favor, and in time she'd realize that, but I knew all too well the heart-searing pain of losing someone you thought you loved. Or even worse, someone whom you really did love. It wasn't my place to say whether she really loved Sean or not. Maybe she did. But if he didn't love her back, it didn't matter. But what if he did? What if they could have been happy and I ruined it by showing up here and throwing the complicated past right in his face?

My heart clenched, and I felt the threat of tears pricking my eyes. I shook it off. It wasn't my fault. I wasn't responsible for everyone's lives and choices.

But I was responsible for myself. And it was time to go.

55

Georgina's head throbbed. She tried to open her eyes, but the lids resisted. Finally, she peeled them open slowly but was met with nothing but darkness. What the hell had happened? She licked her chapped lips and tasted copper. Had she been in an accident? She tried to sort through her cloudy mind. She remembered leaving the festival, getting to her car...then blackness.

Her arms burned. She shifted her position only to realize that her wrists were bound behind her back. *Oh my God. She'd been kidnapped.*

Her pulse pounded. Jim would be wondering where she was. He'd be freaking out right now. And Eli...Eli wouldn't understand! He needed his bath. And a story. Jim couldn't be counted on to make Eli brush his teeth...

Oh my God.

She pulled against her restraints, but she was bound to some kind of pole.

"Don't bother," an indistinguishable voice said in the darkness.

"What is this?" Georgina said looking around the darkness futilely. "Who are you? What do you want?"

"So many desperate questions," the voice said—a low, husky whisper.

Georgina's eyes adjusted just enough to see a figure emerged from the shadows. She squinted against the inky night to make it out, but she saw nothing but the outline of a human figure.

"Let me go!" Georgina yelled. "I'm a mother, please."

"Everyone begs in the end. No matter how self-righteous."

She couldn't see it, but she felt the figure smile.

Georgina's blood froze in her veins. "Please," she whispered again.

"I don't want to kill you," the figure said. It stepped closer.

Georgina exhaled with relief. There was hope.

"Then just let me go. I have no idea who you are. I can't tell anyone anything," Georgina said.

Georgina heard a loud exhale.

"Unfortunately, what I want to do and what I have to do are so often different things."

Georgina's heart sped up. The figure came toward her. A gloved hand gripped her mouth, forcing it open. Georgina tried to scream, but the sound was nothing but a muffled choke against the cold leather. She felt something small and chalky against her tongue. Pills. She tried to spit them out, but the hand forced her mouth shut. Her head was shoved back, and against her struggles, the pills tumbled down her throat.

56

I returned home and sat on the living room couch, trying to process everything that had happened over the past couple of weeks. Trying to reconcile everything against my own actions and the way my life was crumbling around me.

I was suspected of murder, the real killer was tormenting my mother and me, and I was still hopelessly in love with the one person I couldn't be with. And he was likely ruining his life because of me.

I pulled out my laptop and stared at the tiny black cursor on a blank page. I reflected on Father Richard's words. *Your past is what made you who you are today, but your actions now, determine who you can be tomorrow.*

I'd wanted so badly to forget the pain of everything that happened here. I'd run to the ends of the Earth to escape, to become a different person in a different life. But all I'd done was cover it up with more pain. I didn't want to be that person anymore. I didn't want to be angry with mom or with Sean or with myself. I wanted to forgive all of us our transgressions. If I'd learned anything in my time around the world is that you can run as far and fast as you can to escape your problems. But if the problems are fused to your very consciousness, there's no place to go to escape them.

I slid my fingers across the keyboard and let those thoughts take form on the page.

I couldn't control what was happening in this town, but I could control what I did about it. And that was my truth. It was time to let all of this go.

My phone buzzed. I picked it up. A picture had been texted to me. I swiped my screen open and shrieked. Georgina. Unconscious, gagged, on a floor. What the fuck?

Unidentified phone number. I read the message.

Really didn't want to have to do this. She seemed nice. Mother and all. She chose the wrong friend. Just like Ruthi.

I typed back quickly. *What do you WANT?*

Just leave town already, and I won't hurt her.

I can't.

You really going to be responsible for another girl's death? Up to you.

I dropped the phone onto the couch. My mind froze over. This couldn't be happening.

The phone buzzed again.

No police. Tell anyone and she dies. Nice and slow. Stay put tonight, don't make a scene. Leave tomorrow. Get your rest, Clara. Nighty, night.

I RAISED THE GLASS BOTTLE TO MY LIPS. I TASTED THE BURN before it even hit my tongue. Three more and I'd be where I needed to be. I'd be somewhere far away. Five more and I'd be to oblivion. I tipped and let it burn, let it sear away the memories. It was the perfect storm and I was drowning in shallow water. So close to the surface but trapped by the torrential downpour of my failures. How could someone so strong be so weak when it counted most?

Mom stepped into the living room, her fuzzy gray robe wrapped around her small frame. I saw her in my peripheral, but I didn't look at her. I pressed the bottle of Jameson to my lips instead.

"Whatever it is, you can't drink it all away, honey. It won't work," Mom said, coming into the living room.

"I'm going to try," I said. I tilted the Jameson down my throat, bypassing mouth and taste buds. I should tell her about Georgina but how could I put anyone else at risk? I had no idea what the fuck was happening or what this sicko wanted. I rocked back and forth in my seat.

Mom's hand grabbed my wrist and pushed it down.

"Stop this, Clara. What do you think you're going to fix?"

"My conscious state of mind," I ripped my hand away.

"You're better than this."

"Don't tell me what I am. You don't *know* what I am."

"I know you're not a killer."

I shot up. "How do you know about that?"

"Honey, you don't live in this town your entire life and not know something as important as your daughter being a murder suspect."

I brayed. "Maybe you could put in a good word with Lindsey, then."

Mom gently reached out and took the bottle from me. I didn't fight her this time. She set the bottle on the table.

"Be patient, Clara. It will work out. Self-destructing isn't going to get you through it any quicker."

"Says you."

"Clara."

"My patience is spent, mom. I can't stay here anymore."

"You don't have a lot of choice in the matter from what I understand. You can't leave town while the investigation is going on."

"Are they going to chain me up? Because that's the only way they're keeping me in this hell hole."

"It's not so bad here," mom said, smiling.

"Yeah, when your best friend is murdered, your ex-boyfriend is dating Barbie, and the entire town thinks you're the spawn of Satan, you tell me what's not so bad."

Instead of being offended, Mom laughed a little and sat next to me. She picked up the Jameson, examined the bottle for a moment and took a sip. She gagged, causing me to laugh.

"How do you kids just drink this stuff straight like that?"

I took the bottle from her and swigged. "Practice."

She took my hand. "I'm sorry you're hurting, sweetie. I know what it's like to have this town turn on you. But you just have to get through a few more weeks of it. Who cares what they think?"

"You don't get it. I'm not worried about what the PTA moms think of me. I don't want to be here, drowning in the worst memories I have. Don't you know what it's like for me here? And people keep getting hurt."

She exhaled deeply and looked aimlessly around the room. She took my question for rhetorical and didn't respond.

"Mom, I'm going back to Texas. They can chase me down if they want to. They can cuff me and throw me back on the plane. But that's what it's gonna take. I'm not staying here voluntarily."

Mom sighed and shrugged. "If that's what you're going to do, I can't stop you. And I won't try. But don't go getting yourself into more trouble than you already are. If you leave, they will think the worst."

"Let them. I have nothing to prove to anyone anymore."

I pushed myself from the couch and went out the front door into the chilly evening. I was exhausted, but how could I sleep?

Rain clouds rose up from the misty horizon in a veil of hazy periwinkle against the moonlit backdrop. Panic welled up in me. My heart raced, and my lungs struggled to inflate.

I STROLLED DOWN THE SANDY PATH ON A MOONLIT NIGHT. THE waves raged against distant rocks, throwing themselves in a fury against the sharp edges. The pearlescent cast of moonlight spread along the damp shoreline and danced off the ebbing waves.

The sand was cold and soft beneath my bare feet. Where were my shoes? The wind whipped through my long, unruly hair. My legs carried me to the water's edge. I stopped where the damp sand meets the pulsing tide. The icy water crept up to lick my bare toes, numbing my skin. Ice climbed my spine, but I still stood, staring off into the black unknown. I glanced down to the dark water. Debris and seaweed floated languidly in the foaming tide break. I saw something shimmer beneath the surface. Iridescent blues and purples dancing off the water. I reached down to lift the object from its sandy bed. Its eyes shot open—blue and vacant and dead. The pale face turned to me, the hollow eyes rolling in their sockets. I screamed, shrieked, cried out, but the words never left my throat. From her watery grave, Ruthi pressed her finger to her pale lips.

Shhh, she whispered. *Don't tell.*

57

I awoke with a start, gasping, sweating and heaving. Cold air rushed through my throat and lungs as I tried to catch my bearings. The morning was cold and damp beneath me. I looked around. I was outside. What the hell? I was on the front porch, curled up against the wall. Had I fallen asleep here last night? Now, that was a first. My hair and skin were damp and chilled from the morning fog. I peeled myself up, my muscles cramped from the awkward position. I stood and cracked my neck. The realities of the previous night came crashing back into my mind. Georgina. Fuck. I ran inside.

I HAD DEBATED WHETHER I SHOULD EVEN TELL SEAN ABOUT this latest turn of events. Did his proximity to me put him in danger, too? Or did this sicko only go after defenseless girls? I knew he'd try to stop me, but I had to tell someone. And I owed him a goodbye after everything. I couldn't just ghost on him.

He hovered over me as I tried to sort through my things.

"Clara, you can't run. That's what he wants."

"What am I supposed to do? Stay here and wait for Gina to wash up on the beach?" I angrily tossed things into my bag.

My heart was racing. I was flush and on the brink of hyperventilating.

"He's not going to kill Gina."

"Why the hell would you think he wouldn't?" I threw my boots into my bag.

"Because he gave you a heads up. The other victims were all just taken and killed swiftly. No threats, no warnings, no demands."

"I'm not calling his bluff with someone else's life on the line."

"Then let's at least go to the cops. Tell Lindsey."

"He said not to tell anyone."

"Of course he did. Killer 101. Doesn't mean we should be stupid and listen."

"Lindsey won't believe me, anyway. He'll think I just want a valid excuse to skip town."

"You have a cryptic photo and text of Gina bound and knocked out."

"Yeah, and they'll think I did it!"

"You're being too paranoid."

"I think I have every right to be paranoid, Sean. Have you not noticed what's happening here?"

Sean sighed, frustrated, and ran a hand through his hair, making it stick straight up.

"I need to pack," I finally said.

"Clara, don't run. I can't let you."

I spun around, furious.

"And how are you going to stop me? Going to lock me up? Call the police?"

"Of course not."

"Then just stay out of my way, Sean."

His eyes were hurt, pulling at my heartstrings. "I know you want to help me. But the best thing for everyone is if I leave. Just go, before the police have a chance to notice I'm missing. We can tell them about Georgina once I'm safely on a plane out of here."

"And that's just that, then?"

"What do you mean?"

"What about us?"

"There is no us, Sean."

He was silent. I looked up at him. Those piercing eyes, cutting right through me. I bit down on my tongue.

"You have a life here. Regardless of all of this, there isn't a place for me in that life."

"I...thought I was happy here. Had something solid to hold on to. But then you came back, and you shattered every truth I thought I knew. You took a wrecking ball to the life I'd built."

"I'm sorry."

"Don't be. I'm not asking for an apology. I'm asking you to own it. Recognize what we have. What we never lost."

He took my hand. I stared at my belongings scattered on the bedspread.

"Sean, I can't stay here," I whispered. I pulled my hand from his.

"Fine. Be a stubborn coward. Run away, just like you always do."

I ignored the bait.

"Will you please just take me to the bus station?" Frustrated, I threw things into my bag.

"No."

I looked up and raised my brow.

"If you're so determined to run, find your own way," Sean said.

"Get the fuck out, Sean. Go."

He exhaled incredulously but turned to leave. I heard the door slam on his way out, and his truck screech as the tires revved against the driveway.

I lifted the .38 from my bed and cradled it in my palms. I sighed and gingerly placed it in my purse. I'd worry about airport security later. First, I had to get out of town.

My phone buzzed with a text.

Tick tock, tick tock. Such a small neck she has. Won't take much effort.

I ran to the bathroom and expelled everything in my stomach.

I THREW THE FINAL PAIR OF PANTIES INTO MY BAG AND ZIPPED it up. This place had gotten enough of me. I was out. If the bastard wanted to follow me back to Austin, so be it. At least there we had a competent police department. At least I wouldn't automatically be a suspect because I had a high school reputation I'd never live down.

I grabbed my bag and bid farewell to the bedroom I planned never to see again.

"I hope you know what you're doing," Mom said when I walked into the kitchen.

She looked put together for the first time since I'd been back. Her short strawberry bob was styled, and she wore crisp jeans and a short-sleeved blue sweater.

I sighed. "I'm doing what I have to do, mom. I'll lose my

mind if I stay here another day. I'm sorry. I'd be happy if you came back to Austin with me. I can take care of you there. But I can't stay here. You'll be taking care of me." I tried to laugh, but it hurt. It just hurt me from the inside out.

"If the police ask, I'll have to tell them," she said, coolly.

"I wouldn't expect you to lie. It's a sin and all."

Mom didn't smile.

"Be safe, Clara. Take care of yourself."

"You too, mom."

"I do love you," she said. I gave a small smile.

"I know. I'll call you when I get home. Make sure you're okay."

"You don't need to take care of me, Clara. Just take care of you."

58

I bit back tears as I headed out the door and waited for my cab—the one taxi driver in town. I didn't even care that I was getting on a three-hour bus ride to the airport. As long as I wasn't here. My heart and pulse dashed. I couldn't just leave, but I had to, right? I could call the cops once I was out of town. Once the killer realized I'd kept my word and left, it would be safe to call Lindsey.

The taxi dropped me off at the little bus station at the far edge of Main St. I was early, but there was only one direct bus per day that would get me down to Santa Rosa. I grabbed a coffee from the vending machine, pulled my coat around me against the coastal weather and tried not to cry. The main street moved about with summer tourists and workaday locals. Had I not wanted to set the town on fire, I might have found the daily buzz quaint and endearing.

I was sitting on a bench, scrolling through my phone when I heard a short blip. I looked up and saw the police cruiser sliding up next to me. Shit.

Detective Lindsey stepped from the passenger side, suit

and tie and sensible shoes. I swallowed hard. Not what I needed.

"Clara. Going somewhere?" Lindsey asked.

"No?" I tried.

He gave my suitcase a once over and pursed his lips. I shrugged.

"I might be mistaken, but I do believe we asked you to stay put through the investigation."

"I know, and I'm sorry, I want to cooperate, but I have a life 2,000 miles from here that I need to get back to. I have to go to work."

"Your boss was very understanding about this when we spoke."

I rolled my eyes. Kim probably thought it was the most exciting thing to ever happen to her—one of her employees a murder suspect!

"I've been here nearly two weeks, Lindsey. How long do you expect to keep me trapped here?"

"As long as it takes." He smiled placidly. "Speaking of, I'm going to have to ask you to come down to the station."

"What? Why?"

"Some new evidence has come up, and we want to discuss it with you."

"Something about the pictures?" I said, almost hopeful.

Lindsey pursed his lips. "We can talk about it at the station."

"Am I under arrest?"

"Do you want to be?" He said it like a threat.

I started to panic. I didn't know if the killer was watching my every move, but if he saw me go with the police, he might freak out and think I disobeyed his orders. And then what would happen to Georgina? My heart started to flutter. I should just tell Lindsey. He'll have to believe me.

"I can't go," I said.

He raised his bushy gray eyebrows.

"And why's that?"

I chewed my lip and looked around. Fucking hell. I had nothing to lose anymore.

"Because the killer kidnapped my friend and says he'll kill her if I don't leave town immediately," I blurted it out.

Lindsey examined me, a contemplative expression across his face. Trying to figure out if I was just plain insane?

"And why would the killer do such a thing?" There was mocking in his tone.

I threw up my arms. "I don't know! Why would he kill innocent teenage girls? Not a lot of logic to psychopaths, is there?"

"All right. Let's go down to the police station, and you can tell us about it."

"No!" I shrieked. "Aren't you listening? He said *no cops*. And I need to leave, or you're going to find another body on that beach."

"Are you saying you know of another murder?"

"Oh my God, are you serious? Are you listening to how fucking stupid you sound?!" I shouted. I regretted it instantly. Congratulations, Clara.

Lindsey's expression fell. "I'll need you to come with me now." He reached for my arm, and I ripped it away.

"Don't touch me!" I screamed.

"Problem here, Lindsey?" a male voice said behind us.

I looked up at the smug face of Detective Rhodes. Shit.

"No problem," I muttered.

"Clara, can't you just follow directions for once in your life?" Rhodes said, standing there like a puffed-up peacock with his broad shoulders squeezed into a tight uniform.

God, did he buy a size smaller on purpose? I'd love to give that haughty face a right cross.

I sighed and crossed my arms. What choice did I have? I wasn't under arrest, but it would seem I was damn close to being so. I sighed and relented.

"Do I have a choice?"

Lindsey only smiled, thin-lipped, and picked up my suitcase.

59

The cruiser started down the main road leading back into town. I crossed my arms in the back seat, a weight of despair lodged deep in my gut. It wasn't the first time I'd been in the back of a policemobile, and I was certain it wouldn't be the last, but it was the first time I was trapped there while a friend was being held captive. First time for everything.

"Cheer up, Clara," Rhodes said from the driver's seat, hazel eyes glancing back at me through the rear view. I glared to his amusement.

I discreetly reached into my handbag and pulled out my phone and started to unlock the screen.

"Hey! What did we say?" Lindsey snapped. "Put that away, or I'll take it away."

"I just want to show you something. Then maybe you'll believe me."

"When we get to the station," Lindsey said.

I groaned but complied and resigned myself to staring out the window.

A popping sound rang out. Gunshots?

"The fuck?" Rhodes yelled out. The car shook and swerved to the right.

I shot up straight, heart pounding.

Rhodes took control of the vehicle but led it to the side of the road, bringing it to a slow stop.

"What the hell was that?" Lindsey asked.

"Sounded like a gunshot," Rhodes said, uncertainly.

"Your tire's popped," I said.

They both looked back at me accusingly.

"Don't look at me like that. How the hell did I pop your tire from back here?"

They glanced to each other and sighed.

Rhodes and Lindsey stepped out and investigated. Not one, but two tires with bullet holes. My stomach turned. It couldn't be a coincidence. Who the hell was ballsy enough to shoot at a police car in the middle of the day? Whoever was ballsy enough to murder innocent girls, perhaps?

Nerves pressed down on my bladder with uncontrollable force, and it gave me an idea. Just maybe, I could make a run for it and still save Georgina.

"Hey," I tapped on the window. Lindsey glared at me and looked back to the busted tires. I smacked the window again. He looked up with a *what?!* I hurriedly waved him over. He poked his head in through the front passenger side.

"What is it?" He snapped.

"Can I go pee?"

"No."

"Seriously? You want me to pee on your backseat?"

"You have to go all of a sudden?"

I rolled my eyes. "Um, just got shot at. Friend is being held captive. Trapped in a cop car. My nerves are on overdrive."

He didn't find me amusing.

"You can hold it."

"Says the man. You try having a woman bladder."

He sighed and rolled his eyes, exasperated. He looked up and down the isolated road.

"Fine. There's a little public restroom thing over there."

I glanced at the glorified outhouses on the mouth of the running trail and groaned. I'd done more in worse places, I guess.

"Thanks," I said as he opened the back seat.

"Don't you try anything. You're not under arrest now, but you will be if you try to skip out again."

I saluted him. "Aye, aye, Captain. Whatever your command."

"You're a real pain in the ass, Kendrick, you know that?"

"So I've been told."

The smell of fish guts and urine washed over me as I approached the structure and I had to force myself to step inside. Peeing in the woods would have been a more pleasurable option had Lindsey not been watching me with a gimlet eye. I tried not to touch anything as I relieved myself and tried to think of my next move. Would I be able to slip out without them noticing?

As I washed up in the rickety sink, trying to check my reflection in the old, cracked and fogged mirror, my neck hairs came to attention. I listened for Lindsey outside. Silence. A telling breeze swept by. Something was wrong but familiar. I looked behind me in the mirror, and a shadow was beside me. Before I could scream, a searing pain exploded in my head, and everything went dark.

60

I was thrown about in darkness. In and out of consciousness. Cold then searing hot. Winding turns. Blackness all around. My head throbbed in an invisible vice, squeezing. Pressing. I couldn't move my arms or legs. I was an inanimate thing flung about, banging into walls. It smelled of musk and copper. Blood. My blood. My mind slipped away from me.

61

I awoke with throbbing pain in my head, worse than any tequila sunrise. I forced my eyes open, but I was in darkness. A dark room, wooden floor. Musty and damp. Dusky shadows fluttered across the space as my eyes slowly adjusted to the dark. I tried desperately to remember how I'd gotten here but my mind was blank. I had clearly been knocked out... Shit. I had been kidnapped. Holy hell. I almost laughed at the absurdity.

I adjusted my body, but my wrists were tied together behind me and tethered to a pole or rod of some kind. I could make out the shapes of crates against the wall, and it looked as though there were windows that had been covered up, sealing off any light. The place felt strangely familiar. The smell of the wood and the lightness of the air. I closed my eyes and tried to place it. A cool breeze, the lap of waves, the laughter from far off below.

I was in the Lighthouse.

My stomach turned over, and my blood started to race. He brought me here. To my place of original sin. Bile threatened, but I breathed. I wasn't about to give him the satisfaction of sitting in my own vomit.

This shit just got real personal. I looked around to see if by some miracle of stupid killer oversight my purse would have made it. Didn't think so. So, no phone.

I tried not to panic. Someone would know I was missing. Would they? Everyone thought I was on my way back to Austin. Mom wouldn't expect to hear from me until tomorrow, and even if I didn't call, she would just assume I was being selfish and temperamental. And Sean and I had left things...not so great. I doubt he'd try to call or text me. And again, even if he did, my non-response wouldn't send him into a panic. He'd think I was still angry with him. Lindsey? Something must have happened to Lindsey and Rhodes for the killer to have captured me so easily. So basically, I was royally fucked.

I'd imagined a lot of things might kill me over the years. Overdose. Rock climbing. Rotten pork from a shady Cambodian street vendor. Even the odd, strange man in a distant hotel. But I didn't think it would go down in Point Redwood. In the Lighthouse. By Ruthi's killer.

IT'S IMPOSSIBLE TO TELL TIME IN A SITUATION LIKE THAT. YOUR mind goes to strange places, really quickly. But after what I think was a couple of hours of escape plotting and frantic scenarios running through my mind, I finally collapsed into an unwanted, exhausted sleep.

62

Whenhen I woke again, there was a dim light now illuminating the tower. I sat up, startled, and glanced around the iridescent room. Shapes and moonbeams languidly waltzed in and out of shadows. My hands were still bound with coarse rope behind my back, but my legs were free. I was freezing and sweating all at once.

A figure sat on a wooden crate a foot in front of me, shrouded in black, his back turned to me.

"Hey!" I croaked out, my throat dry and parched. My lips tasted of dirt and copper. "What the hell do you want from me?"

There was no response for a few moments. My heartbeat thrummed, echoing in the silence of the room.

Then the figure shifted and turned toward me. He pushed the dark hood down from his head. Blonde hair tumbled loose around small shoulders.

"You must be thirsty," Tabby Gates said, holding out a bottle of water.

"What the fuck?" I said in a near whisper. My head

throbbed. What was happening? Had Tabby come to rescue me? Was I hallucinating?

Her round, tawny eyes looked at me wide and unblinking. The cold menace in that stare answered every question racing through my mind. Oh. My. God.

She raised her blonde, thinly plucked eyebrow at me and shook the water bottle. "Well, are you thirsty or not? It's been hours."

I wanted to spit in her face, but purposefully suffering dehydration wasn't going to help anything. I nodded. She unscrewed the cap and leaned in and tipped the bottle to my lips. I welcomed it, drinking nearly the entire bottle in one swig.

She smiled, satisfied as if my dependence on her greatly amused her.

"What's going on?" I asked, water dribbling down my chin. "Why am I here?"

"You're really not very bright, Clara. I don't know why people say otherwise."

"You kidnapped me?" I said, almost incredulous. This was absurd. Head of the virgin club Tabby *kidnapped* me. I wanted to laugh.

"Kidnapped sounds a little child molester-y, doesn't it? I think of it as having brought you one step closer to your imminent demise."

"You killed those girls," I said, everything coming together in my rattled brain.

She blinked a few times as if registering. Then let out a long, melodramatic sigh.

"I took no pleasure in killing them, I promise you. I let them go peacefully. No pain."

"You strangled the life from them. Drowned them. God knows what else."

She shrugged. "Well, death isn't pretty, no matter how gentle you try to be."

My stomach churned at her flippancy. Who was this person? What alternate universe was this? I was dreaming. Another nightmare.

"I had no choice. You needed to be taught a lesson. Once again," Tabby went on.

"What are you talking about?" I wanted to scream. "What do those girls have to do with me?"

"I blame myself for being naïve. Or underestimating your stubbornness. I wanted you gone from town. Immediately."

"So, you killed them to prove a point? To frighten me?"

She stared at me with amused disbelief, as if I'd asked the most obvious question in the world.

"Well, yes. They were little whores anyway. I wanted you and everyone in this town to see that bad things happen when you're around. I wanted every nasty memory conjured up from that fucked up mess you call a brain. I couldn't have you ruining what Sean and I had. I couldn't have you stirring up old memories and causing him pain."

"And you didn't think replicating his sister's murder would wake his demons?"

"He has me to comfort him, Clara. Don't you get that?" Tabby pressed a manicured hand to her chest. "I'm his safe place. I was there for him after Ruthi died. When his memories get bad, he comes to me. I took care of him after the war. He's the only one I've ever been with. Where were you? Who had you in a bathroom stall?"

My gut clenched. Her words were too close to the truth to be completely contrived. Had the bitch been stalking me in some way? I took a steadying breath.

"You're an idiot, Tabby. You didn't think that the police would want to question me?"

"I admit that was an oversight. I knew they'd question you, of course. I'm not stupid. But I never thought you'd become suspect number one. I figured they'd have just enough on you so you'd high tail and run."

"Who's the dumb one now, Tabby?"

Before I realized it, she had a gun pointed right at my head. A .38. My gun. Real nice, Clara. Way to be a fucking moron.

"Hey, no need for that," I said, scooting back, but trying to look composed. She gave me a pathetic look.

"It's amazing how easy you were to take down. Supposedly you're some kind of badass chick," she let out a roaring laugh. "Maybe you should have been training your common sense instead of punching a bag."

When I got out of this, I was going to string her up as a punching bag.

I suddenly remembered Georgina.

"Where's Georgina?" I snapped.

Tabby smiled. "She's relaxing somewhere quiet."

"If you hurt her..."

"Yes? Did you want to continue that thought?"

I heaved, breathed.

"She's completely innocent, Tabby. She's your friend, God dammit!"

"Clara, Clara. Don't you see how the innocent drown around you? But don't worry. She's just down for a little nap. She's fine. For now."

She stood and paced in a small circle.

"You know, if you'd have stayed out of my way back then, none of this would have happened. Only you to blame, Clara," she went on.

"What are you talking about? Back when? I was long gone when you finally gave it up to Sean."

She narrowed her eyes but didn't react.

"In high school. Sean and I were going to be together, and then you had to ruin it."

"You. Are. Delusional."

"He never told you about it, did he?" She looked so self-satisfied.

"About what?"

"About that night we kissed after the fall dance. Freshman year."

My stomach turned. I thought back on it, so many years ago. Sean was kissing Tabby back then? I remembered that night. Sean had made his first move on me the week before —the first time we'd gone from friends to flirting to something more. And I'd flat out rejected him. Out of fear mostly. And insecurity. I was terrified of losing him because we were stupid enough to take our clothes off together. Okay, so I'd rejected him, and he'd kissed Tabby. Gross, but not that big of a deal.

"So you kissed him twelve years ago. Big deal," I said. Her faced turned sour.

"It was a big deal. I knew we were meant to be together. I would have made him a better person. But then you came along, flaunting your tits and your complete lack of virtue. Really your mother's daughter, aren't you?" Her cheeks burned an angry shade of crimson. Was she for real? My lack of virtue?

"I did everything right!" She suddenly snapped. "You were everything wrong. Slutty and truant, drinking, smoking. Breaking all the rules. I went to church, to confession. I was saving myself for marriage! You get that? Marriage! I listened to my mother. Did everything she told me to do. And he still chose YOU."

"You don't know very much about the world, *Tabs*."

"I guess not," she said on the brink of dramatic tears. "An innocent girl like me didn't stand a chance against that. Of course Sean was going to choose you. He was a hormone-ridden boy after all."

"But you didn't save yourself, did you? I don't see a ring."

I shouldn't have said it. The gun collided with my temple. I grunted but shook it off. She heaved but collected herself.

"I had to, Clara. It was the only way to make him forget you. I sacrificed *everything* to help him get over you. I gave him the most important thing I had." She shook her head, mournfully.

I nearly laughed. Then remembered the gun pointed at my head. How did I play this? Appeal to her morality? Be demure and humble? Play into the stereotype of the wanton vixen?

"You can't blame me for Sean not looking at you, Tabby. You weren't his type."

She glared at me.

"What I mean is," I tried to salvage. "Have you ever thought you were too good for *him*? He was troubled. We both were. That's why we worked together. You had it all together. You were good. We weren't. That's why it was just Sean and Ruthi and me."

"Nice try, Clara. He only thought that way about himself because you and Ruthi were always dragging him down. That's why you both needed to go. He needed no distractions."

A fist wrapped around my heart and squeezed until it slowed to a hard thump.

"What?" I said lowly.

"I'll admit he didn't react quite how I'd hoped after we got rid of Ruthi, but I'm patient. I knew he'd come back. And he did. Meanwhile, you were gone forever. Or so I thought."

"You killed Ruthi," I said, my voice barely audible in the echo of lapping waves outside.

She gave me a nonchalant shrug. "I didn't want to. But she was never going to leave. Such a sickly, neurotic thing. Sean was far too invested in her. She was bringing him down, ruining his potential. I knew no matter where we went, she'd still be there."

I lunged toward her, forgetting the pistol. She shrieked and flung herself back. My bound wrists pulled tight against the pole, and I fell. I screamed at her, feral, vicious. I was ready to bite through the ropes and tear her throat out with my teeth. Anger pulsed through my veins, pounding against my skin. She could see it, and she smiled. A placid, sinister smile. I sat there, heaving, trying to focus. She might kill me in the end, but I would kill her first. I swore it.

"Why did you bring me to the lighthouse?"

She smiled. "Poetic isn't it? It was such a special place for you and Sean. I thought you might like to see it one last time. After all, you were here when she died weren't you?"

My chest heaved.

Then something dawned on me. She'd said *we*. After *we* got rid of Ruthi.

"Who's your accomplice?"

She looked at me curiously. "What makes you think I haven't worked alone?"

Because you're not that smart, you psycho Barbie.

"You said 'we'."

"Oh, did I? Oops, caught me. Nigel was always such a good puppy."

"Nigel? The dorky, awkward pharmacist?"

My head spun. How did *that* happen?

"He's a bit of a goober, I admit. But he's also a bit of a sicko. Did you know he used to dissect animals for fun?" Tabby scrunched her nose. "Caught him once dismembering a cat, the little psycho."

"Nigel helped you kill Ruthi? Why? What did she ever do to him?"

"Nigel will do anything for me, Clara. You think you're the only one men fawn after? He didn't do it because of Ruthi, or because of any feelings whatsoever about you. He did it simply because I asked. He's loved me since we were kids." She shrugged indifferently.

"You sick, manipulative bitch."

Perfect bleached teeth flashed as though I'd paid her the mother of all compliments.

"What happened that night? Tell me!" I said.

Tabby cocked her head to the side and studied me.

"Do you know how drunk she got that night? I mean, really. You guys all had it coming. She'd wandered up the beach—probably looking for you—and I found her sitting on the rocks. Just swaying in the breeze all alone. And you know what she said when I approached her? 'That she didn't need saving so I could move along.' Ha! She was so out of it, only took one swift blow to the back of her head to bring her down. Don't worry. I prayed for her as I squeezed the air from her lungs. Then Nigel was good enough to take her body up and drop it off the cliff."

She'd had water in her lungs. Meaning she'd been alive when she went into the water. I felt like my stomach was coated in barbed wire as images flashed through my mind. I closed my eyes and breathed.

"So, what now? You're going to kill me, too? And you and Sean are going to live happily ever after?" I said.

"No," she said bluntly.

"No?" I said when she didn't elaborate.

"I learned my lesson with Ruthi. Sean cares too much about you—or at least he thinks he does—to suffer your death. But if he knows the truth about you, then he'll hate you forever."

"What truth?"

"That *you* killed Ruthi. And that you killed those girls."

I laughed then, incredulous. "How the fuck do you suppose you're going to pull that one off?"

"Evidence, my dear. You're already a suspect. You tried to leave town when the police clearly instructed you to stay, tried to escape when I shot the car. I knew you'd do that by the way. You're so predictable." She scrunched up her nose amusedly. "Oh, and the blood they found on your clothes in your room. And the bloody rock you used to bash their heads in."

I deadpanned. "You set me up for murder."

"Not really that hard. You did kill your own cat, after all."

"What? No one is going to believe that. I'm the one who found its God damn head!"

Tabby shuddered and gagged. "Cats are such disgusting creatures. I *hate* them."

My jaw dropped and my words caught as I processed this new level of insanity.

"And when I tell them that you actually did it?" I said.

"Why would they believe a murderer over me? I mean, look at you, Clara. You're an absolute mess. You even tried to kill your own mother. Tsk, tsk."

"*What?*"

"By getting Nigel to switch her medication of course. You need help, Clara."

"You tried to kill my mother?" I saw red rage.

"That whole bit was actually just happenstance. There really was a problem with the medication, but not on purpose. Nigel is just a complete bumbling fool. But unfortunately, his mistake brought you back here."

"Did he...was it Nigel who tried to kill me in the cemetery?"

Tabby snorted a laugh.

"Don't be so dramatic. He was just trying to scare you. Did it work?"

I shook my head, ignoring her insane rhetorical question. "So you'll send him down with me?"

She shrugged. "It's not like Nigel and I are going to live happily ever after." She laughed like it was the best joke in the world.

I was going to be sick.

I would not, could not, in a lighthouse. I pressed my eyes shut and breathed. This is not how I die.

Tabby left the lighthouse tower in search of "refreshments" as she said, leaving me fuming, terrified and heartbroken all over again. My head throbbed, and I suddenly feared the blow she'd inflicted had given me a concussion. The warm, viscous liquid that had been trickling down my cheek had dried to itchy clots on my face. I fought unconsciousness as I tried to process, tried to think, to reason. My vision blurred and shards went through my pupils. Stay awake, Clara...

I SNAPPED TO, SUDDENLY ALERT, HEART THRUMMING. I WAS still alone in the tower. I breathed and tried to focus. I shifted around the pole, and something sharp dug into my back. A nail. A beautiful, rusty nail! I inched the rope up to it and tried to hook it over the nail in a way that could catch the point. I moved back and forth, straining my shoulders to their max.

"Goddammit, Tabby," a voice said.

Startled, I shot my head up and spun around. Rhodes was standing in the doorway, looking around the scene as if his puppy had torn up the bed linen.

"Rhodes," I said, breathless and disbelieving. Never thought I'd say it, but thank God for Rhodes.

Rhode's full lips curled up into a subtle smirk.

"That's what the badge says. Must admit I've always wanted to see you all tied up, but not like this. Fuck."

"What the hell? How'd you find me? Who cares, untie me!"

"Fuck, I told her not to do this." He rubbed a hand over his hair.

Realization clicked. "You're helping her?"

He looked at me warily but didn't confirm or deny.

"You helped kill those girls?" I said.

"God, no," he said with disgust. "I'd never hurt anyone. Especially not some innocent teen girl."

"You always did like the young ones," I said snidely. He didn't look amused. "Then why would you help her?"

Rhodes sighed and looked around contemplatively.

"It's a long story, Kendrick. Don't really have the time. Where's Tabby now?"

"How the hell should I know? Little tied up right now."

"Cute. How long has she been gone?"

"An hour maybe. Maybe four. I'm all mixed up. Probably had to get her hair done. Look, Rhodes, whatever's going on, it's not too late to do right here. Let me loose."

"Mmm. Can't. Sorry, Clara Bell."

"Can't? Rhodes! She's fucking crazy, and I'm pretty sure she's going to kill me."

"If I let you off, she'll know. But I won't let her kill you," he said with zero conviction.

I groaned. "Then go get Sean. I won't say you've been here."

He shook his head reluctantly.

"Sorry, Kendrick. Can't do that either."

"What's going on? Why are you helping her? What, you're her partner in all this? She, you and Nigel have some sick threesome going on?"

"Not exactly."

"Rhodes!"

"Look, Clara, I'm sorry, but she's got some shit on me. Bad shit that would ruin my career. Possibly even land me in jail. She said if I didn't go along with it, she'd blow it wide open."

"What kind of shit?" I said. Rhodes chewed his lips. "Rhodes! What could possibly be so bad that you're willing to let innocent people die?"

"Pictures! Okay, very incriminating pictures. She hacked my Cloud. I didn't know what she was planning to do. But she came to me with them one night and said she might be in trouble and she needed me to direct the police to anywhere but her."

"You mean direct them to me. You bastard. You tried to frame me."

"Better than seeing you dead. She wanted to kill you the moment you got back here."

A thought dawned on me.

"And the girl up at the Lost Coast nine years ago? Did you have something to do with that?"

"No! That was a coincidence. Know how many girls get murdered in this country? Shit. Sick country we live in. Maybe it was Tabby's inspiration. I don't know. But you did happen to be up at that same beach when she was killed."

"What? How would you know that?"

"For some school thing. When Lindsey made the connection to you, who was I to argue?"

My jaw dropped. "Fuck. You."

"Hey, it's not like I planted evidence at the scene. I just led the horse to water. Let Lindsey make the connections."

"What kind of pictures are they, Rhodes?"

He hesitated.

"Tell me Goddammit!" I shrieked.

"Of me...and a girl."

"Sex pics?"

He nodded.

"You're kidding? You're letting her blackmail you over some homemade porn?"

"The girl...is sixteen," he said it almost in a whisper. My jaw dropped.

"What? How old are you, thirty? Can't get a woman your own age?"

"The young ones love me, what can I say?" He was trying to be demurely cute but failed. I glared. "Look, I was really drunk. And for the record, I thought she was eighteen."

"Oh, yeah, loads better. You perv," I said with disgust. "And it's obvious she's underage in the photo?"

He scratched the back of his neck and hesitated.

"She's wearing her St. Thomas uniform."

"Oh, what a fucking wet dream for you," I said with disgust, shaking my head.

"Clara, I could go to jail for that. It's rape. Least of all, I'd lose my job."

"Oh, so what? You'd deserve it. Think I have any sympathy for you?"

"Don't act like you weren't throwing yourself at me back then. Every time you got hauled in for some thing or another, you'd bat your eyes and push out your tits."

"Because I was a dumb kid. You were the adult."

"I was twenty-three back then! That's not an adult." He groaned and paced back and forth.

"You're an adult now," I growled and shook my head.

"Fuck, you know what? None of this matters. She's a crazy bitch who's gone too far. I'll put a stop to it," Rhodes said.

"No, you won't," Tabby's voice said. She stepped up behind Rhodes, the .38 pointed at his head.

Rhodes turned slowly toward her.

"Tabby, put that down," Rhodes said.

"And why would I do that when I've just heard your plan to take me down? Detective Rhodes, suddenly having a conscience? I certainly didn't plan for that plot twist." Tabby said, saccharine sweet. She was an eerie juxtaposition of innocent and vile that prickled my skin.

"Tabs, think this through. You don't want to do any of this," Rhodes said.

Tabby shrugged, innocently. "A little late for that, don't you think? You know, Ryan, I'm supremely disappointed in you. I had high hopes for us as friends."

"You're really insane, you know that?" Rhodes said.

Ugh. Don't push her, dude.

Tabby's round eyes narrowed. "I'm just a girl who's willing to do what it takes to get what she wants. I'm not a coward who runs away from the things that matter." Her gaze flicked to me.

"Don't think for a moment that this isn't all your fault, Clara. You will be dealt with," she said.

Tabby turned back to Rhodes. "Remove your gun. NOW. Leave one hand up."

Rhodes gingerly reached under his with one hand and pulled his 9mm from his back holster.

"Set it down." She aimed the gun a little higher, and he complied. "Now get in the corner." She directed him with the gun.

"C'mon, what's your plan here, Tabs?"

She cocked the pistol. "Don't tempt me, Ryan. Really wouldn't want to put a hole through that pretty face. It's rather lovely to look at."

Rhodes held up his hands in submission and backed slowly into the corner near me.

Tabby looked around sharply then motioned to a pole running floor to ceiling.

"Handcuff yourself to that."

"With what?"

"The cuffs in your pocket," she said, annoyed.

"I don't—"

She raised the pistol.

"Okay, okay." Rhodes pulled a shiny pair of metal cuffs from the inside pocket of his coat and proceeded to lock himself to the pole.

Tabby nodded, satisfied. She sat on the crate and rested her elbows on her knees, not setting down the gun. She looked like she was pondering.

"It's not too late to do the right thing, Tabby," Rhodes said, calmly.

Tabby laughed incredulously. "The right thing?"

She looked over to me—*Can you believe this guy, girl-friend?*—as if we shared some girl bond.

"Did he tell you what he did, Clara? Why he's helping me?"

"Banged some high school girl," I said, unaffected.

She arched a manicured blonde eyebrow. "Did he tell you *who?*"

I didn't want to care, but my interest perked. I shook my head. Tabby's pink lips pressed together in a wry smile.

"Hannah. March."

My jaw dropped, and for a minute, I saw stars.

"You fucking bastard," I said slowly. I faced him and glared. "Failed to mention that little morsel."

Rhodes groaned. "Does it make a difference? Sixteen is sixteen."

"Except this particular sixteen-year-old is dead. And they think I did it. And somehow, I'm guessing that attribution has something to do with you," I said.

"Wouldn't be very convenient for Rhodes if the rest of the police department found out the dead girl was the underage girl blowing him in the police station, would it now? Are those the same handcuffs she was wearing?" Tabby said, smiling.

I glared at Rhodes. He was just super drunk, right.

"What is it about your girlfriends that always gets them killed?" Tabby continued.

Rhodes' face paled milky white.

"You cunt," Rhodes said.

My stomach turned. What was she talking about? Tabby tilted her head and grinned at me.

"So much you don't know, Clara Bell. You and Ruthi were supposedly so close." She shrugged.

"What the hell are you talking about?" I seethed.

Tabby sighed and looked to Rhodes. "Should you tell her or should I?"

"What the fuck is wrong with you, psycho bitch?" Rhodes yelled.

"Ryan, Ryan. You really shouldn't insult the person with a gun to your head. Were you taking photographs of your conquests back then too?" Tabby asked.

The pieces started to come together in my mind. The muscles in my arms pulsed and ached to move, to punch something. I slowly turned to Rhodes. His face was beet red with rage.

"What's she talking about, Rhodes?" I said softly.

His jaw tensed, and he took a few deep breaths, then finally exhaled.

"I had a thing with your friend back in the day."

My heart dropped into the recesses of my gut. It couldn't be true.

"No," I whispered.

Tabby giggled. Fucking giggled like a little toy doll.

"Don't you just *hate* being lied to?" Tabby said.

I closed my eyes. Ruthi and Rhodes. No way.

"When? How?" I breathed out. How could Ruthi have not told me that? We shared everything.

"It was just toward, um, the end," Rhodes said, shifting uncomfortably in his bindings. "She came to me."

"Bullshit. You took advantage of her!" I snapped.

"Hey, I didn't force her. She said she didn't want to go to college a virgin or some stupid shit. But didn't want it to be some high school boy who'd tell everyone all over town. She said she knew I wouldn't tell. Couldn't tell." He shrugged as if it were the most sensible logic on the planet. "Hey, give me a break, I was a lot younger then," he said.

"You don't appear to have changed at all!" I screamed, hysteria bubbling up inside me. I heaved and tried to collect myself. Everything I thought I knew about *everything* was collapsing on me. Sean would murder him if he knew.

Thoughts of Sean rushed my brain. Where was he? What had the little witch done to him?

"And Kate?" I asked, suddenly remembering the third victim.

"No. I never touched that girl," Rhodes insisted.

Tabby sighed dramatically. "She was on her way to becoming your next conquest and you know it. I saved her from becoming another one of your little whores," Tabby said sweetly. "Now kids, play nicely. Mommy needs to think."

64

As Tabby stared reflexively into the room, I resumed my subtle attempt at the rusty nail behind me.

Tabby's head snapped toward me. "What are you doing over there?"

"Nothing. I'm just uncomfortable. Think you can put my hands in front of me?"

"Yes, because your comfort is my concern." She rolled her eyes and sputtered a laugh.

The clamor of footsteps up the lighthouse steps halted our banter. Tabby's head snapped toward me, and she glared.

"Who's that?" she snapped.

"How the fuck should I know? This is your master plan, remember?"

Rhodes snickered.

She pursed her little pink bow mouth and sighed as though this turn of events was all so inconvenient.

"I wasn't expecting company," she said. She stood and

straightened out her Catwoman attire and smoothed her blonde curls.

She checked the gun and gripped it firmly. I had to wonder whether she really knew how to use that thing. How did someone like Tabby learn to use a pistol? Well, Clara, how does someone like Tabby murder three people and frame two other people for it? Chew on that.

The steps grew closer, and I heard the murmur of low male grumbles.

The door to the attic burst open, and Nigel came in. He had a limp body thrown over his shoulder. Fucking A, was everyone so much stronger than they looked around here?

"Well, well, the plot thickens. Welcome to the party, Nigel," Rhodes said with amusement.

"Nigel!" Tabby shrieked. "What are you *doing* here?"

Her cheeks burned, and to my pleasure, she started to look undone.

"Change of plans, Tabby," Nigel said. "This one caught me planting the evidence."

He threw down the limp body.

"Sean!" I screamed. My heart pounded, and I pulled hard against my restraints to no avail. Tabby looked equally horrified.

"What the hell did you do to him?" she squealed, her cheeks burning red. Her eyes popped. Did she really love Sean? Some fucked up version of love?

"He's fine," Nigel said. "Just chloroformed him. He'll wake up in an hour or so. I had no choice. He knew exactly what I was doing when he saw."

"And what was he doing at your house?" Tabby said, glaring at me.

"I don't know! I told him I was leaving town. Maybe he

went by to see mom. Where *is* my mom, anyway?" I glared in turn.

Tabby waved her hand in the air dismissively. "Oh, relax, drama queen. She's out with your Aunt Josephine. Some church thing or another. We made sure they'd be gone. I have no desire to kill a helpless lady."

"Little girls do just fine," I snapped.

Tabby shot me a nasty glare but said nothing else. Then she sighed, frustrated and looked to Sean's limp body.

"So what are we supposed to do now, Nigel?" she rested her hands on her narrow hips. "Hard to convince him of Clara's guilt now."

Nigel scratched his hand, looking ever more like a dunce.

"Can we drop his body somewhere else?" Nigel offered.

"He's going to remember you knocking him out, half-wit."

My fear started to lighten. Tabby's plan wasn't so airtight. She hadn't anticipated her accomplice being completely incompetent at pulling off homicide. I could work with this.

"He's not going to love you now," I said.

"Shut up, bitch," she snapped.

I looked up at Nigel and saw the anger stewing in his eyes. Did the little creep do it on purpose? Was he really in love with Tabby? He wouldn't want the plan to go off as she'd wanted. Then she'd live happily ever after with Sean. And Nigel would be...well, in jail, I guess. Did he realize the depths of her deception? Nigel's mouth twisted contemplatively.

"I'll think of something," Tabby said, tapping the gun against her rosy cheek.

Who would have thought little Virgin Queen Tabitha Gates could ever be so creepy?

65

For what felt like hours, Tabby and Nigel spoke in hushed arguments in the corner while I racked my addled brain for a solution.

"Any bright ideas?" I whispered to Rhodes.

"Shut up!" Tabby snapped from their corner.

I thrust my head back against the pole. I rolled my gaze over to Sean's limp body and bit my lip to keep from crying. I envisioned all the ways I'd torture Tabby if Sean didn't wake up.

Suddenly, Sean stirred on the floor. In a moment, his eyes popped open, and he shot upright, coming fully alert. My heart popped.

"What the fuck?" He said, rolling over and up. He winced then, rubbing the back of his head. He glanced around the room, confused. His face sported the green pallor of nausea.

"What's going on? Tabby?" he said. He coughed.

She snapped around.

"Sean," she said with a breathy fawn, scuttling over to him. "I'm glad you're okay."

She knelt beside him and stroked the sweaty dark hair from his brow.

Sean looked at Tabby, then back around the room. His hazy, half-lidded eyes landed on me, tied up.

"Clara? What the..." He shot back to Tabby. "What the hell is going on?"

"Ask your girlfriend," I muttered, suddenly a little pissed off at him for his incredibly idiotic lack of judgment. His face twisted up.

"It's going to be fine, Sean. Don't worry about it. I'm sorry about your head. Nigel, apparently, can't follow directions," Tabby said, continuing to fuss over him.

Nigel did not look pleased with that.

Realization clicked in Sean's face, and an eerie calm came over him. The calm of one who has just realized one wrong move would mean his demise. His harsh blue glare softened to one of convincing understanding, even if feigned.

"Tabby, what's going on?" he repeated calmly, taking her hand in his.

"I'm sorry it had to go like this," Tabby said. "Really, it wasn't my plan. But she just wouldn't *leave*."

Sean's eyes looked tentatively to me. I wasn't sure how to react. How to play this? I tried to tell him with my eyes to play it cool. Play along with her lunacy. Could you reason with crazy?

"You can't do this, Tabs. Clara didn't do anything. She didn't hurt those girls."

Fucking hell Sean, pay attention.

Tabby sat back, affronted. "Of course she didn't. But that doesn't make her innocent. She came between us. She's a homewrecker and a bad influence. She tempts you into evil."

"So...you killed them?" His words wavered between a question and a statement of realization.

Tabby shrugged. "Unfortunate side effect, but there was nothing else to be done. I am sorry," she said, with little conviction.

I saw the horror in Sean's eyes as he ran through the various scenarios.

"Why, Tabby?" His words came out choked.

She tilted her head to the side and smiled. Then she stroked his cheek, caressing him gently.

"Don't worry about any of that now. Just be happy it'll be over soon."

Tabby stood and rested her hands on her hips, gun still in one hand.

"What's your plan, Tabby?" Rhodes said, goading. "Don't tell me it stops here."

She whipped around and glared at him.

"Yeah, Tabs, what are we supposed to do now?" Nigel asked, uncertain. He shifted uncomfortably as he surveyed the scene.

Maybe I could turn Nigel...

"You and Sean could run away together," I said. "Run away, and no one will know that you were involved. You've already set the evidence against me. They won't be able to deny my guilt. And Nigel can back it up."

Tabby glared at me. "Please don't insult me, Clara. Naiveté doesn't suit you, and it's insulting to me. There is no happy ending to this. And Nigel," she pointed the pistol at his head. "Is collateral damage."

She fired.

Nigel collapsed to the wooden floor. I screamed, not able to hold back. Tabby stood unfazed, the gun still smoking in her small grip.

My heart thumped, and I could barely breathe. She was certifiably insane. Sean and I were done for.

66

I was going to be sick. Not that I felt all that badly for Nigel, but I still didn't think he deserved to die.

I saw the fear festering in Rhodes' eyes. Even tough guys shake in their boots sometimes. I fought the irrational urge to laugh. I didn't give a shit about what happened to that fuck wad, but for now, I needed him. Handcuffed or no, he was going to help me out of here.

Tabby, likewise, looked distressed. Her plan was not going by design, and it was starting to show on her peaches and cream face. She paced, tapping the gun against her narrow hip.

"Damn it, damn," Tabby muttered.

Think, Clara, think. I spotted Rhodes, subtly shifting around. I carefully watched him from the corner of my eye as he maneuvered a tiny metal object from his coat sleeve. Hidden pocket? What was he...a KEY! Glory halleluiah, he had a hidden key.

With dexterity, he maneuvered the key into his handcuffs and carefully unlocked them. Then he sat still and silent, watching Tabby with a keen, calculating stare. That's right, Rhodes. Use that brain.

And in a heartbeat, he was free from the cuffs, on his feet and charging at Tabby. He barreled into her but not before she snapped the pistol up and pointed. He collided with her as rapid-fire shots echoed off the walls.

Rhodes went down in a hard thump, taking Tabby with him.

I held my breath, waiting for movement. Tabby twitched beneath Rhode's slumped body and a moment later wiggled out from under him, huffing and steaming. She wiped the disordered curls from her face and flicked her head around the room. I followed her gaze and horrified expression to Sean's body, a pool of blood forming in his abdomen.

67

I shrieked.

"You bastard!" Tabby screamed at Rhodes where he lay wounded on the floor. Without a thought, she fired into his chest.

My blood froze, hardened and cold against my veins.

I stared at Sean's limp body on the dusty wooden floor. I wanted to cry, but I wouldn't entertain those emotions. I had no time for sadness or grief or anger or fear. I only had time for calculation. How were we getting out of this? Because it was not a matter of if, it was a matter of how. This is not my end of days.

One of Sean's eyes subtly fluttered open. So small a movement it was hardly noticeable had I not been staring intently at his face. I sucked in a tiny breath, trying not to react. His eye caught mine for a brief second, and his mouth turned up in a tiny smile. Then he closed his eye again. He was awake. This changed everything. He was down, but he was awake. I could work with that.

Tabby ran to Sean's side and knelt. Her face remained

calm and impassive, but I saw the small threads of her composure fraying at the ends.

"Sean, baby," she cooed. "Wake up. You're not dead." She stroked the sweaty dark hair from his pallid face.

"He needs a doctor, Tabby. You can still save him."

She shook her head but didn't reply. A small tear glinted at the corner of her eye. Then she turned to me with pure, unblemished loathing in her eyes.

"It's too late. And it's all your fault, Clara. There's nothing left now."

I remembered the nail. It might be my only option at this point. Likely she was going to kill me either way, so I at least had to try. Tabby was busy cooing over Sean, so she didn't notice my movement this time. I subtly slipped the twine bindings over the nail and slowly, carefully began to saw away.

I kept sawing. I felt the fibers splinter against my skin. Each one popping and resonating. Then, I felt the release of freedom. I exhaled slowly. Now what? I had no clue. She still had a gun.

I slowed my breathing, trying to focus. I glanced to the pile of bodies. Sean's chest slowly rose and fell. We had time, but not much. Nigel and Rhodes were unmoving lumps. Something caught my eye on Rhode's raised pant cuff. A knife in a thin ankle holster. Gotta love a prepared, corrupt cop.

I took a breath and slowly let my hands unravel from their bindings, my shoulders popping as I set them into a right position. I sprang up and ran for it.

I darted toward Rhodes before Tabby could rise from her position beside Sean. I swiped the knife and pivoted on my heel, poised to attack.

Tabby pointed the .38 at Sean's head, and I stopped in my tracks.

"Don't think I won't," she said, her face a mask of stone.

"You won't," I said, not sure if I believed it. "This whole thing is so that you can be together."

"And you've ruined EVERYTHING!" She shrieked, high and shrill. She stomped her foot. "And now what am I supposed to do? I can't let him be with you, Clara. I just can't."

"So you'd rather see him dead than with me?"

"I'd rather see him dead than with anyone else, but *especially* you. You will ruin every good thing there ever was about him. You will crush his soul, destroy his world."

I knew it was the ramblings of a mad woman, but some remnant of truth nipped at me. If we survived this, I would have to let him go.

"You don't have to do this, Tabby. Sean and I won't be together. You're right. I'm not good for him. Don't you want him to be happy?"

"The only way he'll ever be truly happy is with me." A glint of tears shone in her eyes. Did she believe her own illusions? She must.

"That's the thing you've failed to realize, Clara," she said coldly. "I hate you more than I love him."

She cocked the pistol and pointed at Sean.

My world went red.

68

I charged at Tabby, no longer caring that she had a firearm. She spun around before I reached her and braced for impact. I sliced through the air with the knife, but she managed to deflect. I caught her arm though, and she growled as the knife tore through black cotton and flesh. Her eyes smoldered with rage. She came at me full force, sending me flying backward. I knocked my head against the wall, and my previous head injury sprang to life. I saw stars, so dizzy I nearly vomited. The knife fell from my hand. She came at me again, and I sent a quick jab, then a fast right cross right into her creepy Barbie face.

She stumbled back, and I knocked into her, sending the gun flying across the room. I barreled into her. We tumbled to the wooden floor. My right cross came into her face again, hard. Once, twice, ten. I didn't know. She wriggled and writhed under me. Then I felt a sharp pain right in my kidney. I yowled. Girl had learned a thing or two in self-defense class. I faltered just enough to where she kicked me off her. I rolled onto the floor, pain rippling up my side, through my brain. But the anger overrode the pain.

I grunted and quickly turned over. She was running for the gun. I jumped up and leaped toward her. I kicked out her legs. She went down with a shriek, her chin hitting the floorboard. I pushed up, ready to knock the bitch out. She flopped over and thrust a two-by-four at my head, cracking me square across the temple. I stumbled back, my ears ringing and the room turning to swirls of blurred shadows. She came toward me, the board still in her hand. My vision focused. Blood was splattered across her face. Her eyes bulged from their sockets. She was heaving and grunting. I forced composure and readied. My head spun, but I planted my feet and found balance. Bring it, bitch.

She came toward me, and I ducked. The board caught my side as she tried again to catch me. I dodged her and brought an elbow to her side. She went down. I bolted for the gun. As my hands closed around the cold metal, the board came onto my side. I went down, feeling my ribs splinter. I spun and fired. Click. Nothing. Tabby smiled menacingly.

It wasn't empty, but it was jammed.

I hesitated just long enough for her to grab ahold of my hair and slam my head down. I buzzed and rattled with pain and confusion. But this was not how I went down. Tabby Gates did not take me down. I swung the butt of the gun and clocked her in the head. She fell back.

"Clara!" Sean called my name. I nearly collapsed from those simple decibels of sound on the air. I glanced to him. He tossed me an old crowbar. I grabbed it up. Tabby came toward me, and I thrust it right through her gut. Her brown eyes jutted out, and she gasped. Blood bubbled up through her mouth. She choked on blood and air, trying to speak. I fell back against the wood, and she fell on top of me, her blood gushing onto my chest. I grunted and thrust her limp body from me. I lay there, eyes closed, heaving, crying, spinning.

I heard a shuffle. I opened my eyes. Sean stumbled to me, clutching his stomach. Blood seeped from the wound in his abdomen. I came to attention immediately and sat up.

"Sean!" I stood and embraced him. He collapsed against me, and we fell to the floor.

"Oh my God," I said, frantically pulling his hands from his stomach so I could see the extent of his wound.

"I'm okay," he gasped.

"Like fucking hell you are. We have to get you to the hospital."

He glanced to Tabby. "Is she dead?"

"Better be. There's a goddamn crowbar through her gut."

"I'm not sure she's human, better double check." He smiled through the pain, which made me smile in turn.

"Let the police check. C'mon," I pulled him to his feet and set his arm around me. I winced but let the adrenaline lubricate the pain coursing to every extremity.

We started to walk, and I saw Nigel's body on the floor in the corner. Poor bastard. Poor stupid, lovesick bastard.

He helped murder three innocent girls, Clara. And he would have killed you. Save your sympathy. Ahh, but the idiotic things we do for blind love.

"Do you have your cell?" I asked Sean.

He shook his head. "No, Nigel took it when he knocked me out."

"Here, hold on." I pulled away from Sean and went to search Nigel's body. Sure enough, Sean's iPhone was in Nigel's pocket. I sighed with relief. I handed it to Sean, and he proceeded to call 911.

I saw the gun on the floor and picked it up. I dislodged the magazine, and the jammed bullet came out.

"Had to make it hard on me, huh?" I asked the gun.

"It just knew you could do it on your own," Sean said, winking. Then he winced as though even the smallest bat of an eye sent a shock of pain through him.

WE SAT ON THE LIGHTHOUSE FLOOR, LEANING AGAINST EACH other while we waited. I kept the gun pointed at Tabby's body for good measure.

Suddenly her body twitched, and a low guttural cough and groan erupted from her mouth. I jumped and cocked the gun and pointed.

"No, Clara, don't," Sean said, setting his hand to my wrist and slowly pressing my hand down.

I heaved, anger swirling and bubbling inside me.

"Cops and medics will be here any second. You're not a killer," Sean said.

On command, footsteps echoed up the lighthouse steps. The door burst open, and a handful of paramedics rushed in. They stopped short when they saw Tabby on the floor, a crowbar protruding from her gut, her coughing and gagging on her own blood. They rushed to her, and I screamed.

"No! Him! Attend Sean," I said.

They turned and saw Sean, giving a split-second assessment.

"Attend to the girl first, she's critical," the medic said.

"No. You. Don't." I said, raising the pistol toward the medic.

"Clara, don't!" Sean said, gasping and falling back. Blood had soaked his shirt.

"She's the fucking killer. She can wait. Attend him NOW."

The medics hesitated for all of a split second, then rushed to Sean.

"Keep her stable," the lead said to another, nodding toward Tabby as they brought the equipment to Sean. The lead spoke into the radio on his shoulder.

"Three victims, one gunshot wound to the abdomen, one critical stab wound, and one badly beaten." The medic's mouth dropped when he noticed Rhodes and Nigel. "Shit, make that five victims. Goddamn bloodbath. Backup bus needed immediately."

I lowered my gun and fell back down.

A moment later, I heard sirens below. More footsteps and then the lighthouse attic flooded with police.

I suddenly felt every blow to my body erupt anew. I knew my ribs were broken and I likely had a concussion. I lay down and the world blurred.

"Miss," I heard a commanding voice. "Miss, stay with me. Clara!" I felt a gentle tap to my face, but my consciousness left me anyway.

69

I awoke in a bed with tubes running in and out of me and a smiling nurse checking my vitals. Everything hurt. Every single inch of muscle and skin ached and burned.

"Hey, you. Nice to see your eyes," the smiling nurse said.

"Where am I?"

"Point Red clinic."

"Am I okay?" I choked out, finding my voice.

"We think so. You've been roughed up pretty good, but you're going to be fine in a few weeks."

"Weeks?"

"Well, you have three broken ribs, multiple contusions, and a decent concussion."

"You should see the other guy," I said, with a graveling laugh.

She smiled lightly but didn't seem so amused.

"I have. She's dead."

"Oh," I said, both relieved and confused. Tabby was a nurse at this clinic. They would have known her.

"Sean?" I asked.

"He's recovering. He lost a lot of blood, but the bullet missed vital organs. Like you, he's going to need a LOT of down time to recover, but he'll recover."

I lay back against the pillow and shut my eyes.

TABBY HAD DIED A FEW HOURS AFTER ARRIVING AT THE CLINIC, but not before she rambled on about how she'd kill me next time, as though she were a Scooby Doo villain. She really was delusional.

Sean had gone into surgery, and I was going crazy not knowing how he'd fared.

A shaken, but intact Lindsey came to my room that night.

"We don't know exactly how it all went down for certain, considering everyone is dead, shit, but it appears that after Rhodes saw Tabby attack you, he knocked me out and left me tied up in the cruiser," Lindsey said. "Woke up with a pretty nasty headache." He smiled thinly under his mustache.

Other than being a little groggy and shocked, Lindsey looked otherwise unharmed.

"You alright?" I asked, adding him to the list of people my actions had hurt.

He rubbed his jaw. "Physically, yeah. But I'd be lying if I said I wasn't rattled. I owe you an apology, Clara."

"Oh?"

"We searched Tabby's house. We found evidence that supports everything you and Sean said. Including your hacked Cloud photos. Plus, an eight-year-old yearbook with your face desecrated throughout, and Sean's and your senior prom photo with her face superimposed over yours."

Jesus. I almost felt bad for the little psychopath. Almost.

I forced a smile, my busted lip cracking with the movement. "It's alright. She did her best to turn everyone against me. Nearly worked." A thought struck me. "Georgina? Have you found Gina?"

Lindsey nodded. "Georgina was discovered drugged and unconscious in Tabby's bedroom closet. Slightly traumatized, but mostly physically unharmed. She'd only been administered a heavy dose of sleeping pills. She'll be fine, at least physically." Lindsey stood. "Get some rest, Clara. Then I'd head down the hall and see that boy of yours. He's awake and he's asking for you."

70

I gnoring my nurse's orders to stay in bed, I wobbled down the hall as fast as I could in my broken state. I spotted Sean through the small window on his room door, and my heart contracted. His eyes were closed, but his chest rose and fell with the gentle cadence of life.

A tear slipped down my cheek. I reached for the handle, then hesitated. I had no idea what I was possibly going to say to him.

"Go in," a voice said. A nurse was standing beside me with an easy smile. "I think you're the best medicine for him right now."

I took a breath and stepped in.

I crept slowly to the bed. He was so peaceful in a languid slumber. I gently brushed the hair from his forehead. He stirred, one eye fluttering open.

"Now that's a sight," he said.

"Hey you. I hear you pulled through like a champ."

"As if there was ever any doubt. Thanks for saving my life, Kendrick."

"I guess it was about time I repaid the favor. How do you feel?"

"Like I have a hole through my stomach."

"You do." I took his hand and squeezed.

"Clara, I—" I felt the edge of a confession in his tone and I pressed my finger to his lips.

"You need to rest. I just wanted to see you with my own eyes. I'll let you sleep."

I turned to go, but Sean grabbed my hand and held me in place. "Don't make me chase you to Austin with a bullet hole, you siren."

I laughed. "What have I always told you, Killarney? You're my anchor. Without you, I'm adrift at sea."

EPILOGUE

I n the end, at least we all got some closure on a lot of things. Kendra Killarney finally knew what happened to her daughter, not that I thought the knowledge would bring her any peace.

I don't think it helped Sean's trust issues, either.

We had all expected Ruthi's killer to be a stranger in the night. A dark shadow creeping through town. A menacing transient hiding in the woods. Not one of our own. You never expect it to be one of your own. Not that I had ever liked Tabby all that much to begin with, but you never anticipate the nerdy, church-going virgin was secretly stalking you and planning to steal your boyfriend and murder anyone in her path to do it. Try wrapping your head around that one.

~

TABBY'S FAMILY HAD A MEMORIAL SERVICE A FEW WEEKS later. Although Sean and I didn't officially attend—not many did—we stood at the edge of St. Thomas grounds and watched, hand-in-hand, trying to understand. There is no real understanding, Lindsey told us. She was sick, deranged, delusional. There is no rationale behind her actions. That's the way it is with true psychopaths. They don't realize that there is anything wrong with them. They believe every action is justified because their wants and desires are the only things that matter. They are the ultimate narcissists. They can never be reasoned with or fixed.

I will forever live with the guilt at having taken a life. I will forever live with the image of her life slipping away at my hand. I know I had no choice. It was her or me. But in the end, I was the one who had to snuff out the candle. Taking Lola's advice, I went home that night to write it out. I wrote until my hands cramped, and my emotional dams broke free, flooding until their reservoirs were completely dry. For the first time, I think I finally wrote down the honest truth.

Lindsey told me to try to think of it as having saved countless lives. Likely Tabby would have never stopped. Even if she had succeeded in getting what she wanted, it would have only fueled the twisted justification that murder was a means to an end.

How long had she been this way? Who can say? Some children exhibit psychosis as early as they can put thoughts into actions. Some are triggered much later in life.

It's not for us to understand, Father Richard would say. And it's not for us to decide.

I WAKE TO THE SOUND OF LAPPING WAVES AND THE SOFT caress of a loving hand running down my shoulder. I don't open my eyes but savor the sensation of his touch in darkness. Sean stirs beside me. His arm slides over my side to rest on my stomach. He pulls me into his body, and I can feel the hardness of him pressed against me. He nuzzles his nose into my hair, and I lean back into him, utterly in bliss for the first time in nearly a decade. His lips press down on my chilled skin, sending tiny prickles up my spine. I finally roll over and face his blue gaze, no longer cold ice but a warm summer sea. I wonder if this is what every morning will be. After so long, waking in safety.

Where we go from here, I don't know. We could try to rebuild here in Point Redwood—replace the pain with good memories. In some ways, knowing now what happened to Ruthi, it brings us some level of closure. Ruthi can rest, and we can move on, knowing. And I can finally stop running. Maybe that makes Point Redwood a better place for me than it's ever been. Sean has a life here, and I have a life in Austin. But what does that mean for both of us? All I know is, whatever life we lead from here, it will be together.

The End.

Thank you so much for reading *Shallow Water*!

Want to be the first to know about new releases and get a FREE story? Sign up for my insider book list at amandajclay.com/subscribe.

Did you enjoy Shallow Water? It would mean the world to me if you would leave a review.

ABOUT THE AUTHOR

Amanda J. Clay is a California native, currently residing in Denver, CO. When she's not creating fiction, she spends her free time plotting world adventures.

Do you have thoughts or questions? I'd LOVE to hear from you! amandajclaybooks@gmail.com.

Connect with me on below or at visit me at amandajclay.com.

ACKNOWLEDGMENTS

To Thomas, for helping me through this project from inception to finish.
I couldn't do it without you.

A big thank you to my editor Teresa Kennedy of Village Green Press, and to my critique partners and beta readers who helped mold this book into a fantastic story!

Cover Design and formatting done in house at Florence & Reynolds.

ALSO BY AMANDA J. CLAY

The Redemption Series

The Redemption Lie

All That Glitters

The Cat's Reprisal

Rebel Song Series

Rebel Song

Rebel Rising

Rebel Fire

Stand Alone

Lies in the Darkness

Hollowbrook Haunting: A Paranormal Gothic Romance

Shallow Water

Made in the USA
Monee, IL
25 January 2020